A Very Irish Curse

A. D. Graham

Copyright © 2014 A. D. Graham
All rights reserved.
Edited and published by Strict Publishing International
via the CreateSpace Independent Publishing Platform
ISBN: 1500884669
ISBN-13: 978-1500884666

CONTENTS

Prologue	1
Chapter One	11
Chapter Two	21
Chapter Three	23
Chapter Four	41
Chapter Five	49
Chapter Six	61
Chapter Seven	65
Chapter Eight	77
Chapter Nine	85
Chapter Ten	91
Chapter Eleven	113
Chapter Twelve	123
Chapter Thirteen	135
Chapter Fourteen	141
Chapter Fifteen	149
Chapter Sixteen	157
Chapter Seventeen	171
Chapter Eighteen	183
Chapter Nineteen	187
Chapter Twenty	195
Chapter Twenty-One	209
Chapter Twenty-Two	219
Chapter Twenty-Three	227
Chapter Twenty-Four	239
Chapter Twenty-Five	261
Chapter Twenty-Six	281

PROLOGUE

The flickering torches burned in the darkness as the procession slithered its way along the track, the ground sodden after recent rain. Men guiding carthorses were illuminated by the yellow light, their eyes reflecting the flames as the fire made plain the fear on their faces.

Columns of men, many of them armed with swords, some with simple farming implements, trudged through the mire of the treacherous passage, the clatter of their weapons and the heavy grating of the wheels on the laden cart disturbing the quiet of the night. Aboard the shuddering contraption, the human load was almost oblivious to the heaving motion, despite the severe jolting over the large stones left in the makeshift road.

The old woman was clad in the remnants of a filthy cloth, with a hole torn at the top for her head. The pathetic garment, barely covering her wasted and wrinkled body, lifted intermittently in the night breeze and the violent lurches of her mount. She had no choice but to suffer the rigours of the journey, tied as she was to the rough wooden post lashed upright amongst the bundles of brushwood that lined the cart. She snarled curses and moans of complaint at the shuddering motion, but these were muffled by the twisted thorn branches that wound tightly around the back of her head and between her lips, preventing her ranting at her captors.

The straggling column moved slowly yet deliberately toward the outlines of a hill. The rise was framed in a pale glow from the moonlight. On its brow stood the ruins of a church, topped by the dark outline of a Celtic cross.

"Hold!"

The shout came from ahead. Men stopped, some afraid, others reaching for weapons in answer to their own concerns. The procession threatened to degenerate into disarray as panic began to seize those whose courage had limits and who had counted fear of their leader as their prime motivation up to this point. Torches flickered, as men lifted them high to determine what lay ahead, to find the source of the shouted command, their minds playing tricks on their eyesight.

"Demons," some said. "Conjured by her... to take her back to hell!" Whispers and stuttered shouts punctuated the commotion as the better-armed soldiers tried to maintain order amongst those farmers whose fear of the unknown was gradually overcoming their bravado.

"Hold, I say!" the native Irish lilt was now discernible in the shouted order.

The procession began to dissolve into small knots of men. Muttered, anxious questions filled the air, until a man at the head of the group strode forward. He was tall and bearded, wearing a steel breastplate, the only armoured member amongst them. There was a torch in his left hand, and with his right he drew a finely crafted sword from its sheath. The tartan of a Scottish Plantation settler was distinctive below the breastplate as torchlight flickered against the burnished areas of its dented surface. His heavy breath formed clouds of vapour in the freezing night.

"Why do you stop us?" he shouted into the darkness.

"You know me. I am Sir George Hamilton! A fair and just guardian of these lands, which I own. This witch must be destroyed. As decent folk and good Christian men, you know that we must do our duty."

The men in the column nodded their heads, muttered grunts of agreement, Hamilton's words apparently having the effect of re-establishing the modicum of bravery that had persuaded most of them to accompany him on this terrible journey. Some even looked at their charge aboard the cart who, growling behind the thorns that bloodied her wrinkled features, tore her mouth as her gums worked at them. Blood trickled down her wizened chin, dripping into the cart. Men backed away, terrified.

"Speak, damn you!" shouted Hamilton, into the darkness, his fear slowly wearing away his patience.

With neither a sound nor displaying the degree of dread now present amidst the Scottish immigrants, three figures entered the pool of radiant light created by the torches. Clad in plain Irish Gaelic style and carrying only staffs, two of the figures had thick red hair, now tossed gently by the wind. The third man was older, greyer, and wore plain sackcloth. He too carried a staff, though its design was intricate, more ancient, ornate. The Scotsmen, as a group, began to draw their swords, before Hamilton could speak.

"Wait. Wait!" Hamilton raised the torch.

"Let them speak," he said, more softly.

The central redheaded figure stepped forward. The burning torches revealed a stern and troubled face.

"I am Padraig Maguire of the clan Maguire," he said, his voice deep and distinctive, reminiscent of Hamilton's, yet with a pronounced Gaelic accent, so clear as he spat the words, loud enough for all to hear.

"You know me, Hamilton, as a just clan leader," he grated, and frustration and anger, just discernable beneath the surface, betrayed by his enunciation as he spoke.

"Aye, I know you, Maguire," Hamilton replied icily. "These are religious proceedings. Why do you interfere?" Hamilton stared at the Irishman, confused, unsure of where his words might lead.

"You can not burn this witch!" Maguire said with venom.

Hamilton stepped back, astonishment clear in his expression.

"You won't be telling me what I can and cannot do on my own land, Maguire. Leave, before we come to have a disagreement."

There were snarls of assent amongst Hamilton's men. It was clear that the time for talking had passed all too quickly.

"Your land?" Maguire barked, unable to contain his anger.

His countrymen looked at him, aware of his temper and the situation that they found themselves in, yet recognising the wisdom of his words.

"My people were here a while afore you set foot on Ireland, Scotsman. Have a care to remember that! You can tell..."

He reared his head back as the sound of Hamilton's blade hissing through the air curbed his speech, and the tip of the weapon swung toward his throat, stopping inches from him.

Hamilton stared at Maguire as he spoke. Though his words were slow and deliberate, his anger was palpable. The sword was held firmly in his hand and his grip was steady, enough to give him the power of life and death over the Irishman standing in front of him, in but a brief and bloody instant.

"The Witch killed my people," he said, his voice trembling with anger. "She killed children, women. You have no grasp of what she is capable of, Maguire! You'll not be telling me what I can't do, Irishman!"

Maguire did not move, his eyes merely looked at the tip of the sword, his expression unyielding.

Hamilton's men, still far from settled, began to look around once more. Mutterings of ambush were heard amongst the Scots. Men looked nervously at the roadside and the Irishmen. Both groups stood poised for action, until the older grey haired figure, standing beside Maguire, stepped forward. His voice was clear and his words seemed to have a calming effect.

"There is no need for violence here, Lord Hamilton," he said, raising his hand as if in hope of placating the two men.

"Peace be with us this night. We are not each other's enemy on this day. The enemy is the witch. You both know this."

He looked steadily from Hamilton to Maguire.

As the old man pointed to the pathetic figure still bound aboard the cart, Hamilton gradually brought the sword down from its threatening position.

"Agreed," he replied. "What do you suggest?"

For a moment, the old man stared at him in silence.

"You must give her to us. She is inhuman, an abomination in the sight of our gods. She can only be destroyed through our rituals, the ways known only by the Druids, with the use of the proper incantations."

He paused, trying to gauge the effect that his words might be having on Hamilton.

"It is the only way."

As he spoke, the old man had begun to rave, drool dripping from his quivering lips, his dread regarding the entire situation only too obvious. He became unsteady, and his companions clasped his arms to hold him up.

Hamilton stared at him incredulously.

"You want us to give her to you?" he replied, alarmed at the prospect of losing this foul creature that he had fought so long to capture. He shook his head at the thought.

"No, she will be burned and go straight to hell. She'll suffer justly and that's the end of it. Now get out of our way."

He paused, nostrils flaring in anger and fear.

"No!" the old man screamed, shedding the restraint of his companions and clasping the Scotsman's arm in an apparent effort to convince him of the error in his judgement.

Hamilton, in desperation and without warning, plunged his sword through the old man's chest. Darkness clouded his mind, affected his judgement, and undermined the inhibitions that had stopped him from removing this babbling impediment to his progress. As the sword struck home, scraping bone and spilling blood over Hamilton's hand, the victim collapsed to the ground, his breath hot against his killer's hand, gasping in his death throes.

The two Irishmen stood, confounded for a brief moment, then with a cry, drew daggers and attacked. Dodging the thrust from the assault of one man, Hamilton misjudged Maguire's own thrust and the dagger caught him in the shoulder, as he attempted in vain to pull the sword from the old man.

Hamilton's men, who by now were eager for a fight, drove toward their leader, battering and stabbing at the Irish, before they could cause further harm. The struggle lasted seconds, then it was over, and three dying Irishmen lay bleeding in the mud of the path.

"My Lord, you are injured," Hamilton's lead swordsman shouted, rushing to his master's side.

"No! Leave me. We do this now, before more of these bastards turn up. Move!"

The column re-organised itself as frightened horses were calmed and the bodies were brutally cast into the ditch by the side of the road. The procession moved on once more, the steady creaking of the cart the only sound now.

The Druid shuddered, opening his eyes with a start. Breath came in short wheezing efforts as he tried to raise his head. He lay in the mud and stagnant water of the ditch where his body had been unceremoniously tossed. They had assumed that he was dead. If only he had listened to Maguire's advice and had not convinced him that they should go alone, without reinforcements or aid. He had believed that his word would be enough to convince Hamilton of the error of his ways. How wrong that notion had been. He had not reckoned with the Scotsman's determination in the face of his own fear. Perhaps he even now laboured under her spell. Hamilton could never realise what he was doing. Not now. It was too late.

His eyes were failing, death was close, but the flames at the top of the hill in the distance were unmistakable in their brilliance. He saw the burning figure atop the pyre, writhing. He could hear the noise plainly, a terrible high-pitched screeching. Hamilton's men could never understand the implications; never begin to comprehend what would now take place. There was no hope, no hope at all. Only the knowledge that he too would die, soon. He would never witness the fate that all Ireland would suffer at her hands. Sobs wracked his body as he lay in the mud, his life leeching away.

The Druid dwelt on his final thoughts, fleeting notions passing quickly in his dying moments. He could... he would, bind her to this place with a curse. The hill and the surrounding land had been the burial site of his ancestors. The church had been built at its centre, the architect scarcely aware that his designs were directed by something more powerful and ancient than he could ever possibly imagine. The sacred ground marked the epicentre of the circle of power. It was possible that he could prevent her escape from this place of death, with the help of dark Gods and ancient words.

If only he could perform the ritual in time. He would, with his dying breaths. He could use his knowledge and the old ways to call upon the dark Gods, with his own death and sacrifice as his bond. He would offer himself to them and prevent her escape. It was all that could be done now, the only thing that might give his death some meaning.

As the wind increased, fanning the embers to spiralling flame, the hideous yelps of agony that had diminished with the fire became howls drawn from the deepest pit of hell. The Druid watched terror-stricken as the blaze-ravaged figure writhed, still upright and secured to the crumbling remains of the cart. Above that, Hamilton's voice could be heard, as he read from his bible in unceasing rhythm.

"It shall never be inherited, neither shall it be dwelt in from generation to generation: neither shall the Arabian pitch tent there: neither shall the shepherds make their fold there..."

Picking up the cadence, the old Irishman uttered his own curse, while using his blood to inscribe ancient symbols in the wet earth on the bank of the ditch.

"I invoke the spirits of the void, he that destroys all and remains unconquered, he that will rise again, the blood of Lugh, the arm of Nuada..."

His droning went unheard by anyone of this world. Hamilton's ranting bible reading echoed back from the hills.

"But wild beasts of the desert shall lie there; and their houses shall be full of doleful creatures; and owls shall dwell there, and satyrs shall dance there…"

As the life seeped from the old Druid, his head began to rock steadily, mocking the intonation of Hamilton's recital, copying the cadence of the speech while substituting his own words.

"I invoke Cruach, the Wyrm With One Thousand Young, that he might accept my soul as bond for this curse, that he might pierce the heart of the witch should she leave these lands, that he might bind her to these cairns, that his sign might hold her soul…"

As Hamilton continued, the remains of the pyre's victim slumped against the charred wooden stake, roasted hunks of flesh falling from it. Hamilton's voice grew louder as he stirred himself to frenzy.

"And the wild beasts of the islands shall cry in their desolate houses, and dragons in their pleasant palaces: and her time is near to come, and her days shall not be prolonged."

Squirming in a pool of his own blood, the druid raved, his eyes wide as he stumbled over the last few words, before his life might be drained from him.

"Tie her, chain her and muddy her heart, that she might never escape this place, that your mark might hold her forever…"

As he uttered the final incantation in his native tongue, the druid convulsed, as if a force had taken possession of his broken and twisted body. He choked, but the noise he made calmed quickly, turning to a dull exhalation of breath as his remaining life was sucked from him. His eyes widened, in fear of the terrors that he saw at his own end, and his mortal body died.

A VERY IRISH CURSE

Present Day
Newtowncairn, County Fermanagh

James Pollock had never run so fast. His heart was thumping as he sprinted across the slippery grass of the field, his shoes soaked with water. The dense mist, which seemed to have descended so quickly, cut visibility to a few metres. It was hard to see where one field ended and another one began. Where was that damned road? Tremors of panic threatened to engulf him.

He heard them, heard their footfalls behind him in the grass. They were coming. Keep running, keep…

Pollock could never have hoped to see the ditch in his panicked flight, or in his frightened state. He stumbled, fell, and crumpled into the mud. Pain gripped his ankle and he cried out. He struggled to rise; limping painfully into the next rain soaked field. As he moved he saw a shadow in the mist, then another. They almost had him! Lungs feeling as if they would burst, breaking once more into a run, no distance was covered until violent hands snatched at his clothes. A foul smelling bag became gag and blindfold. Arms pinioned, and then bound; there was no escape. A final coherent thought was of Professor Latimer. The prayer had to be silent, though it was intense. Dear God, he hoped that he had done enough.

CHAPTER ONE

Professor Neil Latimer strode briskly across the still damp grass of the University's grounds, his pace dictated by the lateness of the hour. He was about to miss the scheduled start of one of his own lectures, yet again. Lunch had gone on much longer than anticipated and, as usual, he had been keen not to prematurely end the daily lunchtime debate with his anthropologist colleague Dr. Reilly; at least until he had gained the 'moral high ground'. As ever, Latimer was firmly convinced that he was right!

Unfortunately, Dr. Joseph Reilly tended to adopt a similar attitude, but always in his unnervingly calm manner. Many of the restaurants in the area balked at the idea of the two lecturers getting into their little chats, but their tips were always appreciated. A pity though, that things were running late. Latimer's lecture today would cover the Jacobite Wars in Ireland, the period with which he was most familiar and from whose rich and uncultivated research material he had harvested so many works. As he left the lawns behind, he moved quickly into the echoing corridors of the University. Two flights of stairs later and he entered the lecture theatre, expecting to be bowled over by the cacophony of noise that was so typical of his usual body of students these days. He cradled the cold metal knob of the door and pushed... silence! The room was empty, almost.

"Latimer," a voice said from the back of the room. He recognised it immediately, as its echo reverberated around the cold grey walls.

"Professor Moore. Is something wrong? Ah, I have a

class... don't I?"

"Yes, Neil, you do."

Moore got off his seat, his height imposing even from this distance. Professor John Moore was in his early sixties, his hair a grey mop; a man whose knowledge, enthusiasm and drive had at various times gained funding as well as national praise for the University's research efforts. At six foot two, he towered over most of his contemporaries, lending him an intimidating air when he required it, yet at the same time, he inspired confidence in all those who worked with, and for him.

He walked towards Latimer, who remained confused with regard to what the head of department might be doing at his lecture. Moore was usually more forward than this. His movements seemed imbued with a nervous energy, as if something was not quite right.

"What's wrong, John?" Latimer said directly.

"You'd better sit down, Neil." He raised his hand, offering Latimer a nearby chair, his gaze insistent.

Latimer sat, placing his notes and books to one side.

"What's all this about John? I don't..."

Moore found a chair beside him and placed his hand on his shoulder.

"I'm afraid that I have some bad news."

"What is it?" Latimer was intrigued yet concerned now. He was unmarried. He thought about his sister, his brother in America. What the hell had happened? He looked suspiciously at his colleague.

Moore tried to give him a reassuring look, though this only increased Latimer's frustration.

"It's about one of your students," he said at last.

Latimer found himself relaxing somewhat, but guilt made him abruptly sit up again. He heard the slight catch in Moore's voice when he had spoken, a tinge of real emotion.

"What's happened? Tell me for God's sake."

"James Pollock, your PhD student. There's no easy way to say this. He..."

Moore paused. Took a long, deep breath.

"He was murdered last night!"

"What?" Latimer recoiled in disbelief. His head was swimming.

"Murdered! Why, that's impossible. I spoke to him two... no, three days ago. I spoke to him, John. How did this happen?"

Moore, still visibly shocked, had difficulty finding the appropriate words. "I know, Neil. Look, I only heard this morning. I sent your class home. I just wanted to let you know. Very... unfortunate!" Moore cleared his throat.

Latimer looked at him expectantly.

"Unfortunate? Jesus Christ! Understatement of the century!"

He paused, sensing something that he had missed.

"Is there something more?"

"Yes." Moore was uneasy as he stared at the floor. "His body was found in his car, near the area that he'd been looking at."

"Newtowncairn in County Fermanagh, John. That's where he was," Latimer croaked, his voice beginning to fracture.

Latimer could not believe that this had happened. He had spoken to James a few days ago. He had been working on the battle that had been fought around the town in 1689 between the militia of Enniskillen and a small Jacobite force. His work was excellent, no question of that, and would have seen publication, had he lived. Worse than that, Latimer had known Pollock since he had been an undergraduate, and the young man's interest in the period matched his own. Ever since their first meeting, Latimer had felt that there was something about this particular student that showed an almost unnatural depth of knowledge. At times he displayed the wisdom of someone twice his age, in some ways like an old researcher who had studied the relevant texts and primary source evidence for years, looking for clues, insights and conclusions. James Pollock had been able to display an awareness of the source material related to the period that surprised even Latimer. His insight bordered on genius. At times, Latimer remembered, it had almost been frightening. His depth of knowledge had been that good.

They had debated the period frequently, Pollock always convinced how different things might have been, had France been more supportive of King James II's pursuit of the English throne. Latimer silently cursed himself that he had seen so little of him in recent months. He had not even spoken to him, aside from his recent phone call, knowing that he needed little guidance. Perhaps if he had taken more of an active role in the PhD? Perhaps matters might have turned out differently. He closed his eyes to think.

"How was he killed?"

"I don't think that you need to hear the details…"

Latimer turned his head.

"You've just told me that one of my best students was murdered! That doesn't happen every day, now does it? Don't you think I have a right to know what happened?" he snapped.

Moore paused before speaking.

"His throat was cut. Apparently, his body had been left for some time before it was anonymously reported to the police. Terrible; a terrible event."

Latimer had rarely seen Moore show emotion, but the murder of one of the students, and under such circumstances. It must have hit home. Of course, it would be a shock to the entire university.

Latimer stood up. "Look, I'm sorry I shouted, ok? It's just…" Pausing, he sensed Moore's unease.

'There's something else, Neil," he said. "And it won't be easy for you to hear."

Latimer sighed. "Go on."

"When the police searched the car… they say that they found drugs at the scene. In the car, Neil."

'Drugs?' Latimer replied in wide-eyed disbelief. 'I don't know what has happened here, but one thing I am absolutely sure of, no matter what the circumstances, is that there is no way Pollock was involved with drugs. He was a brilliant student and lived only for his studies and his...'

Moore looked up as Latimer stopped speaking.

"Oh my God, his girlfriend. I'd completely forgotten. They'd talked about getting married, you know. What she must be feeling now. I must go and see her, offer my sympathies. I've met her a few times, charming girl. I feel like I know her...' Latimer flailed for words. "Oh dear God," he said at last in consternation. Moore broke the awkward silence. "Yes, perhaps you should talk to her. That would be best, perhaps tomorrow. Look, we'll need to talk to the police later."

'Understood, call me whenever you're ready.'

Latimer turned to leave.

His colleague spoke again: "You might need to take some time off." He paused.

Latimer stared at him, sensing that he was hunting for some answer to the whole affair.

"I don't know any more about this than you do, you know," he said. "This is all totally unexpected." He strode towards the door.

Doctor Joseph Reilly scratched his head, pushing back the greying hair in a vain effort to look nonchalant and relaxed before walking down the corridor that would take him to Latimer's office. With the news of the murder, he knew that his friend would be shocked and words of comfort would be needed. These situations were never easy. He always felt awkward at times like this, anxious, as if he could only be making the situation worse. Having said that, it was not every day that a PhD student studying under one of the university's Professors had his throat cut! As Latimer's closest colleague, Reilly had to make sure that his friend was at least coping with the situation, and offer his condolences. It was the least that he could do.

He was also aware of how Latimer had felt about his

young student. They had developed a dynamic teacher-student relationship, where they could play off each other's strengths and weaknesses. He had been like a breath of fresh air, to both Latimer and his department. Everyone had liked Pollock. In all likelihood, he would have been destined for a lecturing and research post after his PhD. He had been quietly talked about as important to the university's future.

The student's reputation had all been quite recent, for Reilly, at least, who had spent many years travelling in Europe studying anthropology and the occult. It was an interest that Latimer not only shared but also had become increasingly involved with after discussions with Reilly over the last few terms. Latimer had always had his curiosity piqued when he read of European attempts at Alchemy and how such attempts had been recorded behind the veil of accepted history. He had been fascinated by the influence of the occult in such hallowed institutions as the court of Queen Elizabeth I, a part of the past that conventional history, the stuff of boring academics as Latimer had called it, tended to shy away from. Reilly had helped him fill in the blanks through his own knowledge. The pair had collaborated on research, and had even talked of writing a book. All that seemed a little distant now, Reilly considered as he walked. Now that Pollock had been so brutally murdered, their research would be the last thing on Latimer's mind.

He marched on down the corridor toward the office.

"Come in," Latimer found himself responding automatically to the knock on the door. He moved his chair toward the desk, upsetting his concentration on the task that he had been involved with, that of staring across the city skyline of Belfast, lost in thought.

"Neil. What can I say? I'm sorry to hear about James Pollock. He was one of the best." Reilly fidgeted nervously.

Latimer looked up at the thin figure in front of him, as Reilly engaged in anxiously brushing away wisps of grey hair from his forehead.

"Joseph, come in, sit down for God's sake. You're making me jumpy." Latimer faked a smile and kicked the back of an office chair, which acted predictably by shooting across the floor toward Dr. Reilly.

"Time for a drink." Latimer smiled as he reached into his desk, pulling out a half empty bottle of Bushmills whiskey. Reilly grabbed the chair and moved toward the desk, sitting down.

"No really, Neil, are you sure? I mean…"

"It wasn't a question, Joseph," Latimer insisted. "I need a drink because I'm pissed off right now. You need one… well… you look like you need one all the bloody time.'

Both men laughed nervously. The familiar sound of tinkling glass resounded through the office as Latimer dug into a nearby drawer. The mood became sombre once more.

"What's all this about drugs?" Reilly said. "Moore told me. I've never heard anything like it. Certainly not with a research student."

Latimer moved his thumb and forefinger to the bridge of his nose and closed his eyes, as if he was suffering from a blinding headache.

"Joseph, he was a brilliant student, brilliant. You're a social anthropologist. You know when a chap that just 'fits' the field of cultural research, gives insights into areas that he hasn't been taught. Things that you'd never even thought of. Talks as if, well, for example, he could speak at length about diverse rituals between tribes of people on opposite sides of the world as if he's lived his life with them. You've told me stories about students like that, met them during your travels in Europe. It's uncanny, yes?"

Reilly agreed, tasting his drink.

"Yes, I know the type, but they're few and far between, Neil."

"Well," Latimer continued. "They're even less common in history, especially these days. History has lost its *pizzaz!*"

"Lost its what?" Reilly looked at the contents of his glass.

"Popularity in mainstream media if you like. It isn't taught the way it used to be. That's fine in some respects, but I think that government sometimes forgets the fundamentals. James Pollock was different, not a product of the system. He made me want to get into arguments with him. I'd speak to him sometimes and it was like conversing with a seventeenth century nobleman. His insight was that good. It didn't come from his reading or research. It was as if he could think seventeenth century. For a historian, that's pure genius."

Latimer rested back on his chair, put his feet up on the desk and took a swig of whiskey.

"And I simply can not believe that he was involved with drugs in any way. In fact…" he paused, considering the glass in his hand. "In fact, I think that someone is trying to throw the police off the scent!"

Reilly abruptly looked up from his drink.

"What do you mean? Do you know something, Neil?"

Latimer put his glass down, and then loosened his tie.

"Two weeks ago, James Pollock did a paper, as part of the PhD. He knows that two things fascinate me. An interest in the occult, which of course you and I share."

Reilly agreed. Most of their conversations during these past two years had centred on the very disparate issues of Irish politics and the relationship of the occult to both their respective fields.

"And…" Latimer continued. "The 1689 campaign in Ireland. Before the big guns arrived and it all went pear shaped for the Jacobites. Pollock was convinced that he'd found a connection."

"Between what?" Reilly asked, puzzled.

"The 1689 campaign, when the whole thing kicked off, hinged on two things: the siege of Londonderry and the actions in Fermanagh, around Enniskillen. This resulted ultimately in a battle at Newtowncairn. The Jacobites lost heavily there. It could be argued that it was the turning point in the whole war."

"I still don't get it, Neil," Reilly replied, swishing the

remaining whiskey in his glass from side to side.

Latimer clasped his hands together, trying to hide his frustration.

"Pollock was convinced that something happened at Newtowncairn," Latimer paused. "Around the time of the battle, something that doomed the Jacobites. He wouldn't tell me all of the details, or about the research he had based the findings on, but he alluded to…"

"What?" Reilly replied, suddenly more interested.

His colleague looked up. "He said that it was something to do with the occult!"

Reilly was visibly shocked. "What did you say to him?"

Latimer continued, his voice quivering a little. "I told him, as a challenge mainly, to prove it to me. It would have made a PhD by itself, for goodness sake. Even if there was no evidence, the fact that the soldiers of the time had been so influenced by their belief in the supernatural… it would have been a revelation."

"Yes," Reilly considered the premise. "From a purely anthropological perspective, it would have had a dramatic bearing on how we view the history of Irish culture."

"Exactly," Latimer gesticulated. "It would have turned everything on its head, absolutely no question. So I told him: prove it! I told him to go down there." Latimer paused.

"So, what did he find?"

"That's just it. I don't know," Latimer muttered. "Three days ago he called me here and told me to be ready for the discovery of a lifetime. He said he'd be back in Belfast in a few days. He wouldn't give me any more details. He sounded nervous on the phone, though. Well, not nervous."

"Scared?" Reilly suggested.

"Yes!" Latimer agreed. "Scared out of his wits.

"And what tears me up inside, what really eats away at me, is that now he's dead and I'm the stupid bastard that sent him down there in the first place." Latimer snatched the half-full whiskey glass, and drained the contents, setting it down on his desk again with a thud.

CHAPTER TWO

He had been watching the house for a while now. It was dark. The time of year meant that the cover of early evening darkness could be used to his benefit. He rubbed his hands together to ward off the cold. The location had some advantages. Most of the houses in this area of Carrickfergus were part of larger developments, hard to approach, even more difficult to watch from a vehicle and remain inconspicuous. This was perfect, however. The building sat off the main road, down a country lane. It was an old townhouse, part of a terrace of three dwellings. He had pulled the car off the road a few hundred yards from the building, extinguished the lights, and remained hidden from view. Though a muddy track led to the houses, the roadside was gravelled. No tyre-tracks would be left here. That was important. She had told him that would be important. The other houses showed little activity, some light, but no movement. He rubbed his hands again as he waited.

Pollock's girlfriend would be gone for most of the night. If the timing was right, the body would be taken to Belfast. It would take time to get there, sort out the paperwork, identify the body... then they would have to give her time, to comfort her. It would be hours before she would return, and there was work to do, much work.

He had been patient for long enough, waited for half an hour after the lights in the neighbouring houses had gone out. He zipped up the black coverall, tightening the elastic of the hood, and put on the latex gloves. It was important not to leave a trace. She had told him that too. False soles were taped into place on his boots. They could be destroyed later, and the police would have a hell of a time trying to track down the bootprints that he intended to leave in the mud nearer the houses. He got out of the car, closed the door quietly and moved toward the house, treading lightly on any areas of gravel, watching for signs of life from the buildings. Picking the lock and getting in was easy. She had shown him how to do that, shown him so easily. He removed his boots on the rough matt. The military coveralls covered his feet too. The police might find fibres from them, though she had assured him that they would remain untraceable, as the clothing would be destroyed. He remembered her final words to him as he moved toward the living room.

"Find the book!"

CHAPTER THREE

Latimer stared at the outside broadcast van, parked awkwardly in the narrow street beside the university. Typical, he thought. All they care about is the damned story. He had faced rooms full of external examiners and government representatives about to award grant money, with less trepidation than he currently felt for the interview that he was about to face. The fact that the small, inoffensive looking woman to his left seemed to be threatening him with a microphone was bad enough, but the situation was made worse by the presence of the annoying man with the large camera to his right. He prayed that this would go well.

"Yes, thanks Nick. We're here with Professor Neil Latimer, from the Belfast University where this young student worked, and we believe he was actually a postgraduate student of yours, Mr. Latimer?" She pushed the large microphone toward him.

"Yes, Jenny, that's right. James Pollock was a wonderful fellow. It's a real tragedy, this whole episode."

"The police have stated that the incident is related to drugs, that Mr. Pollock himself may have been involved with trafficking. Have you any comment to make on this?"

"Let me say quite emphatically, Jenny… that there was absolutely no way that he would have been involved in that sort of thing… no involvement."

"So you're telling us that he was in fact, in no way connected with crime in the area, and the recent upsurge in drugs related activity at Newtowncairn?"

"I... Of course not... I mean... how could he...? I'm sure you... understand that sort of thing wasn't his style at all!"

"His style, Professor?"

"I mean... obviously. He was a history student."

"But aren't there some students who get involved with this sort of thing professor, even in a small way? And we understand that he spent quite a bit of time down there?"

"No... not... really, I mean yes, some, but..."

Latimer had been flustered from the start. Nerves and the pressure of the whole affair had been agitating him since he had first heard the news. He stared at the camera, not quite knowing what to say, wanting to push the microphone away, wanting to...

"We'll have to leave it there. Over to you, Nick."

Annie Devlin tilted back the driving seat of her two-seater sports car, pulled a cigarette from the pack on the dashboard, and lit it up with the zippo. She inhaled deeply, feeling the buzz from the nicotine as she pushed the control for the electric window. The high pitched ringing tone ruined the morning silence as she stirred, blew smoke from her mouth and lifted the vibrating mobile phone. She glanced at the screen, drawing heavily from the cigarette once more. It was Sean Watt, editor of the Belfast Herald, probably wanting to know exactly where she was and what she was doing. Bloody control freak, she thought as she considered whether to answer the phone or not. The incessant noise of the tone eventually grated on her nerves, and she relented, pressing the answer button with her thumb.

"Sean... Hi."

"Where are you, Annie? Is he there yet? Why haven't you called in?" the voice drawled in her ear.

Sean Watt had been a newspaper professional for thirty years and Annie had been considered one of his young finds. Still in her mid twenties, she displayed the enthusiasm and drive that appealed to Watt; the ability to get to the truth, to uncover the mystery and display the caustic wit that irritated those with something to hide, something that made her shine as a journalist. Sean admired her not only because she had a nose for the truth but also because she always seemed to get the angle on local stories, the viewpoint that made them interesting.

"He hasn't arrived yet, Sean. Gimme a break. I've been sitting here since seven a.m., freezing my ass off. How do you know he's even coming to work today?" she said, taking a long draw on the cigarette and exhaling out the open window, coughing slightly.

"…and such a nice ass too," Watt chuckled.

He changed the subject quickly, aware perhaps of the difficulty of the act which she was about to suggest that he go and perform. He knew that a jibe like that would irritate her, even if she did not take the bait. She was all about being taken seriously by the men at the paper, and Sean Watt knew how good she was. He jumped in before she could answer.

"Latimer will be there. Just keep an eye out. The TV people interviewed him last night, in the grounds of the university. My contact tells me that he takes a shortcut across the grass every morning. You'll find him. Don't mess this up, Annie. We're running the burglary story tonight. I want Latimer's immediate reaction, word for word. Well, as accurate as it needs to be for the story."

"I'm waiting for another ten minutes. He isn't going to show Sean. I've…" She paused, glancing across the grass to her left.

"Annie? What is it?" Watt queried.

She could see the definite stride of a man who was late for something, hurrying across the grounds, wearing slacks, a tweed jacket, overweight, almost bald, definitely a lecturer type. It was Latimer all right, she was sure of it.

"I see him. I'll get back to you."

Annie stubbed the cigarette out in the ashtray and opened the car door, reaching for the button on the phone, hearing the dwindling shouts of Watt at the other end as she shut him off and kicked the door closed.

Blowing smoke from the side of her mouth, she pushed the phone into the back pocket of her jeans, and reached into her handbag for her tape recorder and press ID.

Latimer was late again. The TV interview experience he had undergone the previous evening, regarding his reaction to James Pollock's death, had left him emotionally drained. He had arrived home late and had drunk considerable amounts of red wine, with little sleep. Prior to the interview he had talked at length with Jenny Hendron, a local TV reporter of some renown. She had seemed friendly, even flirtatious, and Latimer had begun to think that she fancied him! He had that effect on women, he reminded himself as he strode through the wet grass. It had not taken him long however, to realise that he had in fact been duped, lulled into a false sense of security. She had given him scant time to answer her pointed and biased questions, no doubt forming an image in the viewers' minds of a bumbling eccentric and barmy Professor, with little control over the apparent drugs warlord in his class, that he had considered simply a 'student'. The build-up had taken hours, the interview seconds, though he was sure that the opinions of the viewers would reflect only on the facts that the newsroom wanted to convey, not necessarily the truth that he had wanted to tell. He cursed as his shoes slid on the mud that had been generated by the recent rain.

He would have run across the damp lawns, were it not for the fact that he was sure he would fall on his arse. He still felt a little tipsy after the wine of the previous evening.

Annie Devlin slid over the low wall and ran awkwardly in her heels toward the figure of the suited lecturer as he strode across the grass. Christ, she thought as she felt the heels of her boots sink with each step in the muck, wrong footwear! She reminded herself that she was usually better prepared than this.

"Doctor Latimer," she shouted, wincing as mud spattered

onto her shoes and jeans.

Latimer turned toward the tall redhead approaching him. He stopped to consider. The boots she was wearing made the already tall woman even taller, while the tight jeans emphasised her long, shapely legs. He liked that. Her auburn hair was a little unkempt, yet cascaded rather attractively about her shoulders. Latimer was singularly unimpressed, however, by the rough black leather jacket that completed the ensemble. The handbag looked particularly out of place. He hoped that she did not see him looking her up and down as she approached.

"Actually it's Professor," he smiled. "But I'll forgive you this time."

He did not recognise her.

"Are you a student of mine, young lady? You have me at a disadvantage. I don't seem to remember you, though I'm sure that I should have." He winked, noticing for the first time that she had both ears pierced – one ear several times, in fact. Was she one of these 'goths' or 'rockers' or something that he had heard so much about but never actually met?

She wanted to cast her eyes to the heavens in disgust, wanted to at least have a go at him for his 'young lady' remark, but she concentrated and found a friendly smile instead. Best not to annoy him before the interview, she thought, instinctively tucking a strand of hair behind her ear and reaching into the bag.

"My name's Annie Devlin, Doc... Professor Latimer," she corrected. "I'm with the Belfast Herald. I'd like to ask you a few questions about James Pollock?"

She thrust a small laminated press identity card forward with one hand, and switched the small recorder on with the other, her handbag swinging on her arm.

Latimer gritted his teeth, and stifled a curse.

"Miss Devlin, is it? I think you should have watched the television last night. There is very little more that I can tell you." He had neither the time nor the inclination to make a fool of himself again, not after the last interview. Latimer glanced at his watch. "Now if you'll excuse me."

He felt in no condition to tackle another journalist, and began to walk on, reaching the cobbles at the university entrance. He heard the strides of the woman keeping pace with him. Dear God, could she not just leave him alone?

"Yes, you said that Pollock was a student of yours. Did you know that his girlfriend's house was burgled soon after his murder?" she shouted.

Latimer stopped dead.

She caught up, moving around in front of him, bringing the recorder up.

"Why do you think that happened? The police say that it was a coincidence. What do you think? Was he involved in something in Newtowncairn? Do you think there was a drugs connection?"

Latimer turned. "Drugs?" he queried. His eyes narrowed as he looked at her.

"Yes, Professor, the police say the whole thing could be drugs related. Do you have a comment to make?" She thrust the tape recorder into his face.

Latimer recoiled and stepped back, before wincing ruefully.

"Miss Devlin. Call me Neil." He glanced at his watch again. "No. I don't think it had anything to do with drugs, and I'm sure that the burglary is wholly unrelated. James was not involved with that sort of thing. I'm sure of that. Now if you'll excuse me."

He attempted to walk away once more.

"What are your thoughts then, Prof... Neil. Why do you think he was killed?"

"I really have no idea," Latimer sighed as he reached the entrance of the academic building and mounted the stone steps.

"Thank you Mr Latimer. I'll give you a call perhaps," she called as he disappeared through the entrance, waving his hand in the air without turning around. She pulled the mobile from her pocket and dialled Watt's number. The tone rang once.

"Annie? What happened? What'd he say? Come on girl, let's hear it?" His voice rattling off questions incessantly.

"Oh he knows something, Sean. His reaction when I told him about the burglary gave it away. And by the smell of him he's been on the 'sauce', so he couldn't hide his emotions very well. He knows what Pollock was up to and he knows it's connected. You still think its drugs?" she said, staring back at her car.

"Oh yes, I do. This sounds good, girl. I can see the headline now, 'University Professor in County Fermanagh Drugs Scandal'. You just need to keep on him. Now get back here. I need the burglary story and Latimer's reaction in tonight's edition. Just think how good the follow up story's going to be."

Devlin put the phone back in her pocket, her heels clicking on the cobbles as she followed the path, this time toward the car. She tried not to think about how frustrated she was with her job. The last opportunity for promotion had gone to a male journalist at the paper and she knew that she was better. She would have made Head of News, but it went to someone older but certainly not as good. Sean had told her that he could not lose her from the field; she had to be out there getting the stories, getting to the truth. It was in her blood and was what she was best at. He told her that she would not want to be stuck behind a desk all day. She had believed his crap, sucked it all up, but she still could not accept it. Maybe this time. Maybe this story would make all the difference.

Something was troubling her about all this, but she would keep talking to Latimer. He had let too much show to avoid her attention now. She smiled, and fumbled for her keys.

Latimer's legs felt like jelly as he climbed the stairs. He avoided the lecture theatre and headed to the next floor, straight for his office. He threw down his briefcase and phoned John Moore.

"John. It's Neil. Listen, you were right, I do need some time off. I'm sorry. I shouldn't have come in for this lecture. Could someone take it for me? I know I'm late, but I think the young man's death is playing on my mind. Yes. Yes… I'm seeing the poor lad's girlfriend tomorrow; if you don't mind covering? I'll stay here then, do some paperwork. Thanks again."

Latimer replaced the handset, and then lifted it again and called Joseph Reilly, his face flushed with a combination of anger and embarrassment.

As he hung up, his mind wandered. He closed his eyes, trying to visualise Pollock, as he had sat in the lecture theatre. God, he thought. Why couldn't he remember what he looked like? He needed a context perhaps. That was it, wasn't it? He closed his eyes, trying to recall, and the past came back to him…

Latimer stood at the front of the room; students tiered in rows in front of him. It was a first year class, the start of a new term. He considered the young men and women for a moment, wondering who was paying attention, whether any minds were wandering. He would find out, in his usual way.

"So. Ladies and Gentlemen," he boomed.

"We've looked at the causes of the war in 1689. What we haven't looked at are the 'what ifs', the factors that could have changed events, led them along other paths at any stage. I'm sure that one of you can enlighten me on a few of these."

He scanned the class. Hands remained stiffly down as thirty students strove desperately to avoid eye contact with him, afraid that they might be made a victim. He hated himself for doing it. They were students after all, not teenagers in a fourth year geography class. They were studying for their degree. Yet, when he felt that they were not listening, he had little option but to test the water.

"Anyone… no? Oh come on now! Haven't you all been doing extra reading? Oh, I am disappointed," he announced sarcastically, surveying the sea of averted gazes.

Latimer turned once more to the slide on the large screen, and opened his mouth to speak.

"Hamilton!"

The cry came from the back of the class as Latimer spun on his heel.

"What? What was that?" he said.

A limp arm waved from the upper row of seats. A skinny youngster who did not look old enough to be at university, clad in a black biker's jacket, unkempt hair tousled roughly on a head that seemed a little too big for his scrawny shoulders.

"Hamilton," he repeated.

Latimer cocked his head to one side.

"Ham-il-ton," the Professor intoned slowly for effect, sizing up the candidate who had volunteered. And his answer had shown that at least he was on the right track.

"What about Hamilton? Tell me more Mr…?"

"Pollock, James Pollock," the youth replied, his voice holding a little more confidence now. He cleared his throat.

"Hamilton could have changed everything!"

Latimer's eyes widened. He mentally stamped on his urge to show the body language that would indicate that Pollock might even be on the right lines with his supposition. He motioned for the student to continue. The boy seemed nervous, and then he took a deep breath.

"We… we dismiss the potential opportunity now. But despite William's newfound position as King of England, he had little interest in fighting a protracted Irish war and he wanted an easy way out of the situation. His capture and subsequent dispatch of Richard Hamilton to Ireland to attempt talks with Tyrconnell could have created a very different situation here, though no less bloody of course, though the traditions and history that we accept today would have been very different. The sources suggest that both parties had wanted peace talks of some kind. One could argue that it was Hamilton that convinced Tyrconnell to continue, despite the odds against success, that it was Hamilton who created a bloodier legacy than even he could ever have contemplated..."

Latimer was amazed as he watched the young man speak, betraying a confidence now that belied his years. He found himself nodding, not in agreement necessarily, but with an awareness of the solid foundations of the points that Pollock was making.

"...the Hamilton brothers themselves are influential in so many ways. After this point we see Richard Hamilton involved in the disaster at Derry, Anthony Hamilton's notoriety at Newtowncairn. It would... it would create a PhD by itself... I think!"

By now the rest of the class had turned toward Pollock, whose complexion had slowly turned a deepening shade of crimson. He cleared his throat and looked down at his notes...

Reilly pushed open the door into the all too familiar territory of Latimer's office. Latimer jumped, almost toppling from the chair, the memories of Pollock vanishing.

He looked sheepishly from the clutter of his desk.

"Joseph... I was miles away. Sorry. Quickly... sit down," Latimer pointed to the chair moving a pointed finger from side to side while moving piles of paper about the desk.

"What's happened?" Joseph asked. "You sounded manic on the phone. I've got about ten minutes before a class."

Latimer was still red faced, almost frantic.

"I was accosted this morning by a young journalist from the Belfast Herald. She told me that Pollock's death is being linked to drugs."

Reilly seemed surprised.

"Well, we've already discussed and dismissed that scenario, haven't we?" he asked, his face framing the question, in case he had missed something obvious.

"Yes. Yes of course. But she also told me that his girlfriend's house was burgled after the murder!" Latimer said, running his hand across his balding head.

Now Reilly was intrigued.

"You don't think there's something to the drugs story, do you?"

"No I don't!" Latimer exclaimed loudly. Reilly recoiled visibly, taken aback by the aggressive reply.

"I'm sorry, Joseph. I'm sorry. Really." Latimer composed himself.

"Listen. Yesterday, after we'd talked about Newtowncairn, I went through my mail."

He produced a package from the desk drawer; the brown wrapping was crumpled at the corners, and thick.

"I received this. The postmark says Enniskillen, posted the day before Pollock's murder!"

Latimer proffered the package to the now intrigued Reilly.

"Look inside!"

Reilly poked a hand inside the thick manila bag, pulling out a decaying leather-bound book and sheets of printed documents.

"What is this, Neil?" He looked puzzled. The book was ancient and smelt of damp, with delicate yellowed pages. The loose notes were more modern, typed or printed with handwritten sections, faced with a letter signed by James Pollock.

Latimer pointed a wavering finger toward the notes.

"Read the letter."

Reilly, still entirely puzzled with this new development, reached into his jacket for his reading glasses before placing the crumpled letter on the desk in front of him.

> Dear Professor Latimer,
> Firstly let me apologise for my brief phone call a few nights ago. I have no wish for you to become alarmed on my account, though I must at this time confide in you with regard to my findings here. I have enclosed what I believe to be the authentic journal of General Justin McCarthy – Lord Mountcashel, from the 1689 campaign in Newtowncairn. I am aware that you must

think this is a fake, since all primary source material from the period is well catalogued and researched (most notably by yourself). I however believe the document to be real!

You must have many questions. Let me try to answer them:

I have posted this item to you since I'd like to get work started on translation as soon as possible and I have too many loose ends to tie up here. I believe that the journal will answer your queries in this regard. As to where I obtained it, I will tell you of this when we are speaking over coffee! (I like to keep a few surprises to myself).

The connection that I spoke of on the phone would appear to be centred on a cult that emerged in this area around the start of the seventeenth century. Mountcashel, who it seems was a bit of a historian himself, alludes frequently to this in his journal. He has, however, written all of the more interesting prose in 'code', which as we know was a frequent feature of much of the material written by the French and Irish at the time of the war.

I believe that I have broken his code, however, and have sent my findings in the accompanying notes, since I do not have time to pursue the translation of the entire journal here. I ask only that you strive to do what you can with this matter in the next few days, and I shall meet you in Belfast soon.

The amazing part of the story is that the locals here still believe in Mountcashel's findings and, of course, the cult. Many of them are truly afraid. If only I could find a little more evidence we'd have a bestseller on our hands! Someone is scaring the local population, and I aim to find out why. There really are some people down here that you should meet.

I have therefore decided to gather the rest of my material tonight and tomorrow, and then make my

way home. Perhaps you'd like to make a return trip with me next week. There is much work to be done.
Sincerely,
James

Reilly removed his glasses, aghast. He stared at the journal in his other hand.

"Oh my God!" he stumbled, opening it. The pages threatened to fall apart, though writing was legible within, words in English, French and oddly sequenced numbers with large inked dots in between.

"Do you think his death has something to do with this?" Reilly shivered.

"I don't know what the hell to think. It sounds mad, totally mad. But like I've said, Pollock knew his stuff. He knew what he was doing. He had absolutely no interest in the occult, however. Truly, none! If anything, he was a complete sceptic. I think he continued to investigate in order to answer the obvious questions that he knew I would have."

There was silence, as if the two men were slowly deliberating, trying to focus their thoughts.

"Perhaps I should give it to the police?" Latimer said at last. He nodded, as if he had just solved a complex problem.

"Wait a minute," Reilly replied rapidly. "Shouldn't you at least look through the thing?"

Latimer regarded his friend, considering his words.

"You're right of course, Joseph. This doesn't prove anything," he fumed in frustration. "The police have already decided what to think. I can't seriously believe they're going to accept any of this as anything more than circumstantial."

He pointed at the book.

"Besides, I'm not giving that away until I've read it."

"I agree, Neil. It could be connected to his death. You… we… should at least explore all the avenues here," Reilly said.

Latimer smiled. "Thanks for the offer of help, old friend. But I'm not sure that you want to get involved with this one.

This is all my fault."

"All the more reason why I should be involved," Reilly replied. "You're starting to blame yourself already. You can't handle this alone. You're too involved, Neil. Let me help. For the young lad's sake at least."

"I suppose you're right," Latimer replied. "I was hoping you would say something like that anyway. I'd be grateful for your input."

"The police will treat this as insignificant, and it'll lie in some Constable's desk drawer for six months. Besides, can you imagine their reaction when we tell them that Pollock's death had something to do with the occult? They'll laugh us out of the station."

Reilly frowned, all too aware of the truth of what his colleague was saying.

Latimer continued. "I'm going to take two days to try to translate the thing, then we'll decide what to do. Agreed?"

"I think that's a good idea," Reilly replied. "You need to look through it, Neil. For your own peace of mind at least," he said, looking back at the book on the desk. He got up to leave, finding it difficult to look away from it.

"Yes, I have that feeling too," Latimer said.

"What do you mean?"

"That there's some sort of clue in there." He tapped the leather cover with his index finger.

Latimer smiled, as Reilly considered the ramifications if he was right.

"Joseph, one more thing, we'll need to speak to his girlfriend, and of course the funeral will be soon." He paused. "And, if I do find something in here, are you interested in going down there next week? I'm not even sure it's a good idea myself... but..." He sighed, and rubbed his jaw.

"I think it's something that I have to do."

Reilly paused at the door. "You couldn't keep me away," he said, leaving the office.

Latimer switched on his computer and opened the notes. It was going to be a long night.

A VERY IRISH CURSE

Lord Mountcashel's Journal, 24th July 1689, County Fermanagh

I have left Dublin with three regiments of foot, some twelve hundred and fifty two men, a regiment of three hundred and fifty dragoons and four cannon, though I am in need of ammunition. Indeed, my men are all, I fear, very poorly supplied and I expect reinforcement. In Enniskillen, the rebellion of Protestants remains unchecked. They even support the besieged at Derry. His majesty King James has talked of sending eight thousand men to curb these rebels in Enniskillen. Though where are these men to be found? The siege at Derry starves us of troops to aid my plans in County Fermanagh, while the rebels cause fear amongst our outlying garrisons. The King has asked that I scour the countryside and enlist those Irishmen that are loyal to us, though what have I to offer them but sticks to fight with? Their knowledge of war and even the most simplistic drill is limited. He promises reinforcement from Sarsfield and Mylord Berwick, though on this matter I remain despondent. Sarsfield I rate, though he has already tasted defeat at the hands of the Enniskillen men and is in a poor position to support my efforts. As for Berwick, bastard son of the King that he may be, I have little faith in his ability to support me. I fear that I will have to fight my own battles with the few competent troops that remain to me.

Stranger still as I pass into Fermanagh, is the climate of fear amongst the populace. Not even amidst the worst depredations of my time spent with the French army have I witnessed such fear in the eyes of the people. But it is not us that they are afraid of. They speak of angels of death following our column and dreams that they have had of my defeat in battle, and that all of this has been foretold. We have our own superstitious folk in Munster, but for these people, fear of the unknown is tangible and I suspect that those who I have pressed into service will fare poorly under my command in the battles that will surely follow.

26th July 1689, North of Belturbet Village

I have marched north from Belturbet and Sutherland's positions there. He has already been driven back by attacks from the rebels, who remain strong. Despite my dispatches to Berwick and Sarsfield, I have received no guarantee that they will support me. Berwick has driven toward Enniskillen with his contingent and fought the rebels at Cornegrade, though I believe now that he is pulling back to Derry. As for Sarsfield, despite his best efforts it will be many days before he can reach me, though I must act now. If the reports of my scouts are to be believed, the men of Enniskillen have received arms and powder from the English landed at Derry. I can not afford to wait for their army to gain confidence and the potential of better arms and officers.

These damned winds blow each night, howling in the darkness. The rain remains incessant, soaking everything: powder, provisions and men. If the rebels attack us now, there is little hope that we can defend ourselves, let alone win a great victory for the King. In the darkness, I wonder at our chances now, and as to why I have so readily agreed to lead this first strike at the heartland of the rebels who dare defy the authority of James. Anthony Hamilton reminds me that the weather in the north of Ireland is ever this way, even during these normally hot summer months. Yet still, a wind, rising at night, blows away men's tents as it chills their bones, and seems uncharacteristic and alien to this land.

27th July 1689, nr. Wattlebridge

Many of the men have become sick during the night. They show signs of fever and can not keep food in their bellies. There is talk of a decrepit old woman, a local, who has visited the camp in the night and has been poisoning the water. Many of the men refuse to drink from the barrels and have formed foraging parties. I have attempted to maintain discipline through hanging some potential deserters, though it seems that many of the less experienced troops fear this place more than they fear me.

Anthony Hamilton is convinced that he has found ancient burial mounds during his scouting missions, around the area of Newtowncairn, citing a story told by his grandfather about the place as proof that all is not well here. I have little time for such talk, though the men listen to him as if their lives were threatened by goblins and pixies and not the Enniskilleners who will soon arrive to support Crom Castle.

I attack the castle tomorrow. The success of this venture will decide what further action I may take 'gainst the rebels. Despite Hamilton's tales of *Newtowncairn*, I will form my army there if all does not go well at Crom. It is an easily defended position if Hamilton's sketch map is to be believed, and I have little fear of 'witchery' or superstition, unlike the majority of my troops.

28th July 1689, Townland of Crom
Hamilton places great credence in these tales that he and his kin tell. That long ago, his ancestors lived here, in this hellish place. That they had dealings with demonic forces and their ilk. Even as I write of these blasphemies, I find myself unable to believe the superstitions that the men cling to. I find, however, that many of them, especially those that I have recruited in Fermanagh, recite stories of those times. I had thought at first that their yarns were used to frighten children, but have since found, upon walking through our camp at night, that it is the men who fear the lands through which we now walk. These concerns, combined with the already fearsome reputation of the Enniskilleners, lend this place a haunted aspect. The very soil seems cold despite the time of year. I think now of how I once laughed at Hamilton's tales and stories, of how I saw them as some scheme of his that would grant any cowardice some form of credence. Even if I still doubt, it is clear that most of the men do not.

We have but one chance to strike back at these rebels who defy the authority of King James. Though they believe, like so many others in the north, that persecution of their religion will ultimately follow. That is a matter for those in power. For my part, I am but a soldier. I will obey orders. Even in France, I did things and carried out tasks that I had no relish for: the sacking of towns, the burning of churches. I questioned nothing. With King James, though, there are inevitable differences with the French; there is at least a chance to secure the isle before Dutch William comes. And that depends upon our attempt to put an end to the resistance at Enniskillen.

We begin the attack on Crom Castle.

30th July 1689, Newtowncairn
I have moved my positions from the well defended walls at Crom. Although scarcely impregnable, I do not have enough men or guns to take

the place. I have deployed my troops outside the town of Newtowncairn. An empty shell now that the residents have fled with news of our approach. The presence of my small army brings life to it. No cattle, no sheep, or any other livestock exists here. Even the very ground seems barren, as if nothing dare grow. It is a strange place, made remarkable only by the presence of ancient stone monuments and aged oak trees. Hamilton tells me again of the cairns of which he has spoken before. He seems quieter now. I pray that he is still able to command, for I will have need of his dragoons.

31st July 1689, Newtowncairn
Two of my men were found dead this morning. I have seen the results left by enemy scouts before, but this is not the work of the rebels. The men that were killed were seasoned soldiers, though I can tell this only since they wear the uniforms of my regiment. I can no longer recognise their features since they no longer have their heads, and some of their limbs are missing. What manner of man would carry out these atrocities? In all my time spent fighting for the French I have never seen such acts. That they have been supposedly carried out in the name of war does little to excuse this kind of devil's work. Mutterings around the camp suggest witchery. I still can not believe in such superstition, yet the very air in this place suggests death, decay and evil. Though I have seen much in my years as a soldier, never did I believe that Ireland held such dread. I fear for my men, and the success of our mission…

A rider has arrived. Hamilton is defeated at Lisnaskea. Ambushed at the river north of the village, and having had many men captured, he has retreated through the mists to Newtowncairn. I must look to my position here and have ordered an ambush north of the village, in the hope of dividing the approaching forces so that I might deliver cavalry charges to them when they lack formation and discipline. Even now, the mists swirl and reform as if alive, as if the very air itself is about to enact some terrible retribution. My fears play upon me. Hamilton's stories toy with my mind. I must be about my task here. There is little time for fanciful tales.

CHAPTER FOUR

Barbara Reilly sipped at her hot tea and walked slowly from the kitchen, carrying a mug for her husband.

"So why do you have to go on another trip?" she asked, innocently, yet in a tone that suggested she already knew the answer she would receive, as she entered the spacious, finely decorated living room.

Joseph put down the magazine article he had been reading. "It's Latimer. Look, darling, I think he's unhappy about this whole thing with his student. He feels, I don't know, somehow responsible for it all," Reilly said, trying to justify the journey that he knew he would ultimately have to make with Latimer. He had to try to make his wife understand how important this all was.

"But wasn't the young man involved in drugs or something?" she replied, handing the mug to her husband. "I'm sure I've heard that on the news."

Reilly raised his eyes. "I don't think so, dear. I'm sure that's just media gossip. Latimer thinks that they're trying to hide the truth, that there's too much remaining unexplained."

Barbara nodded, settling on what was really bothering her as she moved beside her husband on the sofa, reaching for the TV remote and reducing the volume.

"How long will you be away for this time?" she said. Her tone was cold, distinct, holding little comfort for Reilly's continued words. For the last six years her husband had spent time at various universities across Europe, always for long periods, always with little contact. At first she had forced herself to ignore it, to remember that his work meant everything, tried to remember their time as students together as a way of comforting herself. Lately, however, a sense of isolation from her husband had begun to gnaw at her. His long periods away from home had begun to erode her sense of being part of a happy, contented marriage. She had sometimes thought the worst, come to the conclusion that many wives would, that her husband has been having an affair, despite the best advice of her friends that it was unlikely.

"Oh not long dear... I... I'll only be gone for a few days."

"You're not having an affair are you, Joseph?" she looked at him accusingly, nursing the cup of tea in her hands, trying to remain calm.

"What?" He raised his voice as the words came. "Barbara, for God's sake, of course not!"

"Well, what am I supposed to think? You're travelling all the time. You told me when you got this job that the trips would stop, that we could start a family. I'm nearly forty, and nothing has changed in the last five years. It's like Europe all over again! You're away doing God knows what, for months on end. What the hell am I supposed to think?" Her voice was raised. As she finished, however, she began to sob, looking away from him.

Reilly moved toward his wife and placed an affectionate arm around her.

"Barbara, please, don't be like this," he purred. "Look, I promise, this time is the last. This is just a favour for Neil, nothing more. It's not as if I'm leaving the country, now is it? I told you. My travels across Europe for research work are completed. I don't need to do that any more."

He paused, turning her face to his, looking into her eyes.

"As soon as this is over, we'll talk about starting a family. I can't say any more than that now, can I? I promise you, I am not having an affair." He smiled, almost willing her to forgive, to let it all go.

"Oh, you haven't got a bloody clue, have you?" Barbara screamed, droplets of hot tea flying from her mug as she stormed from the room.

Reilly had to admit that he had neglected his wife over the years, even taken her for granted, but it was so that he could excel in his career and his research, and thus provide for her. He had always promised himself that children would come later. They had agreed. Hadn't they? He prayed that he had not left matters too late. The years he had spent in Europe and the Far East, as he worked and researched into his field. Had they all been wasted? He mused silently as he stared at the tea that had spilled on the table. The work had to have been worth something. He knew that. He would leave her for a while. Talking now would make things worse.

The phone rang, its distinctive clamour disturbing the silence and his thoughts, making him sit bolt upright. As he moved toward the hall, he heard the sobs of his wife upstairs. He looked toward the landing, then back at the phone.

"Hello."

"Joseph, it's Neil. Is this a bad time? How's Barbara?" Latimer said, sensing the catch in Reilly's voice.

"Good, she's well," he lied, glancing toward the stairs. "What's wrong?"

Latimer paused, before continuing. "I've spoken to Lisa Fleming," Latimer said. He sounded excited.

"Who?" Reilly replied, now confused.

"Pollock's girlfriend. She lives in Carrickfergus. I said I'd call this evening. Could you pick me up at the library?"

"Well, I…" He hesitated.

"I've got other news," Latimer interrupted. "About the journal! I can't tell you over the phone."

Reilly's face hardened. He turned and stared out the window. It was dark, and the rain had gradually become much heavier.

"I'll meet you in one hour," he said.

"Great, I'll be there. See you."

Reilly replaced the phone in its cradle.

He gave a fleeting look up the stairs, opened his mouth as if to speak, then changed his mind and lifted his coat and car keys.

Barbara Reilly watched as her husband's car left the driveway and began to make its way down the road, lights blurred by the water cascading down the bedroom window. She stifled a cry, biting her lower lip. She felt new tears begin to well in her eyes as she sat down slowly on the bed.

Rain bounced off the pavements of the street facing the university library. Illuminated by the yellow glow coming from the building, the puddles reflected patches of streetlight and the stride of passing students. Latimer was waiting at the entrance, chatting with the security man about football, when Reilly's car pulled up. He placed his brown leather satchel above his head and raced through the rain for the sanctuary of the car, the tails of his raincoat flapping in the wind. He preferred to travel with Reilly than to drive himself. Reilly had a penchant for expensive four-wheel-drive diesel guzzling jeeps! Latimer felt embarrassed whenever he was driving and had to pick up his colleague in his one litre, compact runabout. Of course, Reilly never said much, but watching the large framed, lanky anthropologist squeeze awkwardly into the tiny seat was enough to convince the smaller Latimer that he should either change his car or insist that Reilly do the driving.

A sodden Latimer bounced up into the passenger seat, water dripping onto the vehicle's interior as Reilly winced.

"Hi Joseph. Love the car... or should I say truck. Is it new?"

"Yes, I'm trying it out with a view to buying," Reilly said, glancing in his rear view mirror for a chance to pull out.

His colleague looked around the interior, and peeked over the dashboard. "It's like a bloody tank! You hoping to travel cross country soon?" Latimer sniggered.

Reilly smiled ruefully, ignoring the jibe. "Where are we going exactly?"

"Carrickfergus," Latimer replied. "Along the coast."

"Yes, I've been there." Reilly pulled out, nestling the

large vehicle into the Belfast streets, joining a lane of cars, the rhythm of the noisy windscreen wipers punctuating the darkness. It was the rush hour and, as usual, drivers were impatient. Reilly ignored the blaring car horns as he eased through the night traffic.

"Yes, I have directions anyway," Latimer quipped, fumbling awkwardly in his coat pocket. "I'm sure I'll find them."

He scanned around the car once more.

"You can look down on everyone from up here!" he announced.

Reilly laughed quietly. "For God's sake, Neil. Stop being a bloody peasant. It's just a car."

Both men laughed.

Reilly broke the inevitable silence that followed.

"What about the journal?"

"Ah, yes!" Latimer said excitedly, grateful that one of them had finally stumbled toward the point of the evening.

"Yes, I've been translating it. You wouldn't believe some of the stuff in here. Our Lord Mountcashel wasn't just a Jacobite general; he knew a lot more about the area than anyone has ever hinted at."

"What are you talking about, Neil?" Reilly queried.

"I've translated about ten percent, random passages, sections that look interesting, if you know what I mean." Latimer began to pull notes from the satchel.

"Listen to this," he said as he fumbled with the pages, flicking on a slim torch.

"I have established my defensive positions within the town, and will attempt to create disorder within the enemy's ranks with my ambuscade. Anthony Hamilton has gone ahead with a troop of dragoons in a bid to force the enemy to scatter. I now fear that his doubts surrounding these mysterious cairns may be true, and many of my men now fear for their lives."

"What does that mean?" Reilly said, looking in his mirror and moving into another lane.

"I have no idea, Joseph. Hamilton was one of the

Jacobite officers, later became a writer in France. I find it difficult to find another reference to the cairns issue though. It literally takes hours to translate this stuff. If only Pollock had sent me raw translation instead of a way to break the numeric code. The point is that the passage I've just read matches up with other accounts; at least in terms of the activities before the main battle, but I've never heard of these 'cairns' mentioned before. That's what makes it fascinating. Facts that I already am aware of, to some degree, are being intermingled with something new. If it's a fake, someone has gone to a lot of trouble."

Latimer rummaged through the notes.

"What about the French and English passages? Aren't they relevant?" Reilly asked, as his colleague tried to make sense of the mess of paper and notes in the poor light.

"They're relevant, but tell me very little that I don't already know. They seem to be Mountcashel's record of the events of the battle and movement of troops. They corroborate most of the existing primary material. Don't get me wrong; they're a fascinating find. But Mountcashel appears to have translated French into a numeric code at the bottom of each page. That tells a different story. It's almost as if there's an official version, and then he's coded what actually happened. It takes an age to translate. But that's not all," Latimer muttered, looking toward Reilly.

"What else have you found?"

"I was fascinated by the idea of these 'cairns', obviously linked to the name of the town, Newtowncairn, so I did a little digging."

"And…?" said Reilly, glancing back at the road. "Don't keep me in suspense."

"There is no record of Newtowncairn in the plantation surveys of Ireland, though that's explainable." Latimer paused. "What's really intriguing," he continued. "What is altogether strange, is that every record of the place, prior to the boundary documents of 1826, was destroyed in a mysterious fire in the late seventeen hundreds."

"That could be a coincidence, Neil!"

"Of course it could," Latimer said, nodding his head. "Even stranger, though, is the fact that there is no mention of a 'cairn', nor even an ancient burial mound of any sort, related to the area, not on any map, nineteenth or twentieth century. I've cross checked with the Public Record Office." Latimer paused, as if to let the information sink in.

He continued more slowly. "There is also no mention of this on the Internet. No record in ordnance survey memoirs. No reference on the nineteenth century maps. In my experience, there should be something, a local legend, a street name, a hill. Even the misplaced rantings of the local village expert who thinks that he is an armchair historian would have been nice. Here, there's nothing. It's as if Mountcashel's journal is alluding to something that history has tried to erase!" Latimer sighed, clearly exasperated by the fact that he had found so little.

"You've done your homework, Neil," Reilly replied, nudging the car into another lane as it met the motorway, heading north.

"But do you really think someone has consciously tried to erase this data? It would take years, generations of people. I know that some of these villages are remote, but you're reading too much into it."

Latimer raised his hand to his chin. "You think that a person, even a family, could be responsible for this? I hadn't even considered that, Joseph. I had convinced myself that something else was to blame, some incident perhaps. That the locals had not seen it as important, or that the stories simply hadn't been recorded properly."

"Perhaps we're both jumping to conclusions, Neil. We're seeing something that isn't even there. For God's sake, I'm becoming as paranoid as you are."

Both men laughed as the car sped through the traffic in the rain.

Annie Devlin had little trouble keeping up with the large vehicle. It could be seen from quite a distance. Latimer obviously was not concerned about remaining inconspicuous. She changed gear, keeping one car between herself and the jeep as she sped along the road. Whatever these two were up to, there had to be something bigger behind all this. She nudged the accelerator with her foot.

Mountcashel's Journal, 2nd August 1689, Enniskillen

The battle has gone ill for my fledgling force of loyal Irishmen. I had not reckoned on the cunning of the English officers, so recently arrived at Derry, and now in the company of the rebels. My plans are finished and I am now held prisoner in the town of Enniskillen.

My wounds make it difficult to write, though I have been fairly treated by the Enniskillen rebels. Consumed with rage at the rout of my men, and angered by the actions of Hamilton, I charged the troops that had seized my cannon. My officers tell me that a man of my rank should not die for a petty reason such as re-taking a position that has already been lost. It is an action that I now regret, though still I find the attempt difficult to explain, as I was seized by grief, doubt and ill conceived stratagem. I am sure that the feelings of dread that pervade my thoughts and dreams now are brought about by feverish reaction to my wounds.

My dreams remain troubled, tainted perhaps by the stories told by my soldiers regarding the events around that terrible village on the eve of battle, of strange portents in the sky, and of the old woman who plagued their sleep the night before we fought. They burned the place, for fear of what lay there at night, haunting their thoughts; and now, it seems, she troubles even me, for my nights are filled with dread figures of lore and the dark and bloody practices of what can only be the blackest sorcery. I have heard of such deviltry in France, though scarce believed that such acts would trouble my sleep in my own land. If I interpret these 'nightmares' correctly (for that is what they truly are), she calls to me and offers me my freedom. She speaks of a price. I fear that it may be too terrible to pay...

CHAPTER FIVE

Sergeant Michael McGrath gunned the police car into the gravel driveway. The morning fog obscured the house from the entrance, though the patchwork lines of the old building began to take shape as he slowed, parking in front of the door. Thirty years he thought, thirty years in the Police Service and he was still a Sergeant in Enniskillen. He sometimes wondered if it had all been worth it. And now they had given him the ancillary duties in the biggest murder case of the year. He had been through a lot. He had made it through the troubles in Northern Ireland. Even now, the lightness of the term made him angry. The world saw the wholesale acts of terrorism as 'troubles', because that was what the world's media called them. It was like calling the Second World War a nuisance. In reality, it had been a conflict between two sides of a divided community, whose hatred for each other still lingered on. And now he had the peace to contend with, a peace that, to his mind, tried far too hard to forget the past, and the friends that he had lost. So, it seemed he was something of an anomaly in the new Northern Ireland Police Service, an old timer who would not go away, who still thought that the job was worth doing his way. He knew that his face did not fit any more, but he would be damned if he would go quietly. So, they give him the dregs, the cases that no one wanted to waste their time with, the assignments that should have gone to more junior members of the force, the babysitting jobs for new recruits, the follow up questions on important cases. Never the real police work. It made him bitter, more bitter than he thought that he could ever become in the job. But he would not, could not, give up. Too many people had died for him to go quietly. *"CID is short staffed, though we'll handle the suspects, McGrath, you question this list of people. The slightest detail could make a difference."* He had almost heard the Inspector laugh as he handed him the names. What the hell was this old woman going to know, for God's sake? He glanced over at the young Constable in the passenger seat, still gung-ho and enthusiastic. Officially, the new guy should have been driving while the experienced Sergeant observed, but McGrath was having none of that. He hit the brakes and skidded slightly in the gravel.

"You stay here, Laverty. I won't be long." McGrath turned off the engine, opening the armoured car door with a creak, the surrounding fog-drenched silence seeming to make the noise even louder.

The fresh faced youth stared back at him, still a little overawed with his first week in the force. Laverty was in his early twenties, young and naïve. But most of all, he had absolutely no idea how to deal with the cynical, sarcastic, overbearing and overweight figure that was McGrath. He also had a distinctly Fermanagh style border accent, which under any other circumstances might have been considered lilting and musical. McGrath hated it.

"Keep me up to date on the radio, remember the call signs and if anything happens…" he said, staring intently at Laverty. "For God's sake don't shoot anybody!"

Laverty quickly moved his hand away from the sidearm holstered at his waist, smiling nervously. McGrath scratched the thinning hair on his head and put on his hat. He left the car, zipping up his jacket against the cold morning air.

The house was large and old. The once clean plaster of the walls was now an ugly, dirty white, cracked in some places, covered in dark pockmarks in others. The gardens had not been maintained, yet there was patchy grass and no plants to tend. Large clumps of weeds made up for the gaps in the ragged lawns. The house needed a makeover, McGrath decided. It should be the subject of one of the shows on TV, he thought, as his boots crunched on the loose stones.

The driveway was untended and covered in gravel. Dismal weeds poked their heads out here too, though even these looked doomed to expire in the freezing cold of the winter morning. The sharp construction of dreary looking bay windows jutted out from the ancient architecture, standing like impregnable towers in the cold silence. As McGrath stood on the first step, mortar crumbled beneath his boot. Twin pedestals on either side of the entrance, riddled with decay and watermarks, formed an archway as he strode toward the door.

McGrath could hear the distant tone of the doorbell inside the house. It took three rings before the oak door began to slowly open.

The decrepit creature that stood there was the last person he had expected to see. The bald, spectacled man was emaciated, thin and sallow. He must have been in his seventies or eighties, dressed in a dark suit, with a shirt collar and necktie that surrounded rather than clung to the folds of wrinkled flesh around his scrawny neck. His mottled hand trembled as he pulled open the heavy oak door.

McGrath looked past him into the entrance as the smell of mould wafted from the dark hall beyond. He wanted to gag.

The man looked at him through large, round lensed glasses, which made McGrath think of a mad professor from some old horror movie. Under other circumstances, he might have laughed.

"Hello Sir. I'm here to speak to…" He quickly pulled the sheaf of papers from his breast pocket, searching frantically for the underlined name, "… Miss Sorcha Ballantine. Might I be able to see her?"

The creature's head began to wobble a little, as if his brain was taking its time to decide what to do next.

McGrath waited for a response.

"Wait here." The voice sounded like the noise made when standing on broken glass. McGrath watched as the man hobbled across the hall toward a dark, open doorway.

"Miss Ballantine," he rasped. "Police. Police are here."

The croak of the feeble voice grated on his nerves. McGrath was at least thankful that it was not dark. Pull yourself together, man, he thought.

He heard a voice from a nearby room, a woman's tone to it, and then she appeared. McGrath had to say he was impressed. The woman was in her fifties perhaps, but she had plainly looked after herself! Her hair was greying and short, though it had a sheen to it. She wore a thick, multi-coloured sweater, presumably to keep warm in such a large old house, and a pair of comfortable jeans, which still managed to betray her shape to the now more interested sergeant.

"Oh hello." Her voice was like silk. The accent was not local, McGrath thought. It sounded English, though with a lilt of Irish brogue. This woman had obviously travelled.

"Constable, come in, come in!" she continued in the same bubbly tone, beckoning him into the hall. McGrath barely noticed the damp musty odour of the house that he had sworn he had smelt while standing at the door, as he stared into the woman's eyes. He was considerably happier now that he had left the younger man in the car. He took off his hat as he entered.

"Miss Ballantine, is it?"

"Yes indeed, Constable." She extended a hand, a broad smile brightening her face, betraying a few wrinkles.

"I..." he stumbled, not taking his eyes off her.

"Don't tell me, Constable. You were expecting someone older. A little old woman in a zimmer frame, half blind and unable to leave the living room?"

"It's Sergeant McGrath, actually... and yes," he laughed, shaking her hand firmly. "That's pretty much what I was expecting, ma'am!"

"My secret is out," she replied. "Well, Sergeant, I can only say that a brisk jog in the morning, lots of red wine and a life spent painting watercolours has added extra zest to my life." She leaned closer to him. He could smell the aroma of her perfume. "I'm not a great one for gardening, as you can see," she joked, motioning outside.

"But where are my manners? Forgive me." She closed the front door, as McGrath shuffled nervously about the hall.

"Hamilton, some tea in the study please," she said, raising her voice slightly. McGrath could hear the old man walking slowly across creaking timbers somewhere.

"Let's adjourn to the study, shall we? You can tell me what you're here for."

McGrath followed her into the adjoining room. It was spacious and filled with musty books lying on stained oak shelves. Everything was well ordered, however, and that lingering smell that he had thought was there seemed to have disappeared. The room was, despite the obvious signs of work, well laid out and spacious, with a décor that appealed to him. He was impressed. He really had not expected the place to be so... clean, after what he had seen outside. It was filled with antique, almost rotten, books, though these bore the only signs of anything truly old in the room.

"Are these all yours, ma'am?"

"Oh, call me Sorcha, Sergeant. Oh, you're probably noticing my accent, not Irish and with such an Irish name. I changed it, you see, when I came here from England, many years ago now. Sorcha is Irish for Sarah, my... old name, but of course you know that."

McGrath smiled politely.

"The books. Yes, I inherited the books from my Grandmother. She was quite a historian. Travelled across Europe. I've never had much time for reading myself."

McGrath noticed the easel in the centre of the room, with paints, artist's paraphernalia, brushes and cloths scattered across a low table. An old sofa and an armchair completed the scene. Apart from the shelves, the room appeared to have been thoroughly emptied of any other contents, recently redecorated in white and now offered a home to the artistic equipment of Sorcha Ballantine.

He glanced at the work in progress, but could see only pale blues and greens.

"Oh, I've really just started this one," she said, noticing

his interest. "I have some other works I can show you." She fumbled behind the sofa, producing a number of neatly framed paintings.

"These are excellent, ma'am," he said, admiring the quality. They were landscapes. He instinctively tried to look through the large window behind him, noticing that the blinds were partially closed, wanting to ask if the landscapes could be seen from here. "They..." He stopped, remembering why he was here. He handed the paintings back.

"Yes, ma'am... Sorcha. If I could just discuss another matter with you."

"Of course, Sergeant. You didn't come here to see my artwork, now did you? Please have a seat."

McGrath sat into the old armchair, and immediately began to sink into the leather. As his weight fell into the cushion, he began to wonder if the creaking material would ever stop. Eventually he began to settle in the inviting chair, becoming more comfortable.

Sorcha Ballantine sat on the sofa across from him, looking thoughtful as if eager to answer any questions that he could pose.

"Well, Sorcha. I'd like to..."

"Oh here's the tea!" she cried, as Hamilton entered the room, a silver tray held in his wrinkled, claw-like hands.

McGrath realised that he was sweating. He looked at his hand. It was shaking. What the hell was going on here? He felt like a school-kid talking to his teacher. As he looked up, she was pouring the tea. He thought, just for a moment, that he saw something behind her eyes, something dark. Part of him shuddered. The hairs on the back of his neck stood on end. He could see her teeth, and those eyes, blue and wide; he could vanish in them forever. The smile began to diminish. She was scowling. She was becoming...

He looked away toward the window.

"I said, how do you take your tea, Sergeant?"

"White, two sugars," he stammered.

As she poured, McGrath tried to regain his composure.

He removed his hat, setting it on the table.

"Yes, ma'am, thank you," he said. As he took a sip from the expensive china cup he noticed the smell again, decay, mould, rotten turnips? He really could not place it. It must be the old house. He had not noticed it as much when he came in. He remembered something from the doorway, but…

He tried to clear his head, in vain.

"Yes… you'll be aware of the recent murder in Newtowncairn?"

"Yes of course, Sergeant. A really awful thing to happen near the village. It makes me tremble just to think about it." She put her tea down on the table and nodded. "Have you caught anyone yet?"

"No. No we haven't. Really I'm here to ask if you saw or heard anything suspicious in the area in the night in question. It's routine, you understand. We believe the murder occurred about a mile from here"

She paused, drawing in breath. "So close." She put a hand to her throat lifting her eyes to the ceiling.

"I seem to remember the fog that night. A real pea souper!" She smiled again. McGrath smiled with her despite himself, taking another sip from the cup.

She continued. "This will sound strange, Sergeant, but I do remember hearing a tractor that night, around ten."

"That would be the approximate time of the murder, ma'am, yes. Why do you remember the tractor so distinctly?"

"Oh, Sergeant, please, it's Sorcha. I remember it well. I remember thinking that old Tom Wilson had been out very late. I'm sure it was his tractor I heard. He passes close by, in the lane over there," she pointed to the wall, "as he goes to join the main road."

McGrath pulled a silver pen and notebook from his pocket and pressed the button on top. He began to write. "Tom Wilson, you say. He would have travelled along the main road back into the village then?"

"Why yes, Sergeant. I'm sure if anything had happened on the road, he would have seen it. Anything suspicious, I mean." She gently sipped from the cup.

"He lives well off the main road though." She reached a hand forward and placed the cup on the table. "If you like, I can draw a map for you. Old Tom's quite reliable. He may even think that something he's seen is insignificant, though you of course might see a clue. You wouldn't want to miss out on anything, would you now?"

She smiled again. McGrath handed her the pen and notebook, his hands shaking a little. As she took them from him, her hand brushed against his and her touch made him flinch. She hardly seemed to notice, merely took the pen and pad. He watched as she began to draw a simple map on the small page.

"This is the main road. You head back toward the village for about half a mile, then follow this track here."

McGrath nodded and looked at her hands. There was something wrong. Something he had missed.

"Follow the track to here, old Tom's just off to the left." She stopped. "What a lovely pen. Was it a gift?"

"Yes," McGrath continued, "from my ex-wife, many years ago."

"Could I have it, Sergeant?"

He looked at her. That smile again. He felt as though he was walking in a dream.

"Yes. Of course."

"Oh thank you, Sergeant." She pushed the notebook toward him. Her hand… there was something…

"No paint," he said, a tremor in his voice as he said it, as if it was not his place to make such a remark.

"I'm sorry?" Her smile cracked, the voice deepened, as if he had said something wrong.

"There's no paint on your hands." McGrath was in a daze. He felt as though there was something he could just see, on the horizon. Something he should say, but he could not say it.

"No, of course not. I cleaned up a few hours before you came." She stood up and began to clear the cups back onto the tray.

"If you'll excuse me, Sergeant. I do need to get on. Is there anything else?"

"No. No, Sorcha. I think that just about covers everything." He felt a little drunk. He lifted his hat and made toward the doorway.

He could sense her following him. That feeling of dread returned. He moved toward the front door where the decrepit Hamilton appeared to be eagerly awaiting the chance to usher him out, as he pulled open the heavy timber door.

She accompanied him, shadowing his movements.

"Goodbye, Sergeant. And I do hope you catch the terrible person who did this."

He paused, swaying slightly. "Yes ma'am. I'm sure we will." He doffed his hat and made his way down the steps, hearing the door close behind him with a dull thud.

McGrath felt sick as he moved towards the car. He opened the door. "Slide over. You're driving." Laverty nodded and moved across the car as McGrath got in, looking back at the house. It seemed shrouded in mist. It had become much worse during the time that he had been inside.

The younger man started the car. McGrath's head was pounding. Something was wrong. He tried to make the dull throbbing in his head go away and fumbled for his notebook. The map was there. The name was there. He could remember her writing it, could he not? He felt ill.

"You all right, Sarge?" Laverty asked, looking across at him as the car sped down the gravel driveway.

Sorcha Ballantine swept an arm across the table. Cups, saucers and brushes flew onto the floor causing splintering crashes against the timbers and furniture. Hamilton pulled the curtains, darkening the room, lending it the look of a crypt as the white walls became dark. She pulled the thick, black, candle from beneath the table, lighting it with a match. Her breathing became ragged, desperate. Hamilton stood in one corner, motionless, light from the single candle reflected in the round lenses of his thick glasses.

She rolled up the sleeve of her left arm with claw-like fingers, scratching the flesh on the underside, again and again, until it bled watery, dark, ink-like blood. She grasped the pen in her right hand. The arm shook in response to the pressure. The hand became gnarled, tree-like, old. Her face sagged, eyes widening, teeth chattering as she intoned guttural rhythms. She placed her left arm over the candle, lowering it to the flame until it burned and cooked the flesh. Her incantation became louder, rhythmic intonation, repeated over and over and over. Her head shook, her eyes widened, the skin on her face aged and wrinkled. Her bones seemed to suck her very flesh onto their surface. She gripped the pen as the words became louder, more distinct, their power a tangible thing.

"Maybe we should stop, Sarge?" Laverty asked as he glanced across the car. "Is it a migraine?"

McGrath moaned. He was trying not to move to much, trying to make the pain in his head go away.

"No. There's something... something..." he muttered between breaths.

"Sarge?" Laverty was getting worried. They were on the main road now, heading back into the village. Do we head back to Enniskillen? Sarge?"

The smell of burning flesh filled the room as drops of dark blood mixed with the wax at the base of the candle. The visceral chanting had become quieter, more restrained. Her arms had stopped shaking. The sounds became a murmur, then a drop of blood put the candle out, smoke rising in great wafts, and the noise stopped. Hamilton hurried forward as Sorcha Ballantine collapsed in an ugly heap in the chair.

A VERY IRISH CURSE

McGrath sat back in the seat.

"You ok now, Sarge?"

"Yes. I think so." He was sweating, but the pain had gone.

He glanced at the notebook.

"We need to check out a local farmer. Head back toward the village. I'll give you directions."

Laverty pulled over and began to reverse into a nearby farm track.

"Was that lady helpful, Sarge?" he said, innocently.

McGrath glanced across at him, noticing his distinct accent. This time his gaze softened. "Oh yeah. Yes indeed, Laverty. Very helpful, and a charming lady." He glanced forward. "Go through the village and take the next right." He looked at the notes again and began to fumble in his jacket. "Where's my pen?"

Mountcashel's Journal, 3rd August 1689, Enniskillen

My surviving officers tell me that on the day of the battle, Hamilton complained of the wound that he had received at Lisnaskea, before an aspect of dread overtook him at seeing the Enniskillen host. He muttered of ghostly images, demonic features on the officers of the enemy and of his mind being plagued by nightmares, before ordering his dragoons and cavalry to flee the field.

The Enniskillen officers have allowed me to keep my journal and writings. I am thankful for this, since I have found that as time goes on, and I remain in these lands, my memory begins to fail me. I have only my journal to remind me of that which pervaded the minds of my men, and ultimately my own mind. My dreams remain tainted with bouts of euphoria punctuated by hellish nightmare. She is here. Her spirit is here. I am unsure whether my convictions are brought about by the insecurities of my own mind, in turn brought on by my wounded state, or by the power of the strange dreams that threaten to engulf and control me. Yet I feel that still I am at the centre of some devilish stratagem. What she wants, or where my destiny lies, I know not. I know only that I would prefer to face the full weight of rebel cannon, the most impetuous cavalry charge, or the worst wounds that could be inflicted by their musketry, rather than remain at her whim…

CHAPTER SIX

Carrickfergus was cold and wet when Latimer and Reilly arrived, and looked likely to stay that way while they were there. A northerly wind, blowing the hedges and small trees near the houses by the main road, reminded them that they were in the cold depths of an Irish winter. Lisa lived in a relatively quiet neighbourhood, off the main road and along a narrow lane. The terraced houses had been built more than thirty years before in a secluded spot that seemed to have remained untouched by the recent spate of development in the area. In the darkness, with only the lights from the dwellings to guide him to the spot, it reminded Latimer of a scene from a cheap horror movie.

They offered their condolences to the young woman upon being invited into the house. Reilly always had difficulty in such situations, not knowing what to say, concerned at how he should behave. He hated this kind of thing and always felt like he should not be there. Latimer on the other hand, was able to provide a degree of comfort to the poor girl, reminding her of James's sense of humour, his humanity and the fact that although he had died tragically and unexpectedly, he had lived his short life to the full. Reilly had to admit that Latimer brought a sense of ease to the situation, so much so that Lisa now seemed much calmer than had been the case when they had first been invited to sit down in the living room.

The girl's mother, who had opted to stay with her since the burglary, made tea and chatted about James, frequently checking on her daughter to make sure that she was not about to collapse into tears again. Reilly hoped that his presence would not make matters worse.

Noticing a degree of calm, Latimer could not help but investigate matters further.

"I was sorry to hear that your home was broken into recently?" he asked quietly.

Lisa looked up.

"Yes. I wasn't here at the time, but yes. I was staying with a friend in Belfast. It was the night that I had to identify the... identify James. So much has happened at once," she murmured, casting her eyes downwards, tears beginning to form.

Lisa's mother stepped in, putting an affectionate arm around her daughter.

"Perhaps we should go," Reilly said, lifting the cups and saucers and arranging them neatly on a nearby table, as the older woman nodded, smiling apologetically.

"They didn't even take anything," Lisa sobbed, continuing. "They went through James's filing cabinet, emptied the shelves and bookcases, upended the furniture. They left the DVD player and video. Why would they do that?"

She looked at Latimer. "That's why the police think he was involved with drugs? They asked me all about it? If they'd known James the way I... the way we do, Professor, they'd have known that he had nothing to do with all that, wouldn't they?" She looked pleadingly at Latimer, tears streaming down her face.

Latimer bounded from the seat, taking her hand in his. He wanted to tell her what the burglar might have been looking for. He wanted to say how responsible he felt for James's death, that the men who had killed him were merciless fiends capable of anything. But none of that would help. Lisa continued to cry.

Her mother spoke. "They haven't released his remains, Professor Latimer. James had no surviving family. We want to give the poor boy a proper funeral. Why won't they release the body?" In her arms, Lisa began to cry again.

Latimer felt helpless. "I don't know, Ma'am. But I'll do everything that I can to find out." He paused. "And... I won't rest until I've done everything I can to help find whoever did this." He looked at Lisa. "I promise you that." He nudged Reilly. "We should go," he muttered.

"I'll phone tomorrow, if I may. Let you know if I can find out anything from some colleagues at the mortuary. I'm sure that's where he'll be." He stood up to leave. "I'm truly sorry for your loss, Lisa."

The two men made their respectful exit. Latimer was in a morose mood as they left the house, heading toward the main road.

"That was terrible," Reilly said.

Latimer nodded. "It's almost a godsend that he had no family, no surviving relatives anyway. His mother and father died years ago in a car crash, as far as I'm aware. He grew up in foster homes, mostly. It's amazing that he got as far as he did." Latimer punched the dashboard. "That's why it's so bloody unfair!" he yelled.

"Steady, Neil," Reilly exclaimed, "I haven't bought the car yet!"

"Sorry, Joseph," he said, looking across the car and rubbing his bruised fist. "I'm sorry. But did you hear what she said about the break-in? They were looking for this, weren't they?" He pulled the diary from his coat pocket, rubbing his fingers on the delicate cover.

"Well, that puts a completely different slant on things from the point of view of even thinking about bringing the police in, doesn't it?"

Reilly frowned. "Well, I would suspect there's little point to that now, anyway."

"Why?"

"Two reasons. Your fingerprints are all over the damned thing for one, if that makes a difference."

"And the other reason?"

"You've got me intrigued. I'd like to go down there and take a look around, perhaps help with the translation. It could be the find of the century and, as you say, we might even locate some evidence related to the killing."

"Good. Then it's decided. We need to speak to Moore about this though."

"Yes," Reilly agreed. "Though we don't need to tell him about the journal, do we?"

"Absolutely not," said Latimer. "He'd take it off me. I'll sell him on the idea that we want to finish the research, drugged up killers notwithstanding, and that we'd be in little danger after the fact. He'll easily buy the anthropological angle, I'm sure. I can concoct a sound enough rationale from Pollock's notes even. I don't see an issue."

"Agreed," nodded Reilly. "I'll oil the shotgun, just in case."

Latimer flinched in surprise, remembering that one man had died for his efforts already. He found himself unable to argue with Reilly's reasoning though. He would ensure that Pollock's death had not been in vain.

CHAPTER SEVEN

LOCAL STUDENT'S DEATH AND THE DRUGS CONNECTION

Annie Devlin - The Belfast Herald

> Recently murdered student James Pollock, could have been connected to illegal drugs activities in the Fermanagh area, it was alleged by Enniskillen Police Detectives today. Although not proven directly after his death, Police experts are now more convinced that local gangs, operating in the wilds of the Fermanagh countryside, saw an opportunity to be rid of Belfast based 'competition'. Professor Neil Latimer, who was a former teacher of Pollock at Belfast University, admitted to having little idea as to his student's activities in the Newtowncairn area, and would not pass comment on any drugs related issues when pressed...

The phone in Latimer's office was ringing. He thrust through the door carrying a sheaf of notes and a manila file stuffed with assignments. Casting the load onto a nearby revolving chair, he made a lunge for the phone, lifting it in time to see the pile of paperwork fall, cascade like, from the spinning seat onto the floor at the corner of his vision. He winced, and lifted the receiver to his ear.

"Hello."

"Neil. It's Pat, at the Mortuary. You wanted information on the Pollock autopsy?"

"Yes. How are you, old friend?" Latimer hoped that the message he had left on Larkin's answer-phone earlier in the day had not been too 'cold'. He also hoped that he had enough favours left with Larkin to gain some valuable information on the case.

Latimer had known Patrick Larkin since they were at school together, where they had practised pranks on the same teachers, gone out with the same girls, supported the same football teams, yet had gone into completely different professions. Larkin was now an assistant to the county coroner. Not an awe-inspiring position in Latimer's view, though one that benefited from a substantially higher salary than his own; a fact that Larkin was only too keen to remind the tweed jacketed history professor.

"Good, Neil. Good."

"How old is young Jill now? Last time I saw her you were bouncing her on your knee!"

"She's fourteen, Neil!"

"Oh hell. Has it been that long?"

"It's been that long. I've only had about twelve promotions since then. You?"

Latimer sighed.

"I enjoy my job, Pat, and though it involves dead people, like yours, they've been dead a lot longer." He wanted to laugh triumphantly, but found the humour a little too black, even for his tastes.

"You've got me. I'll remember that one when I'm on holiday in Miami this year," Larkin replied.

Latimer sighed in defeat.

"Enough of this. Let's be serious. You know that Pollock was a student of mine? Let's cut to the chase."

"Ok fine. I am, of course, very sorry. You do realise, however, that you owe me for this, don't you? And I will collect." He paused. "Susan's sister is in town next month. Well, I need a favour. Make up a foursome for dinner? You've met Tracy, haven't you?"

"How could I forget her? Does she still go to the loo every five minutes?" Latimer replied.

"Neil, that's not nice!" Larkin pretended to be shocked.

"Ok. I'm sorry. I'll do it; I'll go. Now, let's talk."

"Ok," Larkin continued. "This was a strange one. The pathologist has some very unconventional conclusions."

"Do you mean weird?" replied Latimer, always one for plainly spoken English.

"Ok then, yes. Toxicology report came back with nothing. That's the only… non-weird bit."

"Go on," said Latimer, intrigued.

"His throat was slit. He bled to death after his carotid artery was severed with a sharp instrument, undoubtedly a knife."

Latimer could hear pages being flicked backward and forward on the other side of the phone. Larkin continued.

"The problem in this instance is that with cases like this, if the victim has not been restrained in some way, we normally see signs of a struggle. If he wrestles with his attacker, we usually see bruising on the arms or hands. If the throat is cut while sleeping, we normally see evidence of blood around the hands and fingers as they reach for the wound, attempting to staunch the flow. That's a natural reaction of course, and there were no signs of restraint to prevent such a reaction – in this case."

As Larkin spoke, chanting the bloody details in a sermon like manner, Latimer bit his lower lip, imagining Pollock struggling in his death throes, sprays of dark red blood spilling across his clothing. He could almost sense how he must have felt as his life ebbed away.

"Neil, are you still there?" Larkin's voice shouted.

"Yes. Go on."

"Well. In this case, there was nothing."

"Nothing?" His voice betrayed his emotion.

"There were no signs of restraint, no sign of a struggle, no attempts at movement after the throat was cut, and no evidence of poison or anaesthetic. It's as if he just sat there and watched as someone cut his throat, then did nothing, just remained still and bled to death. Even a suicide doesn't follow this pattern. The body's natural response is to react."

"And this isn't normal?" Latimer queried.

"Well, you're the Professor, my friend? How the hell does it sound to you?"

"No, you're right, quite strange."

Larkin continued. "Look. I have to go. You didn't hear this from me of course. Wasn't the young chap involved in drugs?"

Latimer sighed. "No Pat, he wasn't."

"You'd be surprised, Neil. You never know. Well, look, I'm sorry about all this. Terrible I know." He paused. "But you're free for next month then, yes?"

Latimer sighed again. "Yes. I'm available. Thanks for your help, Pat. But there's one other thing."

"All right, go ahead."

"Yes. You haven't released the body yet?" He had almost forgotten to ask.

"No. I don't quite understand that myself. I believe it has something to do with the pathologist's findings, related to the lack of a struggle, I mean. I'm sure they're looking at the toxicology report again. You know, to make sure they haven't missed anything. To make sure he wasn't drugged prior to the slaying."

Latimer rubbed his chin. "And you can't tell me when the body will be released then? I need to inform the poor fellow's girlfriend. Do what you can for me, Pat."

"I'll see what I can do, Neil, but obviously, I can't promise anything at this stage." Latimer listened to the pause at the other end. "Look, I have to go."

"Thanks, Pat. Thanks again."

Latimer put the phone down.

Dr. Joseph Reilly slipped into the lecture theatre just as his colleague was finishing. About twenty attentive students took notes, or pointed to a classmate's findings in their hastily scrawled handwriting or on the screens of their laptops, all seemingly fixated with the lecturer's booming tone and the giant scribbled points that lit up the wall, courtesy of the overhead projector. He wished that his own students could be so rapt in his lecture notes. Latimer did have a way of grabbing his student's attention. Reilly did wish, however, that his colleague would bite the bullet and get to grips with modern technology and use a laptop and projector for his presentations. Latimer was one of the dying breed of academics at the university who still used the overhead projector. He would use the 'I can remember when we had nothing but a blackboard' speech on him every time that he brought it up. Reilly was convinced that it must have taken Latimer twenty years to get used to a projector in the first place. That would have given him some hope, were it not for the fact that the University I.T. Department despised Latimer, and the feeling was entirely mutual.

"And so, ladies and gentlemen, in summary," he thundered, "Was the so called Glorious Revolution truly glorious? Or, did the events of 1688 simply spell the end of James II's naïve dream that he could hope to change the attitudes of his countrymen in the face of the apparent renewed threat from France? Matters of religion, political expediency and the threat of war would coalesce to galvanise European attitudes against Louis's power in France. As to how matters would be decided in Ireland, we will adjourn… until next time."

A cacophony of noise shattered the stillness as the students began to rise from their seats, putting books away and even, to Reilly's amazement, discussing the points that Latimer had raised, with apparent enthusiasm.

His voice boomed again. "Remember, ladies and gentlemen. Assignments are due next week. No exceptions!" The students smiled dutifully and Reilly waved as Latimer noticed him in the high-rise upper seating of the lecture theatre.

As the throng of young people cleared, Latimer began to take the stairs, two at a time, before slumping down beside Reilly, who produced a plastic cup filled with black coffee.

"You read my mind," Latimer replied, his voice hoarse. He took an obnoxiously loud slurp from the cup.

"You said you had some more information?" Reilly asked.

"Yes," Latimer said, taking another sip from the hot coffee. "Firstly, we're meeting John Moore in ten minutes for a presentation."

"What?" Reilly exclaimed. Latimer chuckled hoarsely at his normally emotionless colleague's reaction.

"Yes. I forgot to tell you." He drank as Reilly's mouth opened and closed slowly.

"I've made no preparations. I… Moore will see right through me," he said gruffly, as his mouth began to dry.

"Don't worry, chum. I'll do most of the work. Just chip in when you feel an anthropological point coming on," he said, beaming. "I have a few slides that I want to show Moore, related to Pollock's research, and some points from the journal. I knew if I'd warned you, you'd have got all flustered and done too much. It would have thrown Moore off the point. I want to grab his interest quickly and get a decision." Latimer glanced at Reilly. "Don't get me wrong, Joseph. I'm not saying that you're boring or anything."

Reilly shook his head and laughed. "Well thank you, Mr. Diplomatic!" He took a sip from his own cup. "A decision?" he queried.

Latimer nodded.

"Related to what?" Reilly asked.

"I'm asking for a week for us to pursue and complete Pollock's research. It will be difficult to convince him, no question, especially so close to the murder. That's why I need to hit him with Pollock's PhD notes." He looked particularly smug. Reilly had seen the look before, when he was not being told the whole story.

"But Pollock didn't send you any…" He looked across at the now beaming Latimer. "What have you done, Neil?"

Latimer pointed to the main points on the slide, made

large on the white wall of Moore's office.

"And so, John, to sum up. The tragedy of James Pollock's death is in what he left us. Again, if I go over the main points of what he sent me in his last research notes, you'll see that he cross-referenced a number of primary source locations with regard to the battlefield. He has gained some local knowledge and folklore, and basically determined not only the battlefield's location but also gained quite an insight into the character of our man, Lord Mountcashel. Pollock's work points to the circumstances surrounding his defeat, the location of the Jacobite rout and details of what essentially became the turning point of the war!"

John Moore glanced at the slide, with text outlined in succinct points. He rubbed his jaw. "And you say that Pollock posted this to you, before he died?"

Latimer brandished a sheaf of typed manuscript. "Yes, postmarked the day before." He shut off the projector and hit the light switch. "This stuff is fresh, John. We need to finish it. This period hasn't seen anything new in years, but it isn't all there yet. We need a week, maybe two, and it will be complete."

"Can it be published?" Moore asked, aware of the nature of grant aid that universities competed for. New, sound research could make all the difference. But on the back of a student's death? It was a concern.

Latimer looked flustered. "Of course!"

Moore exhaled sharply. "Then why shouldn't I send someone else down there. You're a little… close to this, aren't you, Neil?"

Latimer's face changed. He looked like someone had just driven a steamroller over his favourite puppy while he sat and watched!

"No one else can do this, John. I've worked with Pollock on all of his research. I…"

"Exactly," Moore interrupted.

Latimer paused, before taking a sharp breath and continuing as if the words were trapped and had to escape.

"John. We both know that Pollock was special. He would have ended up with both our jobs in time. His death, I believe, is wholly related to an incident where he's pissed off some local punk. It's tragic and unnecessary but it's happened. In light of that, let me do one thing."

Moore sat back. "What's that?"

"Let me finish his research and publish it. Publish it under his name, John. It's the least that I can do, and it would make me feel better about the whole situation. You can't send someone else down there to do that."

Moore stood still, his face betraying neither emotion nor agreement.

Latimer continued, sensing that the decision he sought might just be in sight. "Also," he paused. "He has no family. The only way his name will live on is in the work that he did down there. Are you going to take that away from him?"

Moore winced and shook his head. "You've got me again, Latimer!" He scratched the back of his neck. "Ok. Do it. But two things…"

Latimer beamed excitedly. "Yes?" he said.

"One," Moore continued. "You take no unnecessary risks down there, you hear me? It may have been a random incident with some drunken druglord, but that doesn't mean that the same thing won't happen to you, and then the University Chancellor will have my balls!"

Latimer laughed. "Agreed."

"And two…" Moore screwed up his face and shook his head, glancing at Reilly who had begun to snooze slightly on a chair in the corner. "Explain to me again why Joseph has to go with you?"

Latimer and Reilly exchanged glances.

Reilly jumped in quickly. "From an anthropological standpoint, the findings are impressive… potentially," he said, trying to find the words as Latimer did not seem to have any for once.

"Look, John, let me be honest with you," he announced, standing. Latimer was perturbed, desperate that Reilly should

A VERY IRISH CURSE

not say too much and get them both in trouble.

"We believe that what Pollock found here is strongly based on oral tradition, not recorded histories. I believe he has uncovered something that may be the last bastion of oral history in Western Europe, which can answer some of the questions that Neil has been asking about this period for the last thirty years. From an anthropological standpoint, it could be groundbreaking. In this day and age of the world-wide-web and a shrinking globe, key questions can still be answered through the literal truth, handed down from generation to generation."

Moore responded with a twisted smile. "Bullshit!" he said.

Reilly opened his mouth, closed it again, and sat down, his face reddening rapidly.

Moore got off the desk that he had been leaning on. "You two want to go down there to investigate Pollock's murder. Let's cut the crap from here on in, yes?"

Latimer lifted his arms, admitting with a gesture that Moore had seen right through him.

"As usual, John, I can't fool you. Yes. I'll admit that's part of it. But he has found something here. You have to admit that."

"I agree, there's work to be done here, but that's not your key reason for going, is it?"

Latimer stared at the floor.

"All right, you can go."

"Sorry?" Latimer and Reilly both spoke at the same time.

"I said all right," Moore repeated. "You can both go down there and finish the research."

"But I don't understand?" Latimer said, confused.

"Well," Moore continued. "You've been honest with me... eventually, I'll give you that," he said, trying not to focus on the still embarrassed Reilly.

"I am more concerned, however, with this," he said, moving toward the desk and lifting a newspaper, rapping a bony finger at the front page.

He tossed the copy of the *Belfast Herald* to Latimer.

"Page two," he continued. "I guess we should count ourselves lucky that there's trouble in the Middle East. We didn't make the front page."

Latimer opened the paper, now intrigued.

He froze, and then began to read aloud.

"Local student's death and the drugs connection!" he said. He looked at Moore. "What the hell is this?"

"That's tonight's edition, my friend. Some local journalist said she spoke to you and you had no idea about Pollock's activities down there. What they're implying, of course, is that since you allegedly knew nothing about his research, he could conceivably have been involved in something dodgy or, worse still, you knew about it from the start and are lying. Either way, we are in trouble," he said, his words framed to place emphasis on the collective responsibility that would lie with the university.

"Needless to say, the Vice Chancellor is breathing down my neck about this, wanting answers. What you've told me today will help, but if you could find the truth, and I was confident that you wouldn't get yourselves killed in the process... Well, you can see where I'm coming from, right?" Moore paused, before sitting down behind the desk.

"That bitch!" Latimer said, biting his lower lip, and handing the paper to Reilly.

"That bitch!" he repeated. "I never said anything of the sort. In fact, I denied everything and walked away"

"That's how they work, Neil," Moore countered. "She's turned a denial into an admission, or the fact that you must be hiding something. Best to say nothing in these circumstances. Was she young and attractive by any chance?"

"Well, yes. But I don't see how..."

Moore put a hand up to silence him.

"Spare me," he said. "I think I can see where it all went to hell." Reilly could not help but laugh. When both men looked at him angrily, he changed the subject.

"So... So you want us to go down there, John?" he asked.

"Yes, and there's one more proviso," Moore replied. "I'm informing the local police that you'll be carrying out research based on Pollock's findings. Yes, they'll no doubt figure me for a fool, try to convince me that there was no actual research, but I'll ask them to assign a liaison officer to you both."

Latimer screwed up his face, as if in agony. "What?" he whined in a high pitched voice. "You're kidding, John?"

Moore shook his head. "No. And I absolutely will not move on this. Though you two probably need some sense knocked into you, I'd really prefer to see you back here intact in a week or so.

"Good day, gentlemen. Let me know when your preparations are complete."

Moore strode toward the door and held it open while Latimer and Reilly made a quiet exit.

Mountcashel's Journal, 14th August 1689, Enniskillen

Mr Connor, who tends to the King himself, together with his surgeon Mr. Hubert, have been sent with wine, provisions and money. As I am held here under terms, the Enniskilleners have acquiesced to these visits and have permitted me to write to both the King and those outside parties who might encourage my release. I am treated well, though I am to be used as a pawn it would seem, destined, they hope, to be exchanged for some prisoner held in France.

Despite my wounds, movement is becoming easier. I have been allowed to walk around the rebel town, talk with their leaders. I fear that my negotiations for release, however, will fare poorly.

I have written to Richard Nagle, the Irish Attorney General and a man I have known since my time in England. I have it made clear to him that both he and King James must endeavour to secure my release from Enniskillen. I can not tarry here while the war continues. It has been made apparent in communication with Monsieur D'Avaux, the French Ambassador, a man of some honour, that should the circumstances and agreed restrictions of my parole prevent me from fighting in the war here, I will be granted command of Irish troops in France. Still then, with God's grace, I can serve our cause to some degree. Monsieur D'Avaux even intimates that this would somehow be preferred. In the deep recesses of my mind, however, I remember the dreams, the compulsion to travel far from here in order to carry out her demands. How is that possible, I ask myself? How could she reach this far, control my very destiny? The very thought is intriguing in some measure. Yet still, it troubles me in the night.

12th September 1689, Enniskillen
I believe that I am enslaved by the blackest sorcery. During daylight I have found myself walking, not of my own volition, but at the behest of some demonic visage that resides in my dreams. She blackens my mind like some devilish wine that muddies the blood and clouds all judgement as I stumble as if in a drunken stupor. Perceiving my irrational behaviour as a pretence at escape, the Enniskilleners have doubled my guard, and restricted my movements throughout the town. What dark magic is this that speaks to me so? Have I gone mad, that I should converse with the devil in my dreams? Who would have believed that this devil would be a woman, sometimes fair, sometimes a hag though more often than these, a goddess of war and death, whose black crows pluck the eyes from the dead and wounded on the battlefield at Newtowncairn. I had thought my nightmares had been some product of the spirits of my body, seeking recourse from my wounds, though they do not stop as I heal, they become worse. I fear that I may become infirm of mind.

CHAPTER EIGHT

Annie Devlin's red sports car skidded to a halt in the car park of the Carrickfergus church. The building sat in the hills, well outside the town, isolated and quiet, almost perfect for the proceedings that were due to take place. The hushed onlookers had not been expecting the screech of tyres that interrupted the calm of the morning. The ground was wet, but the heavy rain had subsided to a damp drizzle.

Devlin pulled a cigarette from the packet, simultaneously freeing a cheap lighter from her handbag and lighting up. She took a long drag and inhaled deeply. I really will have to give these things up, she thought, clearing her throat and taking another drag. She looked innocently from the car window at the solemn procession entering the church. Latimer was there, and another man. The mobile phone in the passenger seat began to tone menacingly. She looked at the screen. Sean, will you piss off, she thought, throwing the phone across the dashboard and opening the car door.

She got out of the car, pulling the black skirt down toward her knees to avoid embarrassment. Not having worn the skirt and jacket combination in five years, it took her a while to become used to the fact that it had an apparent mind of its own. As she checked her appearance once more, she noted the start of a nasty ladder in her tights. She wanted to swear, and then thought better of it while standing in the car park of a Presbyterian Church, silently giving thanks that she did not have to wear the outfit every day. Her heels clicked sharply on the ground as she strode toward the building, taking another long drag from the cigarette before stubbing it out, and entering.

"I don't bloody well believe it," Latimer whispered to Reilly as he glanced toward the sound of heels at the entrance. "That woman from the Herald is here. Don't look round, don't look round!" he whispered.

Reilly immediately glanced behind him, his eyes resting on the slim attractive redhead who had found a seat at the back of the church and was fidgeting with her handbag. He faced forward again quickly and whispered to Latimer.

"I can see why you got flustered when you were talking to her, you dirty old man."

Latimer looked at him sharply, gritting his teeth. "Shut-up!" he rasped, as Reilly suppressed a smile. Easily done, given the solemnity of the occasion. James Pollock's body had eventually been released and the party of twelve that had gathered would see he had a decent burial. Lisa Fleming's mother, being an Elder in the local church had pulled strings and enabled matters to go smoothly, given the circumstances and the fact that Pollock had not exactly been a churchgoer.

The Minister, a man about Latimer's age, had not known Pollock. In fact, most of the people here, excluding Lisa and her mother, had only known James through the university. Latimer considered that so small a turnout for such a potentially great historian was tragic, yet he sensed that Pollock would have little concern were he watching proceedings from a better place.

The Minister began to speak. Latimer forgave him some hypocrisy. He had not known Pollock, but he knew that this was probably best for Lisa. He had volunteered to say a few words himself after the first hymn.

The hymn was dire, its power softened by the muted weeping of Lisa and her mother. The singing was led mainly by the Minister, whose voice made up for any lack of conviction on the part of the mourners. When it was over, Latimer was called forward. He had no notes – he needed none. He strode purposefully toward the desk beside the small pulpit.

As he looked at the congregation, he glanced at Annie Devlin, who smiled broadly in return and winked. He looked away quickly before she decided to totally destroy his composure by waving.

Latimer cleared his throat.

"I knew James Pollock as one of my history students. As we celebrate his life here today I want you all to know one thing. I'm not going to tell you lies about how fine and upstanding a person he was, simply because he is no longer with us. I will tell you that he was one of the finest students that I ever had the privilege of teaching, because he was. I mean that with all my heart. James showed insights into history which, frankly, scared me."

Latimer paused as a number of the seated students smiled courteously.

"As well as that, I counted James as a friend, and I hope he counted me as one. As we celebrate his accomplishments in his all too short life, I hope that..." Latimer stopped. Reilly looked up, sensing unease in his colleague's normally confident tone.

"I hope that I never let him down in any way. That if something could have been done to prevent his death, he would have let me know, and I could have stopped it, done something."

Latimer was beginning to sweat a little, his words stuttering.

"He... he would have wanted us to celebrate his life, not mourn his death. I hope that the memories he and Lisa shared will help her in the long nights ahead, and I speak for us all here when I say that we will be there for her if she needs any help along the way."

Latimer felt hot, as though he was having a panic attack. As he looked toward the back of the church, he saw Annie Devlin, scribbling furiously in a notepad, recording his every word. That cold hearted bitch, he thought. She's probably writing everything down, jumping to the wrong conclusions, inventing more lies to make headlines.

He felt unsteady on his feet and was beginning to have tunnelled vision.

"J-James, as I say, was a good friend, and I think... I think if we can live the rest of our lives, the way he lived his, we can be proud. Thank you."

A red-faced Latimer returned, stumbling, to his seat.

Reilly leaned over to him. "That went well," he whispered sarcastically, as the minister smiled and returned to his service.

Annie Devlin finished her notes, writing the word 'guilt' in large letters under the final entry.

"What happened there?" Reilly asked as the congregation made their way toward the door.

"I don't know," a flushed and red-faced Latimer explained. "I still feel uneasy about this whole thing."

"You're blaming yourself, Neil," Reilly whispered. "It's eating you up, for God's sake. And what's more, I think that you are condemning yourself for something that you had no control over." Reilly was uncharacteristically forthright, sensing that Latimer needed shaking out of this rut of grief that he was slowly falling into.

Latimer had to agree. "You're right, Joseph." He brightened a little. "Yes, I think you're right. I also think that I can get my head sorted out, so to speak, regarding the whole affair."

Reilly looked suspiciously at him. "What?" he asked, narrowing his eyes.

"Our trip down there. Our expedition, you might call it. We're going to find out who killed Pollock. Aren't we, Joseph?" he said, his face displaying a determined look.

Reilly clapped his friend on the back. "Let's go."

As they reached the door, Latimer saw Annie Devlin. The degree of reserve and calm that he had managed to find seemed to desert him. He quickly moved toward her.

"Oh hello, Professor. I just thought I'd come to the service and pay my..."

"What the hell did you print those lies for?" Latimer shouted accusingly. Mourners looked back as they left the church, raised voices so uncharacteristic at a funeral. The Minister gave Latimer a harsh gaze... and was promptly ignored.

"Now, Neil, let's not create a scene..." she responded defensively, looking around her.

"It's Professor Latimer to you, young lady," he said, grabbing her by the arm. "And why the hell are you taking notes at a church service?"

Devlin looked at him sternly. "Let go of me, Prof. Right now!" She gritted her teeth. Latimer was surprised by her menacing tone and was now a little lost for words.

The congregation raised their heads from hushed conversation, eyes directed toward the source of the fracas. Latimer let go of her arm as a panting Reilly reached them.

"Let's go, Neil. Come on. We have to go to the graveyard; come on!" He began to push Latimer toward the car.

Devlin smiled politely and turned on her heel, walking away.

As Latimer watched her open the door of the red sports car, she threw her bag angrily into the passenger seat. He shook his head. "I wonder what crap she'll print now, Joseph, eh?" His heart pounded in his chest as he breathed heavily.

Reilly put an arm around his shoulder. "Let's just go, Neil," he said, remotely opening the doors to the large four-wheel drive vehicle.

The quiet calm of the church was destroyed by the high pitched revving of the red car as Devlin screeched out of the car park.

"She has no respect. For anything, or anyone." Latimer spat out the words in exasperation.

A. D. GRAHAM

Mountcashel's Journal, 18th November 1689, Dublin

Like thieves in the night they came, men who had once served the cause of Enniskillen. They were transformed, visibly transfixed by some higher power which I fear can only have originated in hell, for I saw no contrivance of heavenly origin about their blank fixed stares. Without a word, they unlocked my room and directed me to follow, pausing at times as if listening to silent commands from some invisible, demonic entity that controlled them from afar. They set me free, unlocking gates and helping me scale walls, before setting me adrift on the waters surrounding the town in a small rowing boat. I made my way ashore where a horse awaited me. Joined by another mysterious rider, who, in similar manner to his companions, made no sound and offered no explanation, I was guided south toward friendly forces. I have since reached Dublin where I have been warmly welcomed by Milord Tyrconnel and Milord D'Avaux, who congratulates me on my momentous escape and promises that the French have certain plans for a commander of my calibre. Only my wife senses the change in me, yet she fears to ask what ails my constitution. I have neither the inclination to explain, nor sufficient explanation to offer, with regard to the unearthly means of my escape. My dreams still haunt me, urging, no, commanding that I journey to France and still farther, in order to fulfil my destiny! Despite my fears and the urgent will to disobey, I am somehow compelled to follow the instructions that must emanate from the nether world of hellish nightmare.

Still, even as I sit in deliberation with Monsieur D'Avaux, speaking at length of how the French would like to see me head the Irish contingent of troops that they have negotiated with James for release as reinforcements for the European war, I think of her. Do the French know what they ask of me? That I may do her bidding? That I would travel to lands across the sea and be closer to the goal that she seeks? I must agree with D'Avaux, that taking these men to France will help our cause. Were I to stay here, I would be shot out of hand if captured again. At least in this way, I can not only attempt to regain some measure of honour for those troops that remain to me after the Newtowncairn debacle, but I can fight under the flags of King Louis and show the Frenchmen that their time and effort here is not wasted. Not some ignoble diversion to use up

A VERY IRISH CURSE

the armies of Dutch William. If honour must be served by my fighting on another country's soil, then so be it. Yet, ever does the shadow of her presence darken my soul, as if no matter what my own, or any other officer's decision, my destiny is already mapped out.

CHAPTER NINE

Sergeant McGrath knocked on Superintendent Cowan's open door politely.

"Come on in, Sergeant," the bald headed senior officer grunted.

"You wanted to see me, Sir?" McGrath carried a sheaf of papers, ready for a day of report writing.

"Yes. How's the investigation going? In relation to this Newtowncairn murder?"

McGrath shuffled nervously. Cowan stared at him. "You've something on your mind, Michael?"

He sighed. "Sir. It would seem that I've been given the less choice suspects to interview. The detectives have to have made up their mind as to what's happened. I'm helping them..." He paused. "I'm helping them fill in the blanks. You could say I'm used to it, sir." He smiled ruefully.

"Close the door, Michael."

McGrath turned around and closed the door, returning to his stance in front of the Cowan's desk.

"Look, your behaviour over the last few years hasn't made things easy for anyone, me included. You say what you think. You're too direct. You might get away with that in some jobs, Michael, but you know that in this 'firm' you keep your bloody nose clean and do what you're told. Why can't you understand that, son?" Cowan said, his voice quivering slightly with the effort of holding back his temper.

McGrath paused, considering the fact that he was around five years younger than Cowan and how inaccurate his use of the word 'son' might be.

"Yes, I understand, sir," he said, staring blankly at the wall behind the desk.

"Good, because, believe it or not, your groundwork has yielded results."

He opened a manila folder and began to fidget with typed reports as McGrath raised an eyebrow and looked down at the desk.

"It would seem that this testimony you got from the farmer in Newtowncairn proved useful. This car he describes seeing speeding through the village, it's been linked to a couple of known dealers from across the border."

He held a report in his hands now, shaking it at McGrath as he looked down.

"You did a good job here. Number one, it proves what we thought, that this whole thing is drugs related. Now why can't you perform like this all the time, without annoying the detectives?"

McGrath sniffed, and cleared his throat.

"Because they're bloody assholes, sir," he said.

Cowan, slightly taken aback, shifted uneasily in his chair, but McGrath had not finished.

"They blunder about like they're something special, yet every Constable in this station knows the job and the locals ten times better than they do. In terms of real police work, we talk to the people out in the street instead of sitting behind a desk. We get things done quicker, know what questions to ask and get a lot more results… in the long run… sir." He could feel his face reddening as he said it, his gaze fixed on the wall behind Cowan's desk. He knew he had said enough.

Cowan began to tremble with anger.

"For God's sake, Michael. Will you shut up. That's exactly what I'm talking about." He sighed again, placing his elbows on the desk.

"Look. Against my better judgement, I'm sure, but I've got another job for you." He raised a single index finger. "And I don't want to hear any bloody whining, right?"

McGrath nodded, all of his remaining effort now focused

into keeping his mouth shut.

"Two university professors are coming down here, to finish the... well, they call it the research, that they believe the murder victim was carrying out. You ask me, they're trying to cover up the fact that one of theirs was involved in a little more than local history, eh?"

McGrath smirked sarcastically. "Yes, Sir."

"Right. Well, I'm assigning you and Laverty as their police liaison. If they get so much as a cold, you'll get the blame. You meet them, greet them, show them the sights, let them do their work, then wave politely as they bugger off home. Clear?"

"Yes, Sir," McGrath replied. Oh no, he thought to himself.

"What is that goddamned racket in the background, Annie?" Sean Watt shouted above the din.

Annie Devlin drove the sports car at eighty-five miles per hour along the outside lane of the M5 motorway toward Belfast, with the earpiece of her mobile stuck into her ear, the phone dangling loosely in the passenger seat.

"Music, Sean. They're called Slayer! What the hell do you want?" she shouted.

She had been angry since the events outside the church. When she got angry, she listened to thrash metal and drove fast. Growing up in a house with four brothers had done little to help Annie relax quietly when in stressful situations.

"It's what?" he shouted in her ear. "Turn it off!"

She reached for the volume knob on the CD player, still fuming.

"That's better. What is Slayer?"

"They're a band, Sean. The CD was left in the car by an old boyfriend. I listen to it when I'm pissed off. Right now, I'm very pissed off!"

"What happened?" he enquired quietly.

Her ears were ringing. She pumped the horn at a driver

in the fast lane who had decided to pull out in front of her and then choose to obey the speed limit.

"I was at the church service. Latimer gave a eulogy. Very nervous he was too. He's involved in all this, perhaps more than we thought. I'm on my way back to the office." She proffered a middle finger as she drove past the offending driver who had pulled away toward a motorway exit.

"Well, you won't believe what I just heard," Watt continued. "I got a call from John Moore, Head of History at the University. He's not happy with your story, and he tells me he's going to prove that the drugs angle is all a fabrication."

"How's he going to do that?" Devlin asked, despairing at how inept male drivers were, her ears still ringing from the music.

"He's sending his two best research professors down there to clear it all up." She could almost hear Watt smirking at the other end of the phone.

"You're kidding, and Latimer's one of them, right?"

"Right."

"Who's the other guy?" she asked.

"An anthropologist, Dr. Reilly," he replied.

"I don't get it. Why did he tell you this?"

"I think he wants us to lay off. Thought he'd play to my better nature. But I get the impression that he doesn't think Latimer is linked in any way. You know better, honey, right? Listen, we can't be there in an official capacity, but you could check out the story while you're down there. It would just be coincidence if they were about at the same time, right?"

"Absolutely. I'll speak to you when I get it in. Oh, and Sean?"

"Yes, Annie."

"Don't call me honey, you fat git!"

She pressed the off button on the phone and sniggered, imagining Watt's red faced frustration at the other end.

She pushed her foot down on the accelerator, gaining rapidly on another unsuspecting motorway victim.

A VERY IRISH CURSE

Mountcashel's Journal, 6th April 1690, Cork

I have dined with my officers and left them in good spirits. Ensign Fitzgerald has displayed his hidden talents through the preparation of Irish beef and potatoes served with the finest French wine.

The recruitment of troops has proceeded more easily than I could ever have conceived of. It would seem, that with the disaster at Newtowncairn, we have created a state of, if not panic, then desperation. Many Irishmen now seem less reluctant to risk their lives in a war fought far from their homes in the hope of winning favour with the French. My colleagues, Arthur Dillon and Lord Clare, have both raised strong regiments. My only hope is that King Louis's officers, who despite their friendship toward me are ever arrogant and haughty, agree with my request that more aid must be sent, and quickly.

We sail from Cork on the morrow. Though I will miss my homeland, I am glad for the men. The rains and squalid conditions of the camp here begin to wear them down. I look forward to the warmer climes and better conditions in France. Excitement pervades the camp.

My wounds have healed quickly. Mr. Connor tells me he is astonished at how rapidly I have recovered, citing either the waters of Enniskillen or God's will in this accomplishment.

Yet still am I troubled in my sleep. Should I have endeavoured to stay in Ireland, to ignore the yearning that I have, to lead these men in France against Dutch William? I would scarce have been a man of honour or an Irishman if I had, yet still I remain disturbed by a distinct feeling of dread.

CHAPTER TEN

Latimer and Reilly were invited to Lisa Fleming's home after the funeral. Understandably, it was a sombre occasion. Reilly noted however, how relaxed and in control Latimer appeared to be under the circumstances. He had a word for every awkward silence, for every pregnant pause, and even more unbelievably, those words brought comfort to those present, quite the reverse of his nervous discourse at the church.

Reilly watched as he comforted Lisa, noting that she reached into her handbag and offered some pieces of paper to Latimer, who thanked her. As Reilly mingled with the quiet company, clutching a cup of tea, he made contact with his colleague once more.

"What was that all about, Neil?" he enquired.

Latimer produced the scraps of notepaper. "We've had very little information regarding young Pollock's movements down there. We know from his letter that he had been based in Enniskillen, so I was asking Lisa if she knew where he'd been staying."

"And?" Reilly asked expectantly.

"She's given me the name of the guesthouse. Pollock had rung her several times from there. She says that she'd volunteered the same information to the police, though I don't know if they've followed it up or not. I suppose we'll find out when we get there and speak to our liaison," Latimer said, smirking sarcastically as he mentioned Moore's requested police presence.

In the hour that followed, Latimer and Reilly mingled less

and less, conscious that they should not overstay their welcome. Eventually, they said their goodbyes, Latimer giving further assurances that he would endeavour to clear up the matter. Reilly sensed that the affair was beginning to drain his normally effervescent colleague more than he would ever admit. The days ahead would be difficult for both of them.

Joseph Reilly sat down, and placed both hands around his ears.

Barbara began to shout once more.

"But why? Why do you have to go down there, Joseph? For Christ sake, haven't you been away enough? You're never here!"

Reilly looked up painfully into his wife's tearstained face, then stood, and opened his arms in a vain attempt to show affection.

"Get away from me," she yelled, marching into the kitchen. Reilly followed.

"Look, Barbara, I've told you. It's work! John Moore wants us both to go. It's not just a favour for Latimer!" he rasped, his voice hoarse from shouting.

"Don't give me that crap, Joseph. You know I won't fall for that!" she resounded, her face red, lip quivering.

Reilly shook his head and looked at the floor.

"I... I have to go, Barbara. It's as simple as that." He stood up and walked away slowly.

She came to the doorway of the kitchen, shouting after him.

"Don't expect me to be here when you get back, Joseph! Do you understand that?"

Reilly grabbed his last bag, ready to bring it downstairs and deposit it into the newly purchased four by four vehicle that hogged the small driveway. A final thought suddenly occurred to him, and he turned. He opened the wardrobe, fumbling in his pocket for his keys.

A gun cabinet had been built into the carcass of the wardrobe, attached to the wall of the house through a hole cut in the back of the panel. With careful precision, he inserted the small key into the lock on the steel door and cautiously turned it, then repeated the same operation with the lock on the lower half. As it creaked open, he pulled a brown leather shotgun bag from the bottom of the wardrobe. The double-barrelled over-and-under sporting shotgun nestled quietly in the rack of welded steel inside the cabinet. He lifted it, and opened the mechanism.

"Why do you need that?" Barbara's voice came from the doorway of the bedroom.

She had silently followed him upstairs. She was still crying, but her features showed less anger and more fear now. Reilly was visibly startled at the sound of her voice.

"Barbara, listen to me. We're going down there to… to find out what happened to this young man Pollock."

He indicated politely to let him continue as she opened her mouth to speak.

"With the knowledge of the police… and their protection, I might add."

"Do they know that you're going to be armed?" She folded her arms defiantly.

"No, they don't!" he continued, closing the breech of the gun. Barbara jumped at the sharp click. He hefted the shotgun, sliding it into the case, and then lifted shells and cleaning material, dropping them into a pouch.

"I meant what I said, Joseph. I meant it."

Reilly concentrated on the gun, before looking back at her. How could he explain that he had little choice, that he had to be there with Latimer?

New tears formed as Barbara stared aghast at her husband, before she finally stormed off downstairs.

Reilly calmly continued, reaching for a list in his back pocket and mentally checking off the items left to pack, seemingly oblivious to the end of his marriage. He could feel his heart pounding in his chest.

Grabbing bags and holdalls with both hands, he moved onto the small landing and down the stairs, opening the door and casting his items into the open boot of the four by four. He reached for his coat, and closed the front door.

Barbara sobbed as she watched the car drive off, before falling onto the sofa in despair.

Neil Latimer lived in a well to do area of Belfast, close to the university. His Malone Road address and property was highly prized, especially amidst the property boom of the post troubles era in Northern Ireland. The house was large, old, and had been in the family for many years, seeing its tenure range from the seat of the Latimer family, through the rise and fall of its business empires, until it provided shelter for the current resident, the enigmatic Professor Latimer. Living in such a large house by himself gave Latimer time to contemplate and collect. Classical music records, toy soldiers and, of course, books, were some of his passions. Even aside from the library itself, nearly every room in the house had its bookcases. Despite the issues with heating, the unruly boiler and the perennial damp problems, the house had a lived in feel, and a distinct history, which meant that Latimer would never sell, no matter how good the patter of the local estate agents.

He, unlike Reilly, was not good at packing, or at making lists of reminders of what to bring. He, therefore, always had a suitcase at the ready, complete with blank journals, toiletries, underwear, and brown cords. One of his trademark tweed jackets was always ready at a moment's notice. In this instance, however, due to the importance of his latest expedition, he had also created a large ringbinder, suitably indexed and divided, in order to help with the translation of the journal. Together with important notes and literary references, he placed these in a battered and weatherworn, brown leather satchel.

Reilly was due in around half an hour. It was early morning as Latimer finished his breakfast. He poured himself a drink from the bottle of Bushmills whiskey that he always seemed to have somewhere nearby and sat in the living room, listening to the ticking of the old grandfather clock in the hall. He quietly contemplated whether he could set the burglar alarm and get out the front door before it went off upon Reilly's eventual arrival. Latimer feared the digital age, the alarm being one of his few concessions to the tide of progress and technology. Along with CDs, mobile phones, iPods and computers, it terrified him!

Knocking back the whiskey, the rattle of loose stones in the driveway and the deep tone of the car horn alerted Latimer to Reilly's arrival. He put the glass on the table, stood up and moved to the control panel. He typed in the code, grabbed suitcase, satchel and coat, and made for the door. Throwing his luggage into the porch, he closed the inner glass door and fumbled in his pocket for his keys. He locked it, hearing the warning tones of the alarm setting itself. Made it, he thought, perspiration glistening on his forehead. This is ridiculous, he considered, no way to leave your own home. He opened the front door and stepped back, aghast.

Reilly had decided that the jeep he had tried previously had been too small, and he had opted for the larger version, which was wider, higher, and much more intimidating on the road.

Latimer looked at the silver metal beast parked on, no... *occupying* his driveway.

"Oh good God," he remarked to the sullen driver who even now operated the electric window and hung out the side. "What the hell is this thing, Joseph?"

"It's the new car, Neil. Get in. Throw your gear in the back."

Latimer laughed at first, and then whistled audibly as he saw the expanse of space available at the rear of the vehicle. He threw suitcase and coat inside, but clutched the satchel to his chest. He climbed into the passenger seat beside Reilly.

"Hey, Joseph!" he said across the expanse of the cabin.

"Can you hear me over there?" he mocked, voice raised,

and then added, "I think you might have some issues? This is all very Freudian."

Having achieved little response from his colleague, Latimer cleared his throat as the car moved noisily on the loose gravel and down the long driveway, the thundering diesel engine sounding like a turbocharged lorry.

Pulling into the main road and heading for the motorway, Latimer broke the silence, correctly interpreting its cause.

"So what does Barbara think?"

Reilly glanced across. "About me going away?"

"I meant about the car, actually. But you've answered my next question." He pursed his lips, wondering how to proceed.

"Is she very annoyed then?"

"Let's not talk about it, Neil," he said, changing gear with a shunt. "Where are we going?" he added, changing the subject.

Latimer winced, and then opened the satchel, shuffling amongst loose papers before pulling out an address.

"Enniskillen. Islandview Hotel."

"I thought it was a guesthouse?" Reilly asked.

"Yes, so did I. But when I checked, it appears to be a small tourist place. Thrives on local and international business in the summer. Can't imagine why Pollock gave Lisa the wrong impression. I suppose she would have believed that it would have been more difficult to reach him if she'd thought it was a guesthouse or something. Perhaps he didn't want to be bothered, keep his mind on research. I don't know."

"I see," Reilly said, puzzled.

They began to leave the city, travelling south along the M1 motorway. They would, after an hour or so of driving, leave the motorway and head southwest toward Enniskillen.

"Have you done any more translation?" Reilly asked.

"Yes, a little," Latimer replied, looking across the busy road into the outskirts of Belfast. "As I said before, there appear to be two stories here. What we know, and what Mountcashel has added."

"It's a good two hour drive, Neil," Reilly said. "I've been

meaning to ask you, and I haven't really had much time. Mountcashel's battle, this whole Newtowncairn campaign: give me some background. It would help me to understand when we go over the ground. Give me an insight into what you'll be thinking."

Latimer placed the satchel at his feet and pressed his hands together. He paused for breath, staring into space as if mentally preparing himself for a lecture.

Reilly laughed. "You're not in the lecture theatre now. Just give me the gist, if that's possible for you."

Latimer, ignoring the jibe, began.

"1688 was something of a pivotal year for the British Isles," he said.

"The Glorious Revolution?" Reilly asked.

"Yes. Though historians have more recently pointed to the fact that there was nothing very glorious about it all. In 1685, James II accepted the throne upon the death of his older brother Charles II, despite the objections of much of the English nobility."

"Because he was a Catholic," Reilly added.

"Yes. But there was more to it than that, of course. Many believed that the English Civil War of the 1640s had started in similar circumstances, when James's father Charles I had started messing about with the religious establishment, and no one in the English hierarchy wanted another war fought over the monarchy and religion. Catholicism had been frowned upon since the reformation; it's pre-eminence in England would mean dangerous alliances with Spain and, more dangerously in the 1680s, Louis XIV's France. Even the Pope was concerned by Louis's expansionist policies."

"So why the concern over Ireland?"

"Ireland had always been seen, or at least perceived of in England, as a backdoor to invasion. It is arguable that policies and practices from Elizabeth, James I and the plantation right through to Cromwell and the question of land, are based on attempts to resolve the internal security issue and propagate a Protestant hegemony in Ireland that would absolve the monarchy of concerns over security. Concerns that stemmed from the then more powerful Spain and France. Sidelining Catholicism was all very well in England, though in Ireland matters were not so successful for the English Kings."

"Well, that seems like a bit of a simplification! Then James II, a devout Catholic, succeeds to the throne, and all hell breaks loose," said Reilly.

"Yes. Though one step at a time, I'm building to something here," Latimer said, smiling.

He continued. "Irish Catholics were composed of native Irish and of course the Old English as they were known, who had come across during the plantations and converted to Catholicism. They had found it difficult to obtain military experience in England, due largely to the Test Acts put in place by Parliament, meaning that Catholics could not officially hold important civil positions."

Latimer paused, gathering his thoughts once more. "During the civil war, two gentlemen, one a native Irish noble from Cork, the other an Old English settler from Cavan, worked closely on the side of those loyal to the crown in Ireland. They had each married sisters of the then Lord Lieutenant, the Duke of Ormonde. Both men managed to escape Cromwell's wrath and left for France with their families. Their names were MacCarthy and Hamilton, and their sons would gain most of their military service in France in the 1670s."

"MacCarthy, the son would become Lord Mountcashel, and Hamilton, Anthony Hamilton would be the other son then," Reilly added, nodding his head.

"Yes," Latimer said. "You've been reading. Good," he added, adopting the tone of a lecturer speaking to a keen student.

"There were other brothers, all with noted military service. George Hamilton, for instance, the eldest son at the time led the young MacCarthy and Hamilton in an Irish brigade in French service, before he was killed at Saverne in 1676. James's accession to the throne in 1685 changed everything for Irishmen with military experience, however."

"Why?" Reilly asked, a little confused.

"Well," Latimer continued. "The Irish were convinced that an English Catholic on the throne would herald a change in their fortunes. This was, of course, helped through the influence of the Earl of Tyrconnel."

"And what effect did he have?"

Latimer opened his mouth to answer and then tried to grip the seat as Reilly swerved to avoid some debris on the road, narrowly avoiding a car passing in the outside lane.

"Sorry, Neil, expensive tyres on this thing. That looked like a tin can or something."

Latimer slowly released his grip.

"I think it was a paper cup, Joseph! Perhaps you should relax a little and not worry about the shiny new car. You almost put me off there."

Reilly smirked. "That seems unlikely. Anyway, you were saying?"

Latimer attempted to regain his composure, keeping a closer eye on the road.

"Yes. Well. The Earl of Tyrconnel. Richard Talbot, as he was known before James raised him to the peerage, had known James since 1656 when they had served on the continent together. He was to have a defining influence on him, especially so as he was also to become the champion of the Irish land question. With apparent Royal sanction, Tyrconnel set about re-modelling the Irish army."

"That must have scared the hell out of the English establishment," Reilly said.

"Indeed it did. And for many reasons," Latimer added. "Within two years of James's accession, Tyrconnel had sacked most of the Protestants from the Irish army. This, of course, caused a number of issues. He had replaced average quality troops with poor quality ones at best. Remember, Catholics had been barred from martial office. Simultaneously, he created a sacked officer corps of resentful Protestants. He had very few good officers with which to control the fledgling Irish army, though amongst the more experienced by this time were MacCarthy and Hamilton."

"What was the reaction in England?"

"Panic, Joseph. Pure panic. Questions were asked. Is this a private army for James? Does this herald a new civil or religious war or an alliance with France? More importantly, perhaps, were the purges in the Irish army simply a model for what would happen to the English troops? As you can imagine, the establishment, noblemen and army officers, got quite excited."

"Excited enough to do something about it," Reilly said.

"Yes. William III, the very Protestant stateholder in Holland, had married James's daughter Mary a few years before and this put William in line to the English throne. She also had been brought up a Protestant. William had had his own troubles with Louis's France and desperately wanted English support. He was invited to do something about the developing situation in England. At the end of 1688, he landed in the south of the country, without a fight, much of the establishment and James's key officers deserting his cause. James, although captured for a time, got away and fled to France. It is thought that William allowed this for the sake of his wife."

"What happened in Ireland?"

"Pressure had been building for months. Protestants lived in fear. A repeat of the atrocities that occurred on both sides during the 1640s rebellion was anticipated. Many Catholics believed that the time had finally come to cast the English out of Ireland. There was little early resistance against Tyrconnel; he held the balance of power. That's politics, I suppose. He was in rather a pickle, however. His friend James had lost his throne and fled to France. William even approached him through Richard Hamilton, a captured Jacobite and Anthony's younger brother, with a view to making a deal, though that fell through and he rejoined his old colleagues."

"Then we have the siege of Derry," Reilly added.

"Yes," Latimer continued. "Londonderry could be defended. It had a wall, and rumours of massacre led the citizens to seal it up. The key here, however, is to remember that the same thing happened in Enniskillen in county Fermanagh."

"It didn't become a siege though. Well, not that I know of?"

"No, it didn't. And that's important. Enniskillen was able to build itself a militia, get supplied, and bring in sheep and cattle, while Tyrconnel's Jacobite army surrounded Londonderry. The Enniskilleners raided Jacobite positions with impunity, bested the Jacobite generals and defended the town through proactive and strategic attacks throughout the countryside."

"Becoming a thorn in the side perhaps?" Reilly asked.

"Indeed. James's arrival in Ireland in May helped to delay a solution to the growing Enniskillen problem. Londonderry was seen as more important due to its coastal position. Enniskillen was contained from afar, rather than being dealt with. James sat in the new Irish Parliament in May, a waste of time, you might think, with resistance in the north, but the land question was important to the Irish. Most came away disappointed. There were no hard and fast answers to the question of Irish land. But by now, there was little choice but to follow James and help him get his throne back in the hope of future concessions – a large foreign army was being assembled by William on the mainland to come across and do some serious damage to Irish hopes and dreams!"

"So MacCarthy and Hamilton are assigned the task of sorting out the Enniskillen problem."

"My. You have been listening," he remarked, impressed. "Yes. It's become more serious by July 1689 than anyone could have guessed. The siege in the north at Londonderry needs to be resolved and Enniskillen, the other main centre of resistance needs to be dealt with. They need to have control of Ireland, including the troublesome northern province of Ulster, before William arrives. MacCarthy is made Lord

Mountcashel, and given a few thousand men to sort the problem out. A strategy is dreamt up, where a three-pronged attack using noted Jacobite General Patrick Sarsfield and James's illegitimate son, the Duke of Berwick, support Mountcashel's attack. It never happens. That poor bastard Mouncashel must have known that he would have a tough fight on his hands, and he went on ahead anyway, on his own."

"He entered Fermanagh with his small army then, unsupported?" Reilly queried.

"Yes. At the end of July, Mountcashel's three regiments with Hamilton's dragoons and cavalry attempted to besiege Crom Castle, near Enniskillen, but were beaten off. By this time, the Enniskilleners were led by experienced English officers who had arrived by ship, and they were absolutely determined not to become besieged. Mountcashel decided to make a fight of it with the approaching Enniskillen force, at a small village called Newtowncairn."

"So how did the battle go?" announced Reilly, growing more interested in the developing discourse.

"Hmm, we may have to wait in suspense for that. Is this a diversion?"

A long line of cars with winking hazard lights was blocking the end of the motorway.

"Oh bugger," exclaimed Reilly.

Latimer had insisted on not continuing with the details of the battle until they were clear of both the traffic jam and the diversions that seemed to have been put in place by a planner whose aim, it appeared, was to confuse drivers who did not originate from the area in question. Having taken what must have been several wrong turns, by following drivers who were not apparently following the same signs that Reilly should have been looking for, he was lost. Eager to keep Reilly entertained, or to keep himself in full lecture mode, Latimer regaled Reilly with tales of everything from miscellaneous nuggets of seventeenth century Irish history through to occult folklore from the various regions. Reilly was not sure whether it was more difficult to find their way back to the road that they should have been on or to stop himself from telling Latimer to shut up.

"I need diesel," he eventually interrupted. "I think I know where we are now anyway. There's a sign for Augher. If we reach it, we go through Clogher and Fivemiletown, and then it's around fifteen miles to Enniskillen, if memory serves."

Latimer's discourse on the various beliefs related to Irish Faeries and their kinfolk trailed off as Reilly drove at speed into the forecourt of a garage on the outskirts of a small village.

"Need any help?" he asked Reilly as he turned off the engine.

"I'll be fine, Neil. Stretch your legs if you need to."

"I'll read some more of these notes," he replied, busying himself with the satchel in his lap.

Latimer watched the view in the wing mirror of the jeep as Reilly went to pay for the fuel. We'll have to remember to put that on expenses, he reasoned as he watched the traffic come in to the garage forecourt. Pollock was never far from his thoughts.

"What were you doing, my boy?" he whispered to himself in the silence.

He gathered the notes in front of him, determined to keep busy, not to fall into the ravages of grief or despondency. No, Pollock would not have wanted that now, would he? He had left a trail to follow. Why else would he have sent Latimer, his old Professor, a book of such importance, with the potential to make such groundbreaking changes in the way history in Ireland was not only taught, but also perceived. There was something here, he thought to himself, clenching his fists, and it was begging to be found. The snippets that he had pieced together did more than excite him. Frankly, some of the passages in Mountcashel's journal scared him. That much, he certainly had not told Reilly yet. Was that the real reason he wanted so desperately to get out of Belfast and make his journey to Enniskillen? In case his fears made him blab the whole damn secret of the journal to Moore, out of his own concerns to do something about Pollock's murder?

"Dammit! I'm going crazy. I'll sort this out, boy. I'll sort this out," he said to himself.

The driver's door opened, startling him.

"What?" said Reilly, taken aback by his obvious reaction.

"Oh. Nothing," replied Latimer. "Miles away."

"Right. I bought you a screwball." Reilly proffered a plastic conical cup filled with ice cream, with a red plastic spoon sticking menacingly from the top.

Latimer gazed at the thing, one eyebrow slowly rising.

His colleague tried not to laugh. "Figured that if you have to eat that, you'll stick to the salient points of the history lesson you were giving me, rather than wander."

Latimer grudgingly accepted the gift.

"Careful," Reilly added. "There's a gobstopper at the bottom. It will take ages to chew."

"You, Mr. Reilly," Latimer said, carefully choosing his words. "You are devious, aren't you?"

Reilly feigned surprise, and started the engine.

The long road stretched out before the two men, now silent, in a motor vehicle that seemed a little too big for them. Latimer raised the map.

"Ok, there are a string of three towns before we hit Enniskillen. So that was Augher. Clogher and Fivemiletown to go, and we are almost there."

Latimer broke wind.

"That will teach you to buy me dodgy ice cream," he retorted.

"I suppose I can only beg you to tell me the rest of the story now, rather than face the full impact of your chemical warfare," Reilly replied sarcastically.

"Right!" Latimer shuffled in the seat, his hands held up, priming his mind for the big finish.

"So, where were we? The Battle of Newtowncairn? You were about to tell me how it went for Mountcashel."

Latimer glanced across at him. "Not well. You have to remember that the effects of Tyrconnel's purges were still felt across the Irish Jacobite Army, despite the best efforts of men like Hamilton and MacCarthy, or Lord Mountcashel as he was by then. The Enniskilleners on the other hand, had considerable experience, relatively speaking, from militia training and their own raiding of the outlying positions of the Jacobites. They were being well led, and most of all, they were defending their own homes and families; their morale was unquestionably high.

"Mountcashel sent Hamilton on a reconnaissance mission, with a force of dragoons, north toward Lisnaskea. Hamilton and his men chased a group of Enniskillen scouts near the Colebrooke River. The Enniskillener scouts' knowledge of the local area, however, combined with the experience of English officers, allowed them to ambush Hamilton's force early in the day at a river crossing.

"Hamilton was wounded and his troops routed. They fled south back toward Mountcashel's position at Newtowncairn. History records Hamilton as having been indecisive on the day. He would later face a court martial for his actions, but be cleared of any wrongdoing during the ambush.

"The Enniskillen troops headed toward Mountcashel's positions at Newtowncairn on July 31st. He had, however, posted several elements north of the town in an attempt to upset the Enniskillener lines of march and disrupt their discipline through ambush. As the Jacobites fired and retreated, he hoped to persuade the enemy to break ranks and pursue. You must remember, of course, that seventeenth century warfare relied so much on close ordered bodies of troops, with inaccurate matchlocks for firepower and pikes as a defence against cavalry. If lines of troops could be disrupted, enemy cavalry could then destroy them in piecemeal fashion.

"Mountcashel hoped that the Enniskillener's hatred for his cause would disrupt their lines if he ambushed them, force them to break ranks and rush through the village in pursuit in an altogether irregular fashion, where his cavalry and dragoons could destroy them in detail. His plan was a good one, though fatally flawed."

"Why?" said Reilly, now intrigued once more.

"He had not rated the competence of the newly arrived English contingent. For the first time, the Enniskilleners faced a well-drawn up Jacobite force, with good numbers. William Wolseley, the English commander, must have seen what was developing with the ambushes, the attempts to create disorder, the nightmare of any commander of the time."

"What did he do?"

"He instilled order, commanded that no man would step out of line, no man would pursue outside the ranks and files of his battalion. Basically, he kept order and managed his troops, and on the seventeenth century battlefield, that's sometimes all that was required. Though of course, it must have been all he could do to stop them breaking."

"So Wolseley persuaded his men not to break, not to pursue Mountcashel's troops," Reilly said.

"Yes. He brought a sense of order to the Enniskillener enthusiasm to have at the enemy, and it worked. They held, at least for a time."

Latimer continued, "The Jacobites burned the town to the ground as they passed through, and Wolseley's Enniskilleners pursued until they saw Mountcashel's force of three to four thousand assembled on a hilltop."

"Just south of Newtowncairn then?" Reilly asked.

"Funny you should say that," Latimer quipped.

"What? I don't understand?" Reilly asked, now puzzled.

"No one has ever actually identified the battlefield."

"What? How is that possible in this day and age?"

"The primary sources give clues, some from the Enniskillener side, another from the French ambassador

D'Avaux, though none really gives a definitive location."

"That..." Reilly paused. "That seems, dare I say, highly irregular."

"Interesting, yes," Latimer added.

"Though the sources give an account of the battle, yes?"

"Yes, they do. Mountcashel had chosen his ground well; a hilltop position, surrounded by soggy bogland. Cavalry could not approach him, and the only access was via a raised causeway type road. At the end of this he had positioned his artillery pieces, small in calibre perhaps, but nonetheless effective."

"What happened?"

"Debatable again. A close reading of the texts implies, though barely admits, to an eventual breakdown in the Enniskillener ability to hold back, despite Wolseley's orders, to the extent that their lead battalions of infantry charged across the bogland toward Mountcashel's position on the hill. The shock to the Jacobites must have been palpable, ensconced in their apparently well-defended position. They give off one volley from their matchlocks, those that had them, that is, before being engulfed in vicious hand-to-hand combat. The cannon's position was quickly overwhelmed and the crews killed. At this point, the Enniskillen cavalry was able to charge along the causeway without fear of cannon fire, reinforcing their own infantry."

"And the Jacobites," added Reilly.

"The shock of the charge, or perhaps their inexperience, or the impact of the infantry in their front ranks, perhaps even all of these factors, proved too much for them."

"First Hamilton's dragoons, then infantry regiments began to break, and they fled south of the hilltop. Only Mountcashel's own regiment and a few scattered remnants stood fast, and they were decimated by the oncoming Enniskillen infantry and cavalry, having no time to reload, simply trying to fight and survive. Little quarter would be given."

"What about Lord Mountcashel?"

"Mountcashel, according to the Enniskillen sources, was so devastated by the entire affair, that, having escaped the worst of the fighting, he found refuge with some of his officers, and in an act of desperation, charged the captured guns. He was shot by the defending Enniskilleners, wounded, though a mortal wound was prevented by his pocket watch... allegedly." Latimer shook his head. "I don't know if I believe that one," he laughed mockingly.

"He was almost killed, until his men pointed out who he was, and he was spared. He was subsequently captured and taken to Enniskillen with some of his officers. The soldiers that had fled the field were not so lucky. Most of them were killed while trying to run, and those that did escape drowned in Lough Erne."

"A massacre?"

"Yes, very much so, though such acts were a common feature of the time. You must understand that atrocity went hand in hand with all aspects of warfare in the seventeenth century. Sometimes, even officers were lucky to escape. Mountcashel and Hamilton would have seen worse acts committed in their time in France."

"And what of Lord Mountcashel?"

"He petitioned for his release. He was, by all accounts, treated well in Enniskillen. James even sent his chief surgeon there to tend to him, and he recovered, though he continued to seek his freedom, as part of a prisoner exchange for Lord Mountjoy, then held in France. The point was moot, however. Within days, the siege of Derry had ended. Within weeks, William had landed in Ireland. The war had begun in earnest."

"What happened to Mountcashel?" Reilly asked, as they passed the sign to indicate that were entering the small village of Clogher. He slowed down to the speed limit, trying to concentrate on what Latimer was saying. His tone had changed subtly, as if he was getting to the exciting part.

"He escaped, eventually, the primary sources tell us, apparently with the aid of an Enniskillener sergeant." Latimer went uncharacteristically silent for a moment, his fingers patting the satchel.

"Apparently?" Reilly said, eager for him to continue.

"Yes. Well. If the journal is to be believed, a very different chain of events unfolded."

The car swayed a little on the road as Reilly took in what Latimer had just said. Latimer's face had suddenly taken on a very serious look, as if he was party to some great arcane secret.

"What do you mean by that?" Reilly gasped.

Latimer pulled at his nose and sniffed, patting his jacket pocket. "I've... well, I've been building to this, really. When Mountcashel escaped, the Jacobites in Dublin celebrated widely, though it would prove difficult for him to remain in Ireland. He had besmirched his honour, in the eyes of William and his generals, anyway. Unofficially it made great propaganda, for both sides, perhaps. If he were captured again he would probably be shot out of hand. The French would not allow that to happen. Mountcashel was one of the few Irish generals that they respected. They had requested Irish troops in exchange for French advisors and arms, to fight Louis's enemies on the continent. They wanted Mountcashel to lead that force in mainland Europe."

"I don't understand," Reilly added. "What does that have to do with what you've found in the journal?"

"Mountcashel reached France with six thousand volunteers by 1690. As kings faced each other at the Boyne in Ireland, he was marching toward his destiny in France."

"Get to the point, Neil. The suspense is killing me!" Reilly insisted, frustrated with the apparent lack of progress in what was fast becoming a university lecture.

Latimer smiled. "Mountcashel began to record these notes, in code, from writings he had made in Ireland. I believe that he wrote them while in France, and coded them so that none of his contemporaries could read what he had to say. I also think that he added to these notes in France, though the tone changes. By the time I see the change, he seems driven, compelled almost, as if he has a task to complete, and the earlier notes from Ireland are there to remind him of another time, another life, perhaps."

"And what does this have to do with his escape?" said Reilly, almost gritting his teeth. "Get to the point!"

Latimer pointed to a sign for another garage on the road outside Clogher. "Can we pull in here? I desperately need to pee."

Reilly indicated to pull off the road, sighing slightly. "Can we get to the point now?"

Latimer looked across the dashboard, absently scratching at some stubble on his chin. "Mountcashel describes that he escaped not with the aid of an Enniskillener sergeant, or indeed Jacobite officers, but with the help..." Latimer paused. "With the help of a witch! A witch from Newtowncairn."

Sorcha Ballantine used the iron poker to shuffle the hot embers of the dying fire, moving them over and around each other, the patterns of sparks and embers dying and re-igniting, painting a moving portrait of ash in the grate. A bent old man stood rigid behind the armchair.

"They are coming, Hamilton." She smiled behind cracked lips, the movement wrinkling the greying flesh of her emaciated face. "They are coming, and they are bringing the book with them."

Mountcashel's Journal, 23rd April 1690, Brest, France

We have arrived safely at the French port of Brest. Though the rains persist, it is a great deal warmer than our native land. The men remain in good spirits and I pray to God that their fortunes will change and the events at Newtowncairn can be put behind us.

I have been untroubled by dreams and the sickness of the mind, since we set sail. I hope that my nightmares have finished, yet I remain ill at ease. Does this mean that her power is restricted to the Isle of my birth? I pray to almighty God that it is so, and yet were it true, I could never hope to return home. I must put such thoughts behind me. There is a war to fight and men to lead. I can not let them down... not again.

My escape from Enniskillen has been held as honourable by a French Court Martial. Privately, I had expected this outcome. I am too valuable to the French for there ever to have been any doubt. In conference with his majesty King Louis I have spoken on the great Irish matter. His Majesty, despite his noble attempt at convincing me to the contrary, still holds out little hope for my countrymen at war there, yet urges that the conflict on the French borders might yet alleviate the situation in Ireland. I can only pray that he is right.

I have written to my wife for the final time. I have told her that the conditions of this war may mean that I will not be able to write to her easily. I will forever miss her, since in all honesty I mean not to write at all lest she sees the truth of the dread behind my words, and grow frightened or ashamed. I have little need to drag her into this pit of darkness with me, should the dreams ever return.

CHAPTER ELEVEN

McGrath entered the cramped second hand bookshop and removed his hat, letting droplets of rain fall off the cap cover onto the decaying grey floor tiles covering the entry by the door. As it swung closed, he was struck by the high temperature and the distinctive smell of a paraffin heater. The warmth was welcome after the icy rain outside. The owner of the place must have had serious heating bills, he thought. He had made Laverty wait in the car again, despite his protests. The kid was becoming a problem, asking too many questions. Did he not realise that you had to learn from the experienced officers? If that meant sitting in the car while he asked the important questions, then so be it. The lad would have to learn to keep his mouth shut until McGrath could trust him with something important. And besides, Laverty's accent still grated on his nerves, though he had to admit he was starting to get used to it.

He scratched the short stubble of hair on his head and looked around; high shelves, filled with paperbacks dominated the walls of the shop. Books were literally stuffed into the shelves, to the extent that the space left above by arranging the titles vertically was crammed with novels laid horizontally. It seemed impossible to find anything. He looked around at the subjects, westerns, science fiction, romance and… fishing. Someone must be buying this crap, he thought, the shop is still here.

"Can I help you, Officer?" a voice chimed behind him.

He jumped, startled, turning quickly.

The woman was about five feet four inches. She was

stocky, with short grey hair. Her face had that lived-in look that suggested that her life had had its fair share of disappointment. McGrath guessed that she was in her mid fifties. Her ruddy complexion was no doubt brought about by the heat in the shop. Slightly embarrassed by being surprised, McGrath felt himself blush.

"Why, yes, Ma'am... hello! I'm Sergeant McGrath." He extended a hand then thought better of it, reddening still further as he withdrew the offer. "You must be Ms. Hamilton."

"My God, Sergeant!" she replied excitedly.

"Ma'am?" he asked.

"You should be a detective!"

McGrath was embarrassed, completely unaware of where she was taking him!

She continued. "The fact that you've no doubt noted that it says 'Proprietor, Mary Hamilton' above the door and I seem to be the only person here. You've gone on a hunch, haven't you? One of those gut feelings that they talk about on those American police shows?" She folded her arms and smiled, revealing slightly yellowed teeth.

McGrath tried his best to smile. "It is... Ms. Hamilton then, yes?"

"Actually, Sergeant, it's Miss Hamilton, though I'll forgive you your little faux pas, shall I?" She patted his arm and squeezed past him, shuffling toward the back of the cramped shop. "Now, I was just making some tea, would you like a cup?"

McGrath raised his eyes to the ceiling. Here we go, he thought, contemplating the degree of sarcasm that he might have to wade through in the next ten minutes. He should have sent Laverty in.

"Why, yes, Ma'am, that would be lovely," he grunted, hoping that she heard him as she disappeared behind a curtain.

"What exactly can I do for you?" she called. The clatter of cutlery came from what McGrath guessed must be a tiny kitchen.

He cleared his throat. "We're looking into the recent death in Newtowncairn ma'am, the young lad James Pollock. He stayed in the hotel across the road while he was here," he called, raising his voice so that he could be heard. This was no way to conduct an enquiry, he thought. He would wait for her to emerge. He heard the sound of something metallic bouncing off the floor, but Mary Hamilton made no reply.

"Ma'am? Are you all right, ma'am?" he called. He moved toward the curtain.

As he did so, he saw movement and she emerged once more, a small teaspoon held rigid in her hand.

"Pollock, you say?" She looked flushed, shocked, even scared.

McGrath moved forward. She looked like she was going to faint. "Are you all right, ma'am?" he repeated. He made ready to catch her. She looked frail now, as if the news had shocked her to the core.

"Didn't you hear about the murder, ma'am? It would have been on the news all last week. It's the talk of County Fermanagh," McGrath said, puzzled that the event had passed her by. It was clear that she had known Pollock, however, a fact that he could not ignore.

Mary Hamilton was open mouthed, still clutching the spoon in her hand.

McGrath cleared his throat again. "We think it was drugs related, ma'am, you know?"

She seemed to recover a little. "Oh no, Sergeant, I'm sure that young man had no connection to drugs. You can be assured of that!"

McGrath raised his eyebrows. "You seem so sure... Miss Hamilton."

She placed the spoon on the laminated worktop of the makeshift shop counter. She was close to tears now, placing her hands on the counter in an effort to steady herself. "Oh no, Sergeant. That young man was a student of..." She paused.

McGrath narrowed his eyes. "A student of what,

ma'am?" She suddenly seemed detached, looking into the middle distance, as if her mind was making connections amidst the logic of events.

She glanced back at him. "Why, a student of history. But of course you know that."

It was as if she had suddenly awoken refreshed from a long sleep, McGrath thought, as he watched her straighten and remove her hands from the steadying influence of the counter.

"He was here doing his PhD, Sergeant. He had no connection with criminality. I'm sure of it." She folded her arms and pondered. "Such a nice young man. He spent many hours in the shop here, looking for bargains, I suppose. He'd come in every morning before setting off for the village."

"Newtowncairn you mean?" McGrath asked.

She glanced back at him, suddenly stern. "Yes, that's right."

"And that's how you know him?"

"Yes. I don't really listen to the news. So depressing. I don't leave the shop much you see, and I live upstairs."

"Was he ever accompanied by anyone when he came in, ma'am? Did you ever see anyone with him at all?" McGrath asked, more forcefully.

She pondered, concentrating, as if trying to remember the details of conversations and events.

"No. No, he was always alone, clutching his papers and books as if they were a part of him." She smiled as she remembered. "Such wonderful conversations we used to have."

"About what, ma'am?" McGrath asked.

"Oh… history, mythology, such knowledge and interests he had." She seemed distant again, and moved toward McGrath, grasping his arm suddenly. "You must find his killer, Sergeant. You simply must! What have you found in Newtowncairn?"

She stared at him with water filled eyes. McGrath opened his mouth to reply, to tell her that his enquiries were proceeding well, that he had found…

His head began to throb when he remembered the village. Newtowncairn. He had been there. He had interviewed everyone, had he not?

"I... we're... our enquiries are ongoing there, ma'am," he stuttered.

She nodded slowly, almost knowingly. "I see," she said. As quickly as she had moved toward him, she moved away, releasing her grip on his arm. McGrath felt suddenly as if he had been abandoned, left to drown in an ocean of self-doubt. He was sweating.

"If that's all then, Sergeant?"

He had to concentrate to speak. "Yes, thank you, Miss Hamilton. I'll be in touch if there's anything else."

He moved toward the door, staring at the floor. His head was pounding. Next time, he would send Laverty in.

Mary Hamilton folded her arms in contemplation, watching McGrath get into the car in the pouring rain. She nodded her head and muttered under her breath.

"Oh she got to you, Sergeant McGrath. She got right under your skin, didn't she?"

She began to chew nervously on the nail of a finger. Behind her, the high pitched whistling from the boiling kettle broke the silence. She closed her eyes in an effort to stop the tears that she knew were coming.

Since the silence that followed the revelation that Mountcashel had spoken of a witch in his journal, and the inevitable links that both men made to the mysterious cult that James Pollock had mentioned in his letter, neither Latimer nor Reilly were able to make sense of the situation. It was quite a leap for either of them, despite their interest in the occult, to start talking of the validity of a witch cult in the twenty-first century. Questions over whether the issues were related and what was really happening in the village were put aside until more investigations, both into the nature of the journal's contents and the area around Newtowncairn, could be carried out.

In the interim, and with the intention of delaying discussion and analysis of the real issues until they had reached their destination, Latimer continued to regale Reilly with ironic facts, twists and lesser-known variations on the theme of seventeenth century Irish history for the remainder of the journey. Reilly had initially enjoyed the enlightening yet gentle take on the past that Latimer excelled at. Now, however, after many miles of driving, his colleague was becoming boring. Reilly found that he needed something to drink, his head was throbbing, and the action of nodding to indicate that he understood something that Latimer had said was becoming mechanical and making his neck hurt. He was, however, more than concerned, at the effect that telling Latimer to shut the hell up might have. Nearly there, he thought, as he sped along the road, grateful for the lack of lunchtime traffic and noting with grim satisfaction a sign that indicated only five miles to their destination.

He interrupted Latimer as they entered the outskirts of Enniskillen, the rain becoming heavier.

"Do you know exactly where this place is then, Neil?"

Latimer lifted his satchel and began to rummage.

"I do have a map here somewhere."

Several minutes later, he emerged with a crumpled ball of paper.

"Here we are. Yes. Go through the first two sets of lights, and then head for the town centre. I can direct you from there."

Latimer shuffled in his seat, looking absently through the window.

"You know, of course, that Enniskillen is an island town. The waterways into Lough Erne surround it. It's a fascinating place, one of the few towns you can sail around! It could be argued that this gave the populace their isolationist spirit during the Jacobite wars. They lived surrounded by the waters of the Erne. An enemy would have to bridge their way into the town. They were isolated physically and perhaps emotionally due to the religious nature of the war. Of course, during the plantation in the early part of the seventeenth century many of the settlers that found their way to Enniskillen due to..."

Oh God, Reilly thought absently.

"There, Neil! We're through two sets of lights. Directions, quickly. We're entering a lane system here and I may just be the biggest vehicle in town. Need you to stay on the ball here," Reilly barked excitedly, fuelled by anxiety as Latimer fumbled chaotically for the map in panic.

"Ok, yes. Turn right here, that's it. Then left, and we're in the main street. Down the hill and you can't miss it, apparently."

"Who gave you these directions?"

"Oh, one of the hotel staff, when I phoned ahead. I've also passed all the details to the police that Moore asked for, where we'd be staying and so on."

McGrath sat in the passenger seat of the police car, rain dripping from the peak of his hat on to his raincoat in the dry heat provided by the air conditioning system.

"Sarge," Laverty said.

McGrath stirred, and turned to his partner.

"What? What is it?"

"I said how did you get on in the bookshop?" Laverty repeated.

"Fine. Fine. She knew Pollock. Had spoken with him. Claimed that she'd never seen him with anyone else," said McGrath, lucid once more.

"Claimed?" said Laverty, suddenly more interested.

"Yes. Perhaps she knows more than she's letting on. But I don't think she's involved with the gang that did the deed. She's really not the type."

The blare of car horns further down the street interrupted

the conversation. A large jeep was apparently trying to turn round in the one way street and had, inadvertently, created the traffic jam from hell. McGrath checked the rear view mirror as Laverty looked round.
"You don't think that's…?" he said.
McGrath shook his head. "It's possible, Laverty. It's definitely possible."

The younger policeman began to direct traffic in the pouring rain, stopping cars in one lane while getting others moving around the obstruction.

McGrath, now saturated with water, made his way toward the offending vehicle, which appeared to have attempted to cross into one lane, then reversed, ending up with one wheel on a traffic island and cars around it at various angles of travel, like hyenas surrounding a wounded wildebeest. He knocked on the driver's window amidst the blasting of the car horns. The nervous driver, a thin man with grey hair and a look of obvious shock on his face, pressed a button, and the rear window on the far side of the car slowly went down. McGrath pursed his lips and brushed water from his hat with one hand, while making revolving motions with his index finger. Eventually the driver's window came down. McGrath poked his head through the access.

"We're in a bit of a pickle, aren't we, sir?" he said, looking at the driver and glancing at his passenger, a small well built man, wearing cords and a tweed jacket, with a rapidly reddening face.

"I'm going to go for a long shot here, guys," McGrath said, squeezing his nose and feeling the water drip from it. "Would you two gentlemen be Professors Latimer and Reilly?"

Both men jiggled their heads, in perfect synchronicity.

McGrath groaned.

Mountcashel's Journal, May 30th 1690, Nantes, France

My men remain in a pitiful state having been left in poor quarters for so long. Our expectations with regard to improved conditions when we arrived here have not been fulfilled. My troops do however remain proud and ready, isolated as we are in this small town, awaiting supplies. I have discouraged pillaging and foraging in the nearby villages. Though I can speak French, as can most of my officers, the men find it difficult to understand basic commands and many of Louis's visiting officials consider them unworthy to serve alongside the regulars in battle. I have disputed their requests to disband half of the men as unfit and have them sent back to Ireland. I have also sent letters to the King in order to ensure that we are treated fairly.

I have received dispatches from Marshal Noilles, indicating that I am to serve on the Catalonian border with my brigade. Memories of her, memories of the dreams, engulf me sometimes. Spain... where she seeks her revenge, where the object of her search resides. I have attempted to persuade Noilles' officers that the brigade might be more usefully used on the Italian border, in the fight against the Savoy region. I can but hope that my thoughts are considered, for I imagine no manner in which to tell the noble Frenchmen, or even my Irish countrymen, the real reason as to why I have little care to fight near Spain. My journal remains the only manner in which I can express my feelings on this matter. Our allies would think me mad were I to tell them that only darkness awaits me in Spain...

CHAPTER TWELVE

Eventually, after considerable manoeuvre, embarrassment and raised voices amidst the blare of car horns, Reilly had got moving again, this time with a police escort. They had travelled around the town once more. Following McGrath's car, they ultimately made the correct turn into the Islandview Hotel. Neither party had noticed the red sports car that had been shadowing the group since the episode at the traffic lights. But then, neither Latimer nor Reilly nor the policemen had really expected to be followed.

Annie Devlin drove past the scene, as soon as she had determined exactly where the academics were going to stay. As the road became quieter, she pulled into a space between parked cars, and turned off the engine, reaching for her mobile phone. She called a number on speed dial.

"C'mon Sean, pick up," she murmured. "Bloody voicemail," she rasped.

"Sean, it's me. I'm sorting out somewhere to stay." She adopted a mockery of a polite English accent. "The chaps have found somewhere to stay already!"

"The cops are staying close. Either your friend at the university is telling the truth or they really do suspect something. Either way, I'm going to find out." She paused. "Call me, Sean, ok?"

Reilly's discomfort relating to the situation on the road

was mitigated to some degree by the level of confidence that Latimer seemed to display in his dealings with the two policemen. McGrath and Laverty had stood like drowned rats, dripping in the reception area of the small hotel. Latimer, despite the awkwardness of the situation, had so far ordered tea and biscuits for his new police friends, joked with the girl at reception as if he was a schoolboy playing truant for the afternoon and single-handedly managed to arrange one of the empty meeting rooms for his impending conference, as he called it, with the local law enforcement representatives. Reilly stood almost in awe as he watched him in action. Even the police appeared to be impressed.

McGrath tried not to let his damp clothing bother him as he sipped the tea that had been so graciously provided by the hotel staff. He had to admit he had absolutely failed to intimidate this Professor Latimer. He might become a problem. All he wanted was a quiet babysitting job, with no hassles, no drama and no timewasters. Latimer, by the look of things thus far, could pull matters in entirely the wrong direction.

The four men moved toward a large conference room. The blast of warm air that met their entrance contrasted dramatically with the cold and wet hotel car park.

"Why don't we sit down, gentlemen, yes?" Latimer said, with his characteristic jovial demeanour, which had made a triumphant return since their arrival. "We really need to talk."

Laverty smiled naively, McGrath grunted and Reilly, still red faced, wrung water from his raincoat onto the carpet tiles.

They sat, and drank tea. McGrath, by now a little disconcerted with being organised by the man from the university, was the first to speak.

"Look, Professor Latimer, is it? I'll make this short and sweet." He paused to drink from the cup. "I'm Sergeant McGrath," he said, jabbing a thumb at himself. "This is Constable Laverty. We're here as your liaison, but for the most part that means we're here to offer protection. We do appreciate that you've come all the way down here from

A VERY IRISH CURSE

Belfast to…" he paused, "to continue young Mr. Pollock's work, as you call it, but, should that shall we say, lead you down any paths which could result in potentially dangerous situations, I want you to know that we will deal with them."

"Let's cut the crap, Sergeant," a suddenly stern Latimer cut in. "You believe that the case is solved, correct?"

The larger policeman pursed his lips and leaned back in the chair, folding his arms in what Reilly considered to be a most defensive form of body language. He nodded. "Yes, I do!" he continued. McGrath looked as though he wanted to say more, but Latimer was having none of it.

He sized up the opposition and began to speak, gesticulating wildly with each word so that McGrath could be in little doubt of his conviction. "Believe me when I say that I do not for one minute accept that James Pollock's death was related to drugs…"

McGrath, in an attempt to indicate that his attention was not fully engaged with Latimer's animated words, moved his head to one side and whispered at Laverty, more for effect than for purposes of discussion with the young Constable. "Christ, he's just like her across the road: can't face the truth!"

Latimer paused for breath. "…Indeed, I believe that there is in fact more to his untimely death than anyone will accept. I aim to prove it. If you can help me, that's great, but please, let's not get off on the wrong foot."

McGrath sat forward on the seat, about to speak, but was rapidly interrupted by Laverty, whose lilting country accent seemed out of place in the frosty discourse that was occurring.

"Mr Latimer, as Sergeant McGrath says, we want to help you. Look at it from our point of view. We have a witness statement from a Newtowncairn resident stating that Mr. Pollock was up to his neck in drugs related activities, a witness who says that he saw known suspects in the area. And though it hasn't been officially released to the press yet, there was evidence of drugs in the car. So please, let's not ignore the facts. We understand that you're here to continue the young fella's research. Can't you do that without getting directly involved in the case? Let's face it, that's our job." Laverty stopped, and lifted the teacup.

McGrath was amazed, wondering if he could have had the presence of mind to say what his colleague had. The kid might just be all right, he thought, absently.

"Understood. Now let's get on with the matter in hand, shall we?" Latimer replied confidently. McGrath, still taken aback, looked across at him and nodded.

"We'll spend the day getting acclimatised here, signed in, get some dinner and settle in. Tomorrow, we'll give you a call if we're leaving town and, well, we'll take it from there, shall we?"

The party rose, offering mutual handshakes and overly polite gratitude.

Latimer and Reilly filled out the necessary paperwork and made their way towards their respective rooms on the second floor.

"What do you think?" Reilly asked as they moved down the corridor.

"I think I'm going to get changed and go for a walk," he said, enthusiastically.

"So soon," Reilly asked, puzzled. "Don't you want to get something to eat?"

"Well, I think I'm going to find out about the woman across the road before the curiosity kills me! Are you coming?"

Reilly sighed. "No. I think I'll have a lie down; long drive and all. I might even give... might give Barbara a call. Who is this woman across the road you mentioned? When did that come up?"

"Oh that charming Sergeant McGrath mentioned it during the conversation. I'm betting she's someone that knew James, someone that McGrath has already spoken to. So I'm going to check it out."

Latimer stopped and put his hand on his friend's

shoulder, suddenly connecting with his colleague's comments about Barbara. "Yes, Joseph, of course. You should phone home. Do that, yes. I won't be long." He glanced at his key, then at the door beside him. "Here I am," he said. "I'll give you a shout later, shall I?"

"Right. Yes, I'll see you later."

Reilly moved further up the corridor. He found the room, and sat down on the bed, which at first glance appeared almost too clean. An overuse of white paint made the environment seem clinical, without the slightest oversight in cleanliness or a piece of furniture out of place. He lay down, exhausted from the journey, or had Latimer's lecture and the subsequent discussion with the local police numbed his mind? He realised that he was however ignoring the simple truth: that his marriage was over, unless by some last minute miracle he could find a way to mend it.

He fumbled in one of his bags for a mobile phone and switched it on. He would call Barbara and explain. She had to be rational, to understand why he had to do this, to come down here with Latimer. She had to understand the importance of this trip. His hands were shaking as he dialled the number. He paused, turning the phone around in his hand nervously, and then switched it off, throwing it back into his bag. He lay back on the bed and rubbed his eyes in a vain attempt to stem the flow of tears.

Latimer finished brushing his teeth, left the bathroom and grabbed the hip flask that he had left by the bedside table. Downing the last of the whiskey, he belched loudly and reached for his jacket. Across the street, with the passing of the heavy rainfall, men and women made their way up and down the main road. Latimer pondered the façades of the shops on the other side: a hairdresser, a second hand bookshop and an army surplus shop. The logical progressions in his mind came to one conclusion. McGrath would not have let slip about the mysterious woman unless she had something to do with the Pollock case. Whoever she was, McGrath's comments indicated that she clearly had no belief in the suggested drugs connection, and must have known James, at least to some degree. Pollock had not been the army surplus type, and from what could be seen from here, the shop appeared to be run by a man. Neither had he been one for nattering in the hairdressers. Latimer remembered Pollock's uncontrollable mop of black hair, which reminded him of his own teenage years where vanity took second place to the pursuit of his research interests. His obsessions had made him a bachelor, and at his age that status was unlikely to change.

The only logical choice then, assuming that McGrath was not inventing the whole scenario in order to confuse and disorientate his obvious yearning to solve the case, was that Pollock had made a friend in the second hand bookshop. Given the fact that Latimer loved rummaging in such stores in Belfast, for a bargain or a forgotten first edition of historical significance, it was the obvious choice. He rubbed his chin in thought, lifted the key to his room, and made for the door.

The air outside was crisp and fresh, revitalised by the heavy rain, as he left the hotel and crossed the road. Latimer hummed with satisfaction, noting the name on the sign. The Hamiltons had left their mark since the plantation in Ulster. He toyed with the thought that this woman could be a distant relative of Anthony Hamilton, Mountcashel's senior officer, though disregarded the notion just as quickly.

The door creaked loudly. The shelves were crammed with paperbacks on their sides. Various sized hardbacks were piled on the floor, all covering different subject matter. Latimer resisted the urge to start analysing and classifying the titles. The shop smelt damp and musty, and the windows were filthy. The smell reminded him of some of his favourite haunts at home. It was infectious, the odour of discarded books, yet who could know what knowledge lay inside, awaiting the investigative reader. Movement on the floor drew his attention away from his scattered thoughts. He noticed a spider, the size of a watch face, scuttle across the floor in the direction of its nest of novels as the door closed behind him with a creak. He thought of what Reilly's reaction might have been had he seen it. The irony of his friend's fear was not lost on him. Reilly, whose arachnophobia knew no bounds, had spent six months in the humid heat of the Amazonian rainforest where the spiders were the size of dinner plates. Poor man must have been terrified, he thought.

He looked again at the spider's path. He reached into his breast pocket for his glasses. There was something on the floor. As his vision was made clearer, he could just discern a mark, scratched lightly into the tan coloured tiling on the floor. He bent over to see more clearly, the glasses sliding down his nose slightly in reaction. There were lines extending back under the bookcase that currently formed the spider's home, and marks, letters perhaps, but not immediately discernable.

"Can I help you?" a stern female voice called from the back of the shop.

Latimer stood up rapidly, completely surprised, the act simultaneously making him feel dizzy and nudging his delicate spectacles further down to the end of his nose where they tilted at an angle, lending him the distinct look of a mad professor who had been let out for the day.

He fumbled for his glasses, replacing them in the correct position as the lady at back of the shop covered her mouth with one hand, obviously amused by the incident and conscious that blatant laughter in this instance might lose her a customer. As Latimer brought her into focus he tried to smile. Not his most charming, of course, due to the fact that he had been startled, but, he considered, a winning version nevertheless.

"Oh. Hello there. I'm just going to have a look round, if you don't mind," he continued.

The woman raised her hand, inviting Latimer to peruse at his leisure.

"Please, go ahead. Is there anything in particular you're looking for?" she asked.

She had such beautiful eyes, Latimer thought naïvely.

They were tinged, however, with such sadness, he considered.

"Yes, well, I love shops like this," he said, striding forward in order to get a better look. "My interests tend to be quite broad, rather wide ranging," he announced.

"I see. I'm sure you'll find something here." She seemed to have such confidence Latimer thought. She reminded him of himself! They stood a few feet apart, as she moved from behind the counter to face him.

"I'm sure I can help," she said, maintaining eye contact and pursing her lips. "Give me a clue?"

"Well, I'm a historian. I'm partial to detective novels, and I'm what you might call a bit of a new age devotee, spiritually speaking. I suppose that sums up my interests."

She drew a sharp breath, as if sizing him up. Something in her manner suggested to him that she had not expected his response. They both spoke at once, like embarrassed school children.

Latimer smiled and nodded. "You first."

She looked at the shelves. "We have some historical rarities here," she pointed to the lower shelves. "Some unusual reference books you might find interesting. Detective novels are piled by the door there; quite popular, you know."

Latimer gazed at her.

"What particular aspects of new age work were you interested in?" she asked, the tone of her voice changing slightly, more menacing to a degree, Latimer noted.

He avoided the question.

"I'd be quite interested in local history, primary source material, if you have it. Seventeenth century, perhaps?"

"Well, let's have a look." She began to move toward a shelf, following a filing system that only she knew amidst the piles of unsorted material.

Latimer continued. "The new age material, now that is a challenge." He folded his arms.

"You'll find a few items of local interest, though no primary source material. You'll find that a lot of our local history references were destroyed a few hundred years ago, various fires and such. Not a good area for digging deep, historically speaking," she said.

Latimer kept his arms folded, as if he were sizing up an opponent.

"And where's your new age and occult section then?" he asked, innocently.

She seemed acutely suspicious for just a second. "This way," she said casually, beckoning.

She moved toward the corner of the shop. A bookshelf sat at an awkward angle. It was not obvious to the casual browser. Indeed, Latimer noted, it could not be seen as one entered.

"I have a small collection here; not many customers, you understand; not exactly fashionable in this neck of the woods. Was there anything specific?"

The door to the shop opened as an old woman made an effort to lift her foot to make the step up. She was wrapped up in a brown sheepskin coat against the cold, and carried two worn paperbacks in her hand.

"Hi, Mary," she announced, displaying the musical tones of a local accent. "I'm bringing these two back. They were rubbish. Got any more?"

Mary moved away from Latimer. "Come on in, Agnes. Let me have a look."

She walked away. Latimer's eyes followed for a time, before dwelling on the bookcase. He subconsciously raised a finger, tracing it across the scattered spines. He winced as he saw a dog-eared copy of 'The Beast and the Harlot' by McKay, a well-documented fake. Its conclusions tended to match Gnostic Christianity and formed little more than discussions on a witch cult that was said to have existed in the United States in the 1980s, and from which the erstwhile Mr. McKay must have made quite a tidy sum before being murdered in mysterious circumstances.

He carefully replaced one title after another as the books flowed beneath his hand. Fake after fake, written by charlatans after the proverbial fast buck. Latimer had spent a lifetime researching history, and in the last ten years had taken a profound interest in the history of occult literature, and had thus developed a nose for the illusory and dubious. Temporarily absolved from his own self-imposed responsibilities for solving the case, he continued to browse.

He stopped. The sound of the two women talking in the corner seemed distant suddenly, as if he was listening to the distilled sound of their conversation whilst under water. 'Les Cultes des Ghoules', he mouthed as he read the title. He slowly reached for the book. It was hardback, well kept it seemed, since, if it was real, it had been published in 1703 in France. He pulled it from the shelf, scarcely noticing that the belligerent sounding Agnes had by now left the shop and that Mary Hamilton was watching him silently.

He turned to the inside cover, noting the dates, the author, and the texture of the paper. The book seemed so fragile that he feared it might fall apart. It immediately reminded him of the journal that he carried in his inside pocket, at which he instinctively patted his jacket to ensure that it was still there. But the book he held now he considered equally as rare, sought after by a thousand researchers across Europe. So few copies still existed. It detailed the necromantic activities of French sorcerers in the seventeenth century, and Latimer had at one time fallen in love with the thought of finding it eventually, while reluctantly admitting to himself that he never would.

"Do you know what that is?" she asked, her voice suddenly deeper, more insistent than before.

Latimer looked up in surprise, his lips moving slightly.

"This is very, very rare," he said slowly. "It has to be a fake, yes?" She smiled. How wonderful she looked.

"That's one of the few copies left. You're the first person that's ever noticed it and seen it for what it was. You, of course, realise that it's not for sale."

Like a schoolboy who had been caught stealing sweets, Latimer nodded his head and moved to replace the volume.

She walked toward him. "That's not to say that you can't

read it, of course," she said quietly, stopping as she reached the dilapidated shelving. "For a student of history, you seem to know what you're looking at in the occult," she added.

Latimer, now given what counted as permission to read the book, was delicately turning page after page, reading some sections while dismissing others, trying to establish authenticity based on the articles that he had seen related to the work.

"Oh, I'm a little more that a student," he added absently. "I'm a Professor of History at the University," he added, still closely analysing his find. He noted that her expression changed suddenly. She dropped her arms to her sides. Latimer looked up. It seemed as if she had been hit with a hammer.

She cocked her head to one side. "Is your name Latimer?"

Mountcashel's Journal, July 31st 1690, Nantes, France

I breakfasted with the Marquis de Lee this morning. A trusted Irishman who has fought for the French before. He tells me that the French expect great things of my brigade. I will not disappoint them. Despite the setbacks and conditions, the men remain eager for a fight. Lee also brought new orders. We march to Italy to fight under Marshal St. Ruth.

The heat in the day is becoming unbearable, however, and I fear that our supplies will run short during the march. We yearn especially for fresh water in the drier parts of the country where wells are scarce and the locals, already left with little after the passage of many French regiments, have even less to give Irish troops who have not yet earned battle honours. Though I doubt that such things matter to peasant farmers with little enough food for their wives and children.

I am congratulated on my knowledge of the war, and the benefits of my stratagem in suggesting that reinforcements might be better used in Italy, where a worsening situation is developing.

And yet, as I watch the men make ready, I am reminded of the night before Newtowncairn, before I watched so many men lose their lives, before I first felt that terrible witch in my thoughts. I pray that this time, free, as I seem to be of her influence, matters will be very different and the men at least will earn themselves gloire in the eyes of our French masters.

CHAPTER THIRTEEN

Reilly had called his home number twice already and let the phone ring for five minutes. Barbara had not picked it up. He resolved to call a third time, his heart pounding as he raised the phone to his ear, listening to the tone. He would apologise. That would be all that was required. He would apologise, explain that this would be his last trip away. She would understand. He remembered the good times that he had had with Barbara since university, since living together, getting married. He had taken their relationship for granted, never really thought about what she wanted from their marriage, too wrapped up in his work and his travels across the world. But he had now realised that he had to make changes. She would understand his motivations, wouldn't she?

Lost in his thoughts, the phone rang and rang without answer, until the tone changed and Reilly realised that no one was going to pick it up. What had he done? With a fluid motion, he threw the mobile phone to the ground and got up, becoming dizzy suddenly. He could feel sweat on his forehead. Using a chair near the bed to steady himself, he walked to the window. Moving the curtains and undoing the latch, he opened it, relieved to feel the blast of cold air against his face. A small, decorative balcony had been mounted outside each opening on this floor. Not big enough to walk on, but large and solid enough for him to lean out and hold onto. He moved outside the now open window, looking at the street below as darkness began to fall. He looked over at the bookshop across the street, where a pale glow from an interior light granted an eerie luminescence to the shop-front.

Mary Hamilton's realisation that she had now met the man, about whom James Pollock had so often spoken, had been a shock. Latimer, despite his obvious awkwardness and overbearing belief in his own charming nature, was genuinely interested in what he had found here. He seemed to be the very essence of Pollock's description, she thought. She was keen, however, not to bring up the subject of James Pollock, until he had answered a few questions.

"Did you speak with the young chap before he died?" Latimer asked, feigning a mild disinterest, yet failing miserably.

"That's really why you're here, isn't it?" she asked.

He looked up from the book. She could sense his discomfort, sense his fear almost.

"Yes," he replied hoarsely.

"I understand," she said. She sensed his genuine concerns over the whole matter, unlike her earlier visitor who had merely wanted the quick answer, certainly not prepared for the truth.

"I'll put the kettle on. Please, come through and sit down." She motioned Latimer forward.

"Can we take the book with us?" he asked, excitedly.

"Of course. This way." She stopped. "Let me close the shop." She moved toward the front door, locking it and turning the cardboard sign to the closed position.

She ushered Latimer through the curtain behind the counter.

As it parted, he walked into a large living room with what appeared to be a small kitchenette at the end. The walls had recently been repainted, though the general architecture showed signs of age. The room was apparently created with minimalism in mind. Only one chair and a small dining table completed the scene. A television sat in the corner, the area lit by a lamp at the back of the room. What took Latimer by surprise, however, was the bookshelf that stood against one wall. His eyes were initially attracted by what appeared to be hardback volumes, of some age. As he approached, he found that the books were more than commonplace antiques.

"Monstres and their Kynde," he read aloud, his voice quivering with astonishment at the realisation that the sixteenth century occult masterpiece he had heard so much about, actually existed.

He looked again: 'Nameless Cults', Von Junzt's original text, 'The Pnakotic Manuscript', a 15th century English classic, and, if his eyes did not deceive him, all nine volumes of 'The Revelations of Glakki'. He could find no copies of that eldritch tome, 'The Necronomicon', though. Perhaps even Miss Hamilton would have no access to that, he thought.

He looked at her, his mouth agape.

"How is this possible?" he said, his voice shaking with his disbelief. "Most of these books aren't even thought to still exist. How can you have them here?"

She shrugged absently. "I'm a bit of a collector myself. You could say they've been in my family for many years." She moved toward the old style kettle on top of a cooker in the kitchen area, starting to fill it with water.

Latimer looked at the historic tomes once more.

"Might I have a look at these?" he asked innocently, trying hard to contain his excitement.

"Of course," she said, not even looking up at him as she filled the kettle with water.

Latimer gingerly pulled a volume from the nine books of *Glakki*. He leafed through the pages, the paper desperately thin, the print terribly small, yet the text seemed to shine from the page, to cast his consciousness into whirlwind spirals of other planes of existence as he read. The very fact that the book existed at all was astonishing to him.

He devoured the pages, carefully turning each leaf as soon as he was confident that his action would not destroy the fragile paper.

"But how can you have these?" he asked again. "These things are more than rare." He found it difficult to fully take in the enormity of his discovery.

She stopped filling the kettle and placed it on the stove, turning a dial and lighting the gas with a small lighter.

"Tell me about Pollock," she said, turning around suddenly and folding her arms, ignoring his question.

Latimer, surprised by the response, closed the book, replacing it carefully on the shelf. He sighed, and pulled a seat from the small dining table. "May I?" he asked.

As she raised her hand in permission, Latimer sat down heavily on the wooden seat.

"He was, of course, my best student," he said, clearing his throat. "I'd sent him here to research the battle of Newtowncairn," he continued, looking for a response, though none came.

"I… I heard that he'd been murdered. I wanted simply to establish the facts, to convince the police that he wasn't some sort of common criminal. I had to clear his name," he said, staring at the table.

"And that's what brought you all the way down here," she said, choosing her words carefully.

"Yes, of course," Latimer said.

She nodded, watching him steadily. "Tea or coffee?" she asked.

"Oh, coffee, black, no sugar please," he responded mechanically.

She turned and lifted mugs from a cupboard.

Latimer looked around the room once more. Though it was sparse, it was extremely clean and tidy. Perhaps Miss Hamilton had no more to do than tidy up, he thought. He looked back at the bookcase, considering that he now doubted if he could accurately establish anything about this mysterious woman.

Coffee followed. The pair continued with idle conversation before she began to draw the topic around to Pollock again.

"I used to chat with him every morning," she said,

without warning, seeming to remember his presence, and betraying a distinct sense of melancholy as she spoke.

"Why did he come here?" Latimer asked without thinking. "Oh, I didn't mean that it was necessarily a bad idea, I meant..."

"He was interested in the same thing that you are," she said, pointing at the bookshelf.

Latimer was stunned. "What? That's impossible. He had no interest in books of that nature. He shunned anything remotely supernatural, religious, or otherwise. His utter contempt for the spiritual world, in fact, would almost have been insulting to some, especially in this country!" Latimer said in defiance.

She drained the coffee mug. "I'm afraid not," she said, with conviction, moving to the sink.

Latimer was astonished. He could not deal with this. There seemed to be so much that he did not know. What the hell had Pollock been doing down here?

"Mary, I... I really have to go. This is all too much at the minute. Could I... could we perhaps have dinner at the hotel tomorrow night?"

She flushed visibly, shocked. She had clearly not been expecting the question.

An embarrassed silence descended, and for the first time, Latimer could tell that Miss Hamilton had lost control of the situation.

"I'm sorry," he said. "I didn't mean to..."

"I don't leave the shop much," she muttered.

Latimer wanted to try and reassure her, though was not sure if he could. "Join me at the hotel then. I'll come and meet you here at six, six thirty, would that do? Bring one of the books," he said, laughing heartily.

She broke into a strained smile, like an embarrassed schoolgirl.

"Yes, that would be very nice."

Latimer made for the curtain. "I'll show myself out. Thanks for the coffee."

She watched as he unlocked the door of the shop, turned the sign around, and waved as he exited.

"Yes, Professor," she murmured. "And perhaps then you'll tell me everything."

She picked up the empty mug that he had left on the table.

Mountcashel's Journal, August 26th 1690, Italian Border

I have received news from Patrick Sarsfield with regard to the defeat of James at the Boyne River in Ireland. This is a black day, and I fear that if news of James's flight from the battlefield is true, then Ireland is lost without the help of the French.

My thoughts are for my wife and what family remains in Ireland. In addition, actions that I carried out in the name of the King in the past months will become twisted and manipulated by William's propagandists for their own ends, as will the activities of all those who fought alongside King James. Whether we fought and acted honourably in the name of the King will mean little unless French aid helps wrest Ireland from William's grip.

This adds import to my mission here, that I might show the French how we will fight and how we will die.

The news from Ireland is worsened by the appearance of her black form again in my dreams. Once more has she found me, once more do my thoughts reek of the mire of her sorcery. How can man survive the onslaught of these black creatures of the night, when they live in our very minds? I pray that I am not going mad with some disease that robs me of reason. Will she not leave me?

CHAPTER FOURTEEN

McGrath drained the cold coffee from the mug, the bottom of which was now stained with the dark liquid that had been poured into it so many times that day.

He read the report once more. Recently, his interest in the Pollock case had driven him to request the paperwork, rather than simply interview the suspects that the detectives did not want to waste their time on. Pollock's throat had been cut, slit after the initial puncture wound. Acting like a pump, his heart had effectively made him bleed to death within a matter of seconds. While this had been going on, however, he had not struggled, nor had he left bloody fingerprints across the inside of his car. In fact, McGrath mused for the third or fourth time that day, it seemed that he had not even tried to stem the flow of blood. Surely survival instinct would, at the very least, have pushed him to do something? It did not seem right. Something on the pathologist's report might have indicated a clue at least, but there was nothing there. No poison, no drugs, nothing. McGrath scratched his forehead; neither had he been restrained in any way, and the report made no mention of Pollock having been unconscious prior to receiving the wound that killed him. He had not been knocked out, drugged or otherwise made unaware of the fact that he was having his throat cut.

"I'm going to the kitchen to wash my cup," he announced, as if it were the most important event of the day.

Laverty grunted, typing furiously on the computer as McGrath got up.

"Sergeant McGrath!" a voice shouted from the front

desk.

McGrath glanced across the office, twirling his mug absently in one hand.

A constable beckoned from the sliding window that faced on to the entranceway of the police station.

"Someone to see you, Sergeant!" the Constable announced, winking in perhaps the most obvious fashion imaginable.

"This better not be another bloody wind-up, Anderson," McGrath whispered as he passed, walking slowly toward the window.

"No, Sergeant, no. A young lady to see you."

Laverty, whose attention had, until now, been focused solely on the computer screen in front of him, suddenly became interested, like a hungry predator seeking its prey. Correctly predicting his partner's reaction, McGrath spoke without turning around.

"I think I can handle it, son. Finish the report. Traffic Branch are going nuts after this afternoon's little episode in the town centre."

He smirked, imagining Laverty's frustration. As he approached the window, he saw a tall woman, immediately taking in her figure hugging jeans, tight leather jacket and long red hair. He felt compelled to whistle, and then stopped himself.

"Ma'am, how can I help you?" McGrath smiled as she turned around. He had to admit she was quite a looker. Probably lost her dog or something, he thought as he fought the urge to look her up and down. He imagined how the younger Laverty would have chatted her up for hours. How lucky he got here first.

"You're Sergeant McGrath!" she said, directly, in a distinct Belfast accent. Beautiful until she opened her mouth, McGrath thought, his illusions shattered by her tone.

"Yes, Ma'am, I am. How can I help?"

She produced a wallet, flicking over clear plastic sections until she revealed a press pass, which she presented to his eyes.

"Very good, Miss... Miss Devlin, and how might I help the press today?" McGrath's smile had disappeared as he squinted at the press pass. He needed his glasses. If this was connected to those two idiotic professors, he might just explode, he thought.

She produced a packet of cigarettes, pulling one from the packet, as McGrath considered pointing to the 'no smoking' sign above his head.

"I'm a journalist with the Belfast Herald. I'd be interested in asking you some questions about the Pollock case," she said, sticking the cigarette in her mouth and patting her jacket, searching for a lighter.

McGrath had been in the process of constructing something sarcastic in relation to her obvious flouting of the smoking restrictions. Instead, he stopped himself.

"Ma'am, there's little more to add to what's already been handed over to the press," he said, resisting the urge to display defensive body language.

She lit up, moved closer to the window, and leaned an arm on the counter, blowing smoke as she spoke. "Can you tell me why you're talking with two professors from the University then, at least one of whom knew Pollock directly?" Holding the cigarette between her lips, she fished in her bag for a tape recorder, which she promptly switched on.

McGrath considered telling her where to go. He considered closing the opaque hatch. He even considered letting Laverty loose, raging hormones and all. In the end, however, he gave in.

"I'll talk to you in one of the interview rooms, Miss Devlin. There are, however, two conditions."

Annie canted the cigarette to one side with the two fingers that removed it from her mouth. "And they are?"

"One, you turn the tape recorder off, and two, you put that bloody thing out," he said, pulling a tin foil ashtray from below the counter and pushing it toward her.

Taking two long draws from the cigarette, Annie stubbed it out in the proffered ashtray, blew smoke into the air, and agreed.

The silence in the interview room was interspersed with the patter of rain outside as the early evening darkness of winter began to fall. Laverty, only too delighted to be invited to take part, was already enamoured by the confident and forward journalist.

"So, Miss Devlin, have you been in Enniskillen before?" he began, also beginning to flush nervously. Devlin smiled, coughing a little, desperate for a cigarette.

McGrath put his head in his hands.

"Ok, Miss Devlin," McGrath muttered. "What exactly...?"

"Can I smoke?" she asked.

"Definitely not. We've discussed this, ma'am," McGrath said sternly, trying to remain calm. Who the hell did this upstart think she was dealing with?

She shrugged, and pulled the notebook toward her.

"Let me just hang on to the tape recorder while we talk," McGrath asked. He wanted to get this over with and go home.

Reaching into her bag, she passed the small machine to McGrath.

"Okay," she continued. "Why are you involved with these two men? Is the case still open, with regard to Pollock?"

"First of all, ma'am, " McGrath answered. "How do you know that the two gentlemen are from the university?"

"Sergeant, I'm chasing a story here. It pays me to do my homework." She cleared her throat. "If you must know, my editor told me." She sat in a defiant pose, obviously aimed directly at McGrath's inefficient stalling tactics. "You're not telling me anything then, Sergeant. Can you tell me why you're involved, at least?"

"Ma'am," McGrath continued, leaning on the table and clenching his hands. "Those two gentlemen are acting on behalf of the university in Belfast. They're here to continue the young man's research."

A VERY IRISH CURSE

She began to write notes in shorthand.

"So why are you talking with them?" she asked.

"We're safeguarding their security, ma'am, under the belief, that you must be currently aware of, that there may be a connection to local criminals surrounding Pollock's death."

"So you're confirming that he was linked to drugs," she said, beginning to write furiously.

"That's still being investigated, ma'am," McGrath replied, striving to give nothing away. "What evidence we have does point in that direction, however."

"So this Professor... Latimer, isn't it?"

McGrath nodded. "Yes, ma'am, that's right. Though I haven't told you that. You appear to be well informed?"

She smiled, as Laverty watched the interplay between the two. Devlin was clearly looking for a scoop, and McGrath was having none of it.

She kept her eyes on the notebook. "Do you think that he's involved in all of this?" she said directly.

Laverty also looked at McGrath. He seemed confused. It was the last question he had expected.

He had a bemused expression on his face. "Ma'am, those two can barely find their way around town. You're suggesting that they're some sort of criminal masterminds? That's quite unbelievable, if you don't mind me saying so."

"It's a good cover though, right?"

"You've got to be kidding." McGrath paused, looking at his watch. "I think we're done here."

She finished writing in the notebook. "I assume they'll be going to Newtowncairn then, Sergeant?" she asked innocently. "That's where the murder and the so called research took place, isn't it?"

McGrath stopped, his confidence ebbing away. "Newtowncairn!" He stumbled over the word.

She was surprised by the reaction. "You'll be going there with them, won't you? You don't mind if I do a little digging down there myself, do you?"

McGrath's hands began to shake. "It's a very dangerous

place, ma'am." He got up and began to usher her to the door. "Now if you'll excuse me."

She looked at him again, puzzled. "I see. Well, thank you, Sergeant, Constable."

Laverty began to direct her out into the corridor.

"I need a coffee!" McGrath murmured, heading the other way.

"What the hell's wrong with your boss?" Devlin asked as Laverty led her to the door.

Looking after the departing figure of McGrath, Laverty could only speculate. "I really don't know, Miss. I really don't."

He opened the door for her. "If it's any help, the case is still open while those two are here. We're assigned to protect them. If you leave me your card, perhaps I could call you if anything comes up."

Annie Devlin bit her lower lip and beamed at Laverty. "Sure thing. Thanks, Constable," she said, pulling a card from the back pocket of her jeans. Laverty took the still warm card and watched her as she walked away.

Mountcashel's Journal, Isere River, 11th September 1690

Tonight I will lead a handful of picked men on a daring expedition against the Imperial positions, while other troops attack the flank. They have made a grave error in their deployment. I am thankful that the French have agreed with my stratagem, even if they are against my leading the expedition myself.

The night is filled with a low mist that will help cover our movements and deployment. I feel no fear however and have tried to help the men by walking through the camp and encouraging their efforts to make ready for the battle.

They know little of my real reasoning behind this move, nor do my closest colleagues amongst the Irish contingent. I intend to end these dreams by ending my life. This is not a decision any man can take lightly. It is a sin in the eyes of God to even contemplate such an action. I am left with little choice. I yearn to write to Arabella and tell her of this, of how I have reached my decision, but even she would not understand my motives or the state of my mind. At least if I die in battle I shall be given a hero's burial, perhaps in Ireland, while it still remains partially free from the forces of Dutch William.

The dreams grow worse. I see her now as an old sickly hag, clad in black rags with deformed features, broken teeth and the marks of torture. Her eyes, the piercing red eyes... I can not live with this burden.

CHAPTER FIFTEEN

Latimer was in a daze. Buoyed up with the certainty that he had now found an untapped vein of mystical literature on his proverbial doorstep, he changed for dinner and sought out his associate.

Finding him at the bar, Latimer, initially surprised by Reilly's new found love of Guinness, approached stealthily, conscious that his colleague had gone the way of all men whose love life had decided to go pear shaped on them.

"Joseph. What's wrong? I don't normally find you propping up the bar, old friend," he announced as the barman approached.

Reilly turned, his face a map of unspoken worries and concerns, which had been somewhat diluted by alcohol.

"No, Neil, you certainly don't. I have, however, decided to get pissed tonight!" Reilly slurred in a most uncharacteristic manner, as he swayed gently on the barstool, balancing precariously between staying upright and falling, as he stumbled over his words.

Latimer nodded again at the barman. "A whiskey, and I'll pay for whatever this chap owes."

The barman, whose expression remained tactful throughout, proffered a glass toward a convenient optic. Handing over the cash, Latimer downed the drink and put his hand on Reilly's shoulder.

"Come on, let's get some dinner, yes? I have much to tell you."

Two hours later, after Reilly had vomited most of the contents of his stomach into the secluded toilet near the bar, he sat, pale and morose, in front of his slightly dried melon. Latimer tucked into a medium rare steak, munching noisily as he tried to explain the nature of his finds in the bookshop across the road.

"A charming lady," he announced, between mouthfuls. "The tomes of secret knowledge that she has access to, Joseph. Goodness knows how she got them!" He clamped his teeth down on a large lump of meat as he spoke, watery red blood oozing over his lips.

Reilly wanted to throw up again as he watched. The two remained alone in the dining room, interrupted only by the entrance of the waiter, whom Latimer was convinced was gay. Reilly had tried to get him to change the subject before he created a scene.

"You know how interested I am in this sort of literature. I never dared hope that I would find some of these works. The world of the Mythos, so varied, so full of ancient antediluvian magic and unholy rites."

Reilly mumbled, "Yes. Of course, as an anthropologist with an interest in such things, one man's magic is another man's science. You don't believe in any of the rubbish you've found in those books, do you?"

Latimer swallowed another dripping mouthful. "No, of course not, Joseph. It's the principle of the thing, the belief systems that must have existed for these things to be written. The power that these people who wrote these tomes must have commanded... let's call them sorcerers; the reverence with which their societies must have held them. How she found these books, in Ireland of all places, I'll never know."

Reilly considered his starter, and then looked away quickly. "So how do you aim to find out?" he said at last, as he swayed, almost anticipating the answer.

Latimer took a sip of red wine. "I've invited her to dinner, tomorrow evening."

Reilly tried to laugh. The effort made him want to be sick

again. He felt queasy, light headed, and more than a little drunk.

"I think I'll go to bed," he said, standing up carefully. "Are we driving to Newtowncairn tomorrow?"

Reilly chomped on his steak, nodding vigorously. "Oh, I think we should at the very least do a little reconnaissance, don't you?"

"Ok. Perhaps you should wake me for breakfast?"

Latimer tucked into his dinner, putting on a 'camp' expression in an effort to make Reilly laugh, as he noticed the waiter returning with more wine. Reilly, who was in no condition to pass comment on Latimer's homophobia, or even share the joke, made a face as if he was going to be sick again and walked toward the exit.

Having finished his dinner and exquisite dessert, Latimer also retreated to his room. Placing his satchel on the desk, he patted his belly, belched loudly, and pulled out the notes that he had so carefully been working on. From the inside pocket of his jacket, he removed the journal.

"Now, Lord Mountcashel," he announced. "Let's see if we can unlock some more of your secrets."

He switched on the lamp by the bedside table, adjusting the shade so that its light shone on to the desk, and assembled his notes. Placing his spectacles on the end of his nose, he opened the journal. He reached for Pollock's notes.

Mountcashel had been fiendishly clever, Latimer thought. Cross-referencing phrases in French military dictum with more common French language, he had crafted an almost unbreakable code. Only those who had served in the military of the time, and with an inkling of the general's choice of cipher, could even have had a hope of breaking the secret language. How Pollock had been able to do this had, initially at least, been a mystery to Latimer. As he worked out more of the code and became used to Mountcashel's phraseology, however, the reality of the situation became clearer.

He had always been impressed by Pollock's insight. He had, however, completely underestimated the man's skill. Had

Latimer been given the text, he was sure that he would not have been able to decode the cipher. He would have required pointers and clues at the very least. Too much would have been left to chance had he not been given Pollock's guidance. Far from missing the nuances of Mountcashel's meaning, he might have mistranslated entire chapters of text.

Pollock, on the other hand seemed to have got inside Mountcashel's head. Latimer had always remarked on his student's ability to think like any particular historical figure he chose and to provide insights into their particular manner or the basis of some decision they had made. Latimer had considered the skill remarkable enough, though only recently could he see how truly important it really was.

Pollock could literally think like the general. Either that, or he had had considerable help with the notes that he had prepared for translation. So, unless a wandering seventeenth century history and cryptography expert had happened to be available in Enniskillen these past few months, Latimer was at a loss to provide any other explanation. No, Pollock had uncovered something truly wonderful here, and been able to de-code the writing of the general. As to why Mountcashel had so strictly coded what he had to say, Latimer had yet to fully discern. He guessed that this had something to do with the Newtowncairn Witch, a figure who he found playing an increasingly important role in the text as he translated, and someone who Mountcashel appeared to be singularly afraid of.

In addition, as Latimer continued to read and translate the passages, noting the battles and campaigns within which the general had served the French, it appeared that not only did his reported dreams become worse, but also that his grip on reality became more tenuous. Indeed, as he deciphered more of the writing, he began to realise that Mountcashel was not only going steadily insane and becoming chronically schizophrenic, but that he felt that the passage of time was building to a momentous exit or, at the very least, the termination of some grand design.

As the general descended into some form of madness, it

was also clear that the coding and deception in the writing became more desperate, more complex, as if Mountcashel were striving continually to hide his conclusions so that only the cursory and the more obvious points could be clear. Latter passages and journal entries would have been nigh impossible to interpret were it not for the young student's notes. Whoever Lord Mountcashel had been trying to outwit, he had not reckoned on James Pollock's genius.

Latimer tried turning to the end of the journal. The writings ended mid way through the book, with blank pages following what appeared to be a description of the last campaign in which the general had fought: Spain in 1694. The back page, however, held more secrets. Interspersed with Mountcashel's coded language, notes in this latter case, were symbols that Latimer had never seen before; strange angular graphics that, though he had initially considered them to have some occult symbolism, displayed nothing that seemed familiar in their construction. This section seemed less like the journal entries but more distinct, almost reading like a recipe of sorts. The language referred to substances that Latimer had never heard of. Even the text that he could translate seemed fluid, nonsensical. It reminded him of a nonsense poem of some kind. He believed that these could only have been the musings of a madman, discerning that at the time of writing, it must have been too late for the general to revisit reality.

Latimer considered that he had been living with the journal too long himself. In the early hours of the morning, when he squinted, he felt he could almost discern the symbols moving of their own accord.

Hours later Latimer closed the book, drained his glass of whisky, removed his spectacles and rubbed the bridge of his nose. Outside, dawn began to break. Had he really been up all night?

He moved to the bed with the journal and lay down, turning once more to the back page. As he slumped down, his thumb grated against the back cover. He tried again. He looked at the book, puzzled. Turning to the front cover, he repeated the action. It seemed thinner, somehow, as if...

Latimer sprung up from the mattress and pounced on his jacket, which hung over the chair at the desk. He grabbed a pocketknife and pulled the bedside lamp over to him. Carefully, he began to slice open the inside of the journal's back cover. His eyes ached through exhaustion and the lack of clear light, though he continued to cut. There, on the inside of the leather, paper edges could be discerned, thin and desperately delicate, folded upon each other.

Joseph Reilly was not sure whether the pounding that he could both hear and feel came from inside his head or from outside his room. He was crippled by blinding, throbbing pain, afraid almost to move, lest he should make things worse. No, there were definitely two rhythms at work here, he considered, afraid to open his eyes. One was constant, undoubtedly alcohol induced. The other, rapid, less consistent... and being followed by Latimer's persistent shouting from outside his room.

He heard the door being hammered again.

"Joseph, wake up. Wake up! You have to see this."

Reilly tried to stir, and winced as pain lanced through his head. He heard the muffled voice of another guest telling Latimer to keep it down, 'it was five in the bloody morning'.

He shifted slightly, ignoring his head, and mumbled feebly. "All right... I'm coming."

Minutes later, a dumbfounded and tired looking Reilly opened the door. Latimer, smelling of whisky, which wanted to make Reilly gag, was of little help.

"Joseph... you look like crap! But never mind that now. Come quickly!"

He bounded off down the corridor, expecting the weary Reilly to follow. Reilly retreated into the room and wrapped his nightgown around him, shivering slightly. He thought better of trying to find painkillers amongst his partially unpacked luggage and shuffled down the corridor, locking his door behind him.

Latimer was sitting at the desk, poised beneath a table lamp, carefully unfolding a stained, partially torn, piece of parchment.

He looked up at the still bleary eyed Reilly.

"Look, Joseph," he said excitedly. "It's a map!"

Mountcashel's Journal, Isere River, 13th September 1690

I have been gravely wounded by a musketball in my side. My officers and men, the French officers and Marshal St. Ruth himself have all heaped praises upon me for my actions in the fight. Thoughts of how a man of my rank should not be doing the job of a Captain seem dwarfed by the French comments concerning my bravery. Even my men, desperate that I should not lie wounded in the Imperial trenches, fought off the last of the enemy and dragged me to safety. One of the best French surgeons has done sterling work in removing the ball and has done his best to prevent infection.

When asked of my motivation for such apparently foolhardy action, I can relay only that I looked to the welfare of my soldiers and my ongoing attempts to earn the respect of the French after the reverses of the Irish campaign. St. Ruth, with tears in his eyes, embraced me and told me that never again would he doubt our bravery and our resolute steadfastness, as we had now earned on this day the glory or 'gloire' that the French military hold in such high regard. I yearn to tell him the truth, but I can not.

My force of loyal Irishmen have been bloodied, yet have shown their courage in the eyes of their new French masters. In truth, the French have used us as shock troops, forcing the breach at sieges and holding the rear when we are pursued. My men do not complain about this however. Most of them remain set in their need to rid the regiment of the stink of Newtowncairn, to show once more that they can fight and die for a noble cause, albeit a French one.

For my own part, I remain troubled. She comes to me at night and tells me that I must follow her path, that I am to seek the end of the journey, that I must do her bidding. For that is why I have been released and why I was spared at Newtowncairn where rebel fire did not kill me. I have no knowledge of what these dreams may mean, though I fear that I am losing my mind! I have escaped a jail in Enniskillen, even tried to end my pain, only to become a prisoner of nightmare.

One noble French officer, whom I have confided in, tells me that he has heard of such sorcery before. That he has seen witches and their kin, witnessed the results of their spells and potions, and the effects that they have on the dreams of men. He tells me that men such as myself have been driven mad by the demons in their heads.

Must I then follow the path that she sets out for me? Is this my destiny?

In the night she laughs at me, at my petty attempts to betray her. I will silence her yet.

CHAPTER SIXTEEN

Annie Devlin drank deeply from the coffee mug. This part of the job was terrible. She had been sitting here, eating breakfast, and drinking sweet black coffee with too much sugar, for the best part of an hour. Café customers were not allowed to smoke and it was killing her, though the wait gave her time to mull over exactly what she was doing here. Chasing another damn story. But this time, it would be worth it. This time, Annie would prove to her mother and older brothers that journalism was worthwhile, that she could make a name for herself and not end up in some damned factory as they would have preferred. Demure, sweet little Annie, who wouldn't hurt a fly. She hoped she had proved them wrong by now.

She shook herself out of the daydream. Her view could not have been better. She could see Latimer's hotel, the main gate and the car park. The café was at the end of the street, and sitting here, she could see the comings and goings of the hotel's guests. Unless someone knew her vantage point, however, it was almost impossible for her to be seen. Foolproof, she thought, taking another sip of coffee. Now all she needed was for Latimer and his friend to make a move. What was the point in them having come down here and not going to Newtowncairn? She looked at her watch again: just after eight. Come on, somebody make a move. It was not fair!

Ripping open another packet of sugar and pouring it into the dregs of the sickeningly sweet coffee, she watched the police car making its way through the heavy rush hour traffic. This one way system must be a bitch in the mornings, she thought idly, smiling at the waitress and pointing at the coffee mug. As the hot black liquid slowly refilled it, Annie noted that the car was turning into the hotel car park, missing the clearly disgusted look that the middle aged woman serving her had, regarding the state of the unused saucer, piled high with the remnants of paper sugar packets.

It must be the police escort, Annie reasoned, lifting the cup.

"Would you like anything else, luv?" the woman asked, in a gruff voice, whose undertone was clearly laced with the wish that this customer, at least, would get up and leave.

"No, I'm fine," Annie Devlin said again. She had been saying that since she got here an hour ago. They must be wondering if she was a real coffee lover, or a lunatic, or…

The police car turned violently out of the hotel entrance with its siren blaring.

"Oh bloody hell they've already left!" Devlin screamed, despite herself, jumping from the table, pulling money from her handbag and throwing it near the coffee cup, as she ran awkwardly in her high heeled boots toward the door, then toward the car that she had left parked further up the street.

"Thank Christ for that," the waitress said in a barely audible whisper, scooping up the money and dishes with a sigh.

She was lucky, Annie thought as she ran, gasping. Inadvertently perhaps, but her car was parked well along the road, ready to get further in the morning traffic than the police car was likely to in the next few minutes. Good, it was her turn for a dose of luck. If she moved quickly enough she might just beat the worst of the ever-increasing morning traffic. She ran faster, panting loudly, thinking that someday she should really give up the damned cigarettes.

"I can't believe it," Laverty said, shaking his head and muttering curses, revving the engine in an attempt to gun the car through the rush hour traffic. Chaos ensued as confused drivers, eager to make room for the police car, now with full sirens and headlights flashing, tried to move their vehicles into lanes that were already full. Horns blared, windows were rolled down as drivers leant out of their cars and screamed obscenities at each other. No one, it appeared, was moving anywhere. McGrath watched Laverty trying to negotiate through the lines of heavy traffic.

"This is bloody ridiculous," he said. He began to laugh.

"What's so funny, Sarge?" Laverty exclaimed against the sounds of the siren, desperately trying to make progress amidst the maelstrom of traffic.

McGrath looked up, amused. "Oh, those two might appear to be idiots. They might have seemed to all the world like a pair of daft Sunday School teachers, but they got us this time, didn't they? Look, there's no point in going mad. They're long gone. A few minutes won't make any difference now."

"Right," Laverty responded carefully, still surprised at how well McGrath seemed to be taking the whole thing. "Well, the lady in reception said they'd left about half an hour ago. That was before all this traffic built up, which means that if they're going to the village, they won't have too long to themselves before we get there."

"I'm not sure that this was such a good idea," Reilly said, changing gear as the country road narrowed, and the morning mist became more persistent. "Shouldn't we have told the police we were leaving? This is going to cause some major issues, I'm sure. What if they tell Moore?" he rambled, glancing across at his passenger, whose attention was focused solely on the faded and decaying parchment that he held.

"Hmmm?" Latimer replied, intent only on the map that he moved between his fingers.

"I said: don't you think that we should have let the cops know what the hell we're doing?" The irritation in his voice made Latimer look up this time.

"Oh no. Absolutely not. They'd follow us across all the fields, wondering where we got the map, wondering what we're doing?"

"And what are we doing?" Reilly asked, raising an eyebrow.

Latimer looked at him in disgust. "This map points to five hills, let's call them potential cairns, old burial mounds. The things I couldn't find any reference to before. Well, they're here." As he talked, he jabbed his finger at the fragile map.

Reilly winced at the thought of the potential destruction the finger could wreak on a piece of paper that had thus far survived for over three hundred years. "Five small hills, just south of the town. Don't you think that's a bit of a coincidence, what with the location of the battle being such a mystery and all? Remember? I couldn't find anything about these. Nothing, Joseph. It's all very well talking about these bloody cairns," Latimer continued. "Late Neolithic and early Bronze Age, even later. Usually circular, burial mounds erected in prominent locations to intern important members of the community, but only Mountcashel's map even points to their existence. Don't you find that strange?"

"Yes, well, I suppose…" Reilly attempted to answer.

"Exactly," continued Latimer defiantly. "The police would be tramping all over the area, destroying historical evidence. Look, Joseph, this is the find of a lifetime," he said, balancing the map in his hand. "Let's not screw it up, okay?"

Reilly admitted defeat. "You're right Neil. Okay, you're right!" he whispered.

Both sides of the road remained veiled in mist as they drove on, giving an almost sepia like appearance in the yellow light from the headlamps. It was sixteen miles from Enniskillen to Newtowncairn, with two small villages and the town of Lisnaskea on the way. Latimer had to admit, he had not seen any other traffic for the last eight or nine miles. They had already passed through the smaller hamlets before Lisnaskea. Maybe it was a little early for everyone.

"This place is quite remote, isn't it?" he remarked.

"It certainly doesn't see much in the way of tourists," Reilly replied, noting for himself the distinct absence of traffic.

Latimer looked at the larger Ordnance Survey map that he had unfolded.

"Sign, up ahead," Reilly said.

"You see. Now, this little village is Lisnaskea. This is where the Enniskillen garrison first camped the day before the battle. Look at that! There! There!" Latimer said, spittle flying out of his mouth in his excitement.

"What is it? I'm trying to drive, Neil," Reilly exclaimed, perturbed by the excitement.

"That's Lisnaskea Castle. It was left in such disrepair by the Jacobites that Colonel Berry, the English officer recently arrived at Londonderry; well, he thought it unimportant and chose not to garrison it."

"Is that relevant?" Reilly said, as the car put distance between the remnants of the castle and the rampant historian beside him.

He could feel Latimer's disappointment.

"Well, no. I suppose not. Not if you're a bloody anthropologist or something, no!"

Reilly suppressed a laugh as Latimer folded his arms in disgust.

"I'm sorry, Neil. I know you're excited."

"Well, I talked about the history of the campaign and this battle with Pollock a lot. Never did quite get the chance to come down here in more recent times. I suppose I should have. Maybe if I had, he…"

"Don't even think like that, Neil. You know where it leads," Reilly said quietly.

"During the day the traffic here must be bedlam!" he said, changing the subject.

"Yes, just the one street. And we know how traffic chaos can be. Right?"

"Oh… is this going to be the start of an 'it's all your fault, Joseph' speech?"

"No... I didn't mean it like that... I..."

The car swerved a little on the road as the two occupants began to argue.

"Try and pull out, Laverty. Damn, missed it," McGrath shouted, above the sound of the siren.

Laverty shook his head.

"It's impossible, Sarge. We're right in the middle of what passes for rush hour traffic in Enniskillen, mild compared to Belfast, I'm sure, but that doesn't make it any easier to get through. I still can't believe those two did this. I thought we were in for an easy time with them. Come on!" Laverty shouted, pumping the horn as a confused driver tried to pull out in front of him.

"I'll flash him with the lights, Sarge. Get him to stop," Laverty continued, reaching for the headlight lever.

"Leave it, kid. We've caused enough bloody confusion this morning. Let's just get there when we get there," McGrath sighed.

Latimer broke the lasting silence that had followed the heated discussion in the car.

"Newtowncairn sits at a cross roads. We should stop in the village, get our bearings at least. What we're looking for is just to the south. In fact we'll be re-treading the path of the Enniskillen force that attacked Mountcashel's position in 1689, more or less."

"So you think the fact that you've found evidence of these 'cairns' is some sort of breakthrough," Reilly said wearily.

"Well, you obviously don't," Latimer replied. "Look," he said. "There's something about this map, the way everything's... configured!" he added.

Reilly tried to get his bearings from the road. "I really haven't got the faintest idea what you're talking about, you know. On a different point, have you noticed that this fog seems to be getting worse?"

Latimer looked up, unconcerned. "Could it be that you, the ever cynical Dr. Reilly, are trying to create a form of haunted house mystery from our glorious Northern Irish weather?" He laughed heartily.

Reilly shared in the laughter, straining to see through his glasses in order to try and make out the road-sign ahead.

"If I'm not mistaken, we're about five miles out," he added.

"Good," Latimer replied. "Now we get some answers."

Annie Devlin neatly manoeuvred in front of the two cars that blocked her, snaking through the traffic, noting with satisfaction how far behind her the blue flashing lights of the police vehicle were. If she could just negotiate through the next few lanes, she could take a few short cuts, hopefully break a few speed limits, and get there in time to get some pictures of Latimer, and whoever it was that he was going to speak to in Newtowncairn. She had not come this far to fail at the last minute. There was a story here. She could feel it, and she was not going to let it go.

Reilly yawned.

"Fog's not as bad. It would've been nice to get some sleep before we came tramping out here," he said.

Responding to Reilly's infectious yawn, Latimer put his hand to his mouth to stifle his own reaction. "The map's too important. This has to be done now," Latimer responded, suddenly stern and single minded.

Reilly reluctantly agreed. "I understand," he said quietly.

Annie could no longer see the police. She had managed to lose them in the awful traffic in the town. Horns blared as she shuffled between lanes, though she appeared to be getting the better of the situation, at least. She was cutting through the jam and slowly getting out of the town. More than could be said for the flashing lights that were five or six cars behind her. She would be making good time to Newtowncairn. When necessary, she brought down her driver's window, casting sympathetic looks and flirtatious glances at male drivers, who for the most part did their best to let a pretty face get her way. She made good time.

"Shouldn't we let the station know, Sarge, so that they can send somebody else?" Laverty said, turning the wheel awkwardly, trying to squeeze past two other cars.

McGrath gave him a look of utter disdain. "If you think that I'm going to let those idiots at the station know that we can't even handle a couple of rogue professors, you're mad, Laverty. Are you kidding me?" McGrath spat, suddenly angry at the thought of the repercussions. Yet he also had deep feelings of terror regarding the impending trip to Newtowncairn. These feelings had suddenly begun to prey on his mind. Something, somewhere deep in his subconscious, did not want him getting out of this traffic, getting through to that remote village. He could not explain it.

Laverty relented, raising one hand as a plea of surrender to McGrath. "It was just a thought, Sarge. Let's just forget it, shall we?"

Annie Devlin sped along the main road out of Enniskillen. What morning fog there had been now seemed to be clearing a little and, surprisingly, there appeared to be an absence of other traffic on the road; at least, none heading for Newtowncairn. She smiled to herself. She could almost smell the story that would be unfolding there.

Annie had rounded two of the bends on the narrow country road a little too fast and had to brake to get through without smashing the car into a ditch.

Where the hell do I think I am? she thought. The absence of traffic and the remoteness of the surrounding farmland made the area seem empty.

"If I crashed here, I might not be found for years," she said quietly, only partially in jest. An image of her mother flashed into her head. Stay focused, she thought, staring at the road in front of her.

She saw the sign for the village ahead and did not spend any time trying to read it, her mind registering only the thirty miles per hour sign. All she needed to know was that she was on the right road for Newtowncairn. She braked slightly, having no wish to be caught out by either the police or the speed cameras that she knew had started to pop up even in the most remote areas. As she cleared the village, she accelerated again.

"Here we are!" Latimer exclaimed, as buildings and neatly parked cars became clear in the remaining mist. Older style houses and shops, built around a narrow crossroads, were now clearly discernable.

"You see. A normal little country village, full of church Elders and farmers," he said.

"How quaint," Reilly added, unimpressed by Latimer's laconic sentimentality.

"And, of course... murderers," Latimer continued. Reilly opted not to reply this time.

"Let's park the car, Joseph," Latimer added. "I need to get my bearings. Anywhere here will do."

Reilly turned right at the crossroads, pulled into an empty space near a closed chip shop and turned off the engine.

"Now what?"

Latimer spread out the old map.

"Now, if I'm not mistaken," he murmured, pointing to a road on the map. "We're, exactly, here!" He looked up at Reilly, excitedly.

"And?" Reilly asked.

"Well, that means that these cairns, these burial mounds – they're all around us. Look!"

He slowly pushed the map over to Reilly, without removing his finger. Sure enough, the five hill drawings on the sketch surrounded their current position, if the layout of the village on it was taken into account.

"But we have no idea of the scale here," he said. "We can get an appreciation of it, but look around. Even with the mist clearing, there are no cairns, chambered graves, or otherwise. The road rises to the south. There is some high ground on the way in, but nothing as specific as you're implying here."

"I know," Latimer said. "I think they've gone."

"Gone? Now you're not making any sense."

"Walk with me and I'll show you." He opened the car door. Reilly followed, locking the door behind him. Both men zipped up their coats.

"It's a cold one," Latimer said, putting the map away and blowing on his hands.

"Ok," he began as they walked. "Mountcashel must have drawn the five cairns for a reason, yes?"

"Agreed. Unless he was making the whole thing up," Reilly added.

Latimer winced. "Let's assume that he wasn't. I believe that the cairns were present at the time. Ancient burial mounds, possibly symbols of a forgotten age. There's something about them that I can't quite put my finger on yet, but I believe that they were here, as Mountcashel has outlined. Remember that this entire area was heavily drained in the eighteenth and nineteenth centuries. The place has been changed dramatically. The terrain was re-moulded, if you like, through the need for drainage, the needs of local farming."

Latimer looked up, suddenly aware that something was out of place. As they walked through the village, he looked for people, signs of life. Even the cars seemed to be older models, decrepit and rusting. It was as though the village had become firmly rooted in another decade. As he glanced across the street at a row of terraced houses, he saw curtains being drawn, as if the occupants wanted to hide all signs of life and activity in the village.

"Where the hell is everybody?" he asked innocently.

"I was beginning to wonder that myself," Reilly replied.

They reached the main road, along which they had driven minutes before. Latimer pulled out the map again and unfolded it. The silence that had marked their short walk from the car was punctuated now only by the bleating of sheep in the fields by the road, land that still lay shrouded in a heavy morning mist.

"Look, the cairns lie to the right here. In most historical cases, these roads do not change position in the main, they just receive a generous portion of tarmac. That would put the cairns over there!" He pointed to the southwest.

"In a field?" Reilly asked.

"Yes, remember Mountcashel's position. It was off the main road. Why would he have drawn these cairns if they didn't have some meaning for him, if they weren't right in the middle of his defensive position? It has to mean something. Come on, give me a leg up."

Latimer put one foot on the lower bar of a five bar gate as Reilly grudgingly helped him over. He landed with a thud.

"Are you sure we should be doing this? This isn't exactly our land. Shouldn't we have a look around the village first?" Reilly asked.

"We'll be gone before anyone sees us," he said, dusting himself down and setting off, his shoes squelching in the mud. "Nothing interests me in that village anyway," he said, suddenly appearing to have found new purpose and direction.

They strode across the field, wet grass brushing the bottom of their trousers, making them sodden, as sheep trotted away at the sound of their passing, bleating an alarm to the flock.

"Well. At least there's sheep here," Latimer whispered.

"How comforting," Reilly added.

Annie Devlin pulled her car into the side of the road outside the village. She put on her heavy winter coat, changed into a pair of thick boots, and rubbed her hands together for warmth and checked the camera, small enough to remain inconspicuous but large enough to get a good close up. She walked briskly, entering the small village. There is bound to be a pub here somewhere, she thought, though even as she looked, something struck her as odd about the place, distinctly odd. Scanning the crossroads and the buildings, she noticed the four wheel drive that she knew belonged to Professor Reilly, standing tall amidst the somewhat smaller cars parked in the street. All thoughts of incongruity seemed to vanish as the story beckoned once more. She was excited. Finally something was happening, and she could feel the familiar tingle of a story developing.

They're here, she thought. She was disturbed by the sound of metal rattling up ahead on the main road. She could just see two figures in the poor visibility, climbing over a fence... clumsily. The first of them landed awkwardly. That can only be them, she thought. She switched the digital camera on, bounding across the road and making her way along the tree line. Finding a low point in the hedge, she pushed her way into the neighbouring field, proceeding now at right angles to the field that the two professors were trudging through. She was glad of the old army boots that she had decided to change into, as she made her way through the mud. At intervals she stopped, lining up the camera with the two men, still visible despite the clinging mist. They were obviously here to meet a contact. Perhaps a decent photograph could make the front page, especially if their contact was a known criminal. God, what a story!

Lost in her thoughts, she did not see the figure that followed her, that watched her every move and quietly pursued her.

Mountcashel's Journal, 20th Oct 1690, Chambery

> *I have lost many men in the ongoing campaign here. Now, with winter closing, we can rest. Earning French respect for our earlier actions has made us the choice for many dangerous ventures. The cry 'send in the Irish' is heard more and more frequently on the lips of senior French officers who fear risking their own troops in assaults and breaches of city walls. Many of the men, eager to prove their worth still, in the eyes of our French masters, accept this fate, expecting it to lead to French aid in our homeland. I pray that they are right.*
>
> *Disease has also taken its toll. Unfamiliar food and a lack of fresh water at times has caused sickness within the camp, despite the hardiness of my men. It grows colder and I have requested warm clothing and blankets for those who will be forced to garrison some godforsaken collection of hovels in unfamiliar lands through the winter months.*
>
> *Though the regiments have suffered, morale remains high, the men finally having expunged the ghost of Newtowncairn. If only my own demons were so easily cleansed.*
>
> *I have heard my officers talk of my strained nerves and the death of so many of my countrymen playing upon my mind. Yet these troubles are bearable. Worse is the constant presence of the witch. My fear now is that we will be ordered away from Italy now that the front has stabilised, that once more she will try to make me do her bidding.*

CHAPTER SEVENTEEN

"They're here," the old man said, entering the dark, damp smelling room. He watched as the ragged and stiffened figure sitting cross-legged and floating in front of him seemed to reform, to grow tissue on spindly limbs, and become younger, and more... human, unfolding and moving like some enormous black spider waking from its sleep at the centre of a web.

"I know," it croaked. "Yet they are not ready. He does not have it yet," it said, its voice attaining more human characteristics as it continued, as it stood, in the form of a naked, middle aged woman. Sorcha Ballantine looked at the decrepit figure in front of her.

"You wake me to tell me that which I already know, Hamilton," she said sternly. Taking a few steps toward him, she struck him across his jaw with the back of her hand. There was a sickening thump as it contacted. The old man yelped and fell to the ground. He stayed there, gasping. "I... I am sorry, Milady. I am sorry," he pleaded.

"I've tolerated your family and your pathetic service since your ancestor tried to have me burned at the stake, Hamilton, yet still you do not understand!" she cried, as she stood before him, fully formed.

The old man rose only to his knees, daring to look at the thing in front of him.

"There is something else, Milady," he continued as he knelt on the wooden floor, trembling at the prospect of the punishment he might receive should he continue. There was menace in her dark eyes.

"I assume that you have some good reason for this interruption?"

"A woman has followed them. She is young, some would say beautiful!" he stuttered.

"Some would say?" she quizzed, looking dangerously human as her mind enquired after the facts. "You would say?" she added. "This woman follows them. Why?"

"A journalist, I believe, looking for a story." Hamilton began to find his composure once more. "She has no idea of what she seeks. No concept of the truth."

"I see," Ballantine said. She smiled. "Ensure that she comes here. My time runs short and I will have need of her. Yes, I will need her," she said malevolently. "Leave me to my thoughts."

The crawling figure edged away toward the door as the witch's form began to melt once more into a ragged and evil, skeletal façade of humanity.

She could remember so much, so many years. All that had transpired and all those who had died. And now, when she was so close to her freedom, only she could see how important it was that all should proceed, as she had desired, as had been planned so many hundreds of years ago.

Her childhood had been happy, as the daughter of an English nobleman. Her father had been of noble birth. Important enough that he had made sure she had been noticed at court by the Queen herself. She had never known her mother, who had died during childbirth. Her father, though he had fought against the urge to blame his only child for the death of his wife, had ultimately been destroyed by his anger and grief.

The memories were seared in her mind. Even then, as a young maiden ripe for the plucking in the court of Queen Elizabeth I, she had been an outcast of sorts. A maiden of such stature, who yet showed such interest in the dark arts; the very thought of it repelled many noble suitors; a fact that only further incurred the wrath of her noble father. And then she met the Queen's astrologer, John Dee.

Dee had been the unofficial face of the Queen's interest in the occult. Formally serving the court as her astrologer, he had been so much more. Even today, fools thought of him as simply a man of his time, so consumed in his own belief in the realms of the supernatural that he succumbed to the call of alchemy, in line with famous occultists of the time. She knew better than this.

Becoming an exile of the court, and an exile from her father's heart, Dee had taken her in hand to his house at Mortlake. As an apprentice of sorts, if such a lowly term could be used to describe the nature of her relationship to him, to the man who showed her such sights and opened up the vista of the dark arts and the opportunities of a whole new world. His was a lonely existence, his time spent experimenting or perusing the vast quantity of esoteric books and texts that he had amassed, and she wanted to share it with him. To share the depth of his knowledge, the breadth of his experience and talk to those beings that she knew existed at the edges of mankind's perception. Demonology, witchcraft and alchemy, such secrets were laid open for her, over the years, as she got closer and closer to his work. But ever she felt that he was holding back, showing her the paltry veneer of the blasphemous and arcane formulae that he knew; that he had knowledge but did not dare reveal it all to her.

A venomous rattle emanated from her throat as she remembered. He had been so restrained when translating the texts and showing her the ways, the true methods that she wanted to know. For all that humankind had beheld as sacred, all that it had conceived of as demonic and idolatrous and evil. All of it was a lie. An invention set in stone by ancient religion and the established church, by those who sought to keep man ignorant of the truth. But she knew the power of the old ones, the true way, and Dee had shown her how to use that power.

Yet he could not see it, not as clearly as she was able to. Even those fools who obliged to call themselves his friends and allies were blind to the truth. The plain simple fact was that their search for supernatural power was destined to fail.

The source of the voices in their heads were the sounds of the great old ones, those who walked the earth before the stain of mankind dared to pollute it with its so called civilisations, its progress and technology. Dee would not believe, could not accept it, and he suffered for his lack of faith. The memories resurfaced in the mire of her mind as she considered the events that had brought her to this place.

The inevitable persecutions had followed, led chiefly by those who had believed her long dead father's plea that she had been taken away by some dark magic cast by a black magician. Nothing could be further from the truth. She had left that pathetic society and all that had held her to this spiritual realm.

Faking her own death from plague, she had fled to Ireland, amidst the plantation so forcefully sponsored by King James I, the new man on the throne. She had thought Ireland a quiet backwater, a refuge from Dee, who by now had become so compelled to follow the wrong path that he wearied her. She had expected a dull, lifeless, rain soaked land, but had instead found... paradise! The cults that she had conspired to create in England had existed in Ireland for centuries, believing in their own versions of the dark Gods that she had found. The cults of Balor and the Morrigan gave her refuge and she ultimately became a leader to all of them. She showed them the extent of the power that she had learned, that had been found in the texts that even Dee was afraid to pursue, for he may have translated the fabled Necronomicon, the book of the dead, but she, she had learned from it. The Irish cultists did not even realise the true nature of the dark ones that they worshipped. Granting them titles from their own legends, they had been naïve, ill-educated beasts that they dared not call them by their proper names.

But then, further persecution had come, from this new band of settlers that had been placed in Ireland to protect James's interests and propagate a war between the various sects of their church, for she could scarcely owe any fealty to them and their simple ways. She knew too much to let her will be overtaken by them. The purges were swift and ruthless, and the crown ensured that few survived. Their King's agents were merciless in their actions, and though she had only taken a few sacrifices from their people, they had responded with fire and sword to rend her cults, tear away their beliefs with torture and flame until, finally, weight of numbers had even captured her.

She shuddered, recollecting the pain that they had inflicted upon her. They had sought to break her body and spirit. Hamilton must have thought that he had destroyed her that night, when her fire-blackened body had bucked madly against the burning agony of her death. Yet, they could not kill her. Her guile had lent her armour against their torments and attempts to burn her soul from her old body. Her spirit had fled the carcass and taken on the guise of another, but then she had wanted revenge, sweet vengeance for the blow that they had dealt against her destiny. So she had destroyed them, or enslaved them to her will, one by one.

She scowled, made a guttural snort, the wrinkled flesh on her face cracking and blistering. Even then, despite her preparations and the power she had wielded, they had stopped her. Arcane folk magic had tied her to this place, forever chained her to these vile cairns where the remnants of long dead druids lay in silent testament to the imprisoning wall that they provided. She could not escape. There had been no hope for so long, until years later when the wars came again. Rebellions and insurrections had followed, yet she could not find the right man, the right vassal for her will until she saw the great hosts of armies travel across the land, and she had fed on their lifeblood. Fed on their innocence. She had been old even then, but their blood had revitalised her. And one man, one man in particular, had been strong, strong enough to carry out her desires but not to resist her, she hoped. In him she saw the key to unlocking her lonely cell. And he would succeed, in part.

Lord Mountcashel had been a shrewd man. If she had only known how truly clever a general he was, she would have chosen another. He had been picked because she had sensed his fortitude and determination, yet his will had been too strong in the end. It had taken all her strength to hold his mind in check. He had died a mere husk of a man. Yet even in death, he had escaped her, foiled her, beaten her! Those damned military men. How their minds worked she could never fathom, and yet her power had dwindled, so much so that she could not repeat the effort. She had waited, for hundreds of years. She had waited for a chance. And then it came, so quickly, so fleeting that she had almost missed the opportunity to grasp it.

There had been something that she recognised in Pollock, though even now she could not understand what it was. He had realised too late what she might be, and it had amused her to think of his final moments. His life must have meant something to the beasts, for there was no question that he was gifted, for a mere human animal.

Even now, mankind had no concept of the vast designs that lay in their future, such terrifying new realities. She must be free to exploit and direct the power and knowledge that she had gained. They would descend into madness at the knowledge that would be shown to them, and flee from the night that would be unleashed. A new Dark Age, that she would herald, when her freedom was finally granted.

Annie Devlin lifted the digital camera so that she could see the small screen. She used the zoom to home in on her prey. She was in a perfect position now, with a good view of the two men, who had stopped in the middle of the field and were talking. Perhaps waiting for their contact she surmised, as the hand fell upon her shoulder.

"Miss Devlin!"

She turned in shock, gasping with fright at the sight of the policeman in front of her, his importance somewhat diminished by the wellingtons he was wearing.

"Constable... I..." she stammered, searching for a name, her heart thumping from the fright of having been discovered, and surprised that someone had managed to sneak up on her.

"Laverty, Miss. Constable Laverty."

She rapidly regained her composure, putting the camera into a pocket in her jacket.

"I was just..."

"Making enquiries?" he answered for her. "You really shouldn't be out here, you know?" he said, a degree of comfort in his voice now.

"Should they?" she asked innocently, jerking a thumb into the field behind her, toward the two professors at the far end.

Laverty cleared his throat. "Not without us, Ma'am, no," he said shaking his head and looking back at the police car by the road. "But we'll be seeing to that right now!"

Devlin followed his gaze.

"And where is your esteemed boss?" she asked, looking at Laverty.

He winced. "Back in the car, Miss. I don't think he likes this place much."

"Can't say I like it much myself, Constable, but there's a job to be done." As she moved to step forward, her booted foot slipped in the mud and she found herself hurtling forward toward Laverty, who misjudged her fall entirely, put his hands out too late to stop it, and ended up falling down himself, with Annie Devlin lying on top of him.

Laverty sprawled in the mud, pushing her off him. Immediately aware of how foolish he must look, he scrambled to his feet, tugging at his jacket to straighten it while his cheeks blushed a hot pink.

Annie Devlin chuckled. "I don't usually get the brush off quite so quickly, Constable. Are you gay?"

"What? Of course I'm not... I mean... why would you...?"

Devlin struggled to her feet, suppressing a grin, and reached into her jacket, pulling a flattened pack of cigarettes from her pocket.

"Do you smoke, Constable?" she said, as the struggling Laverty, still sliding in the mud, tried to get up, brown smears now spread across his high visibility yellow jacket and hat cover.

"No, ma'am, I don't," he grunted, scraping muck from his coat and trousers.

Devlin tried to find a lighter in her pockets, then promptly gave up as the policeman regained his composure. He raised one arm in a gesture that indicated not only that she should leave, but also that he had had quite enough of this awkwardness.

Devlin smiled innocently at him, and began to walk along the line of hedgerows towards her car. As she did so, she glanced across the field at the two men who she had so recently been spying upon. They were still there, discussing who knew what. She could just still make them out, despite the poor visibility. She was sure that no third man had joined them, however, and now that the police had arrived, she suspected that none would.

Latimer and Reilly had walked slowly across the field, taking in what they could of the undulating ground in the mist, which still clung to the grass like some parasite that would not relax its hold on the place.

"Do you think that the terrain has changed that much in the past three hundred years?" Reilly asked as they trudged through the mud.

Latimer, the map pulled out in front of him, was concentrating on his bearings, in relation to what he could interpret, and, it appeared, had little time for small talk. A murmur was all that Reilly received in reply.

"I guess you'll answer when you're ready," Reilly said, in exasperation.

"This is it," Latimer suddenly said, stopping in the middle of the field.

"This is what?"

Latimer looked at him as if he was a three-year-old that had just stolen sweets.

"This must be near the centre, the central point between the cairns," he said excitedly.

Reilly looked around. "There's nothing here, Neil. No hills, no chambered graves, nothing!" he said, holding his arms up as if to illustrate the point.

Latimer looked about, spinning slowly as he tried to take in the entire area. "I agree, there's nothing here, it's all gone, but that doesn't mean that the cairns have gone."

"What does it mean?"

"The ground has been levelled, the landscape changed, though I believe that whatever those cairns held is still here!"

"On what basis can you say that?" Reilly asked, confused.

"Joseph… I really don't know, something in the translation perhaps, a hunch, a feeling that there's something I'm missing. If it would just click into place, it would answer all my questions," Latimer replied.

He suddenly looked up from the map.

"Though I wouldn't say there's nothing here," he said slowly.

"What's that over there?" he continued, pointing toward the mist in front of them.

Reilly looked. "I don't see anything."

Latimer squinted. "It's a house!" he said. He looked at the map again, and then looked up, then back to the fragile paper.

"What do you make of this?" he said, showing the decaying parchment to Reilly, his finger pointing to a character. "There, at the centre of the cairns."

Reilly looked. "A scratch of the pen, a small inscription perhaps."

"Could it be a tree, do you think?" Latimer said excitedly.

Reilly looked again. "Yes, though I don't see how that's…"

"An oak tree or a sacred tree. The druids used places like this as points of worship. Do you think that Mountcashel is trying to tell us something?"

Reilly rubbed his eyes. "That's a house, Neil, not a tree,

and..."

"Good morning, gentlemen," Laverty's voice boomed across the field.

"Don't you think that you could let us know the next time you're going to totally disregard any advice that the local constabulary has given you?"

A mud spattered policeman approached them, squelching over the soft ground.

"Ah, Constable Laverty. Dear boy, we didn't want to wake you and your sergeant at so early an hour... we thought it best to..." He paused. "Did you fall in the mud?"

"That's enough crap, Mr Latimer," Laverty replied, his voice betraying the degree of anger that was slowly defining his mood for the morning. "I think we should leave now, gentlemen. You're on someone's land without permission. You didn't make us aware of what you were doing. And... my boss is so pissed off right now that he refuses to leave the car. If I could urge that we all get out of here, please. Thank you."

Latimer smiled, and started to say more, only to be interrupted by the shaking single index finger of Laverty held in the air in front of his face. He began to move, considering that the Constable was beginning to find confidence in the face of adversity. Perhaps he was upset. He would consider suggesting later that the young man should find something less stressful to do. Or perhaps he might leave that for another time, he decided, as he looked once more into the youthful face of the Constable and was a little afraid of what looked back.

The trio sloshed back across the route that they had just taken. Reilly was instructed, in no uncertain terms, that he was to follow the police car back to Enniskillen, any deviation being used as grounds for an arrest. He agreed politely. Latimer spotted that McGrath had not left the car, but thought better of going over to speak to him. He also noticed that Laverty appeared to be glancing back and forth along the road, as if looking for something... or someone.

The trip back was quiet, solemn even. Reilly seemed in

no mood to talk, so Latimer continued to study the map. There was something about the layout, the thin inscriptions that Mountcashel had made with his quill, hundreds of years ago. It was as if he was trying to tell him something, but it just would not quite 'click' in Latimer's mind. The bumping movement of the car did not help either, he thought, staring so hard at the map that he was beginning to feel sick with the motion. He closed his eyes, sensing that even Mountcashel had wanted him to get this. Something obvious. Something... deliberate.

They eventually stopped at some traffic lights outside Enniskillen.

"I have it!" Latimer cried, bouncing up and down in the passenger seat.

"What?" Reilly was alarmed at his colleague's outburst. "What is it?" he snapped.

Latimer looked at him, thrilled, and shaking with joy.

"What I've been missing," he shouted. "I have it!"

He poked his finger at the map, again and again.

"The cairns. Mountcashel's cairns. They mark out a pentagram!"

Mountcashel's Journal, 2nd April 1691, Versailles

I leave the court of his Majesty. My conference with King Louis was unexpected, and has proven fruitful. He will dispatch St. Ruth to Ireland to lead the forces there. I am thankful for this act, for it means that Sarsfield and Berwick will at last have some hope of progress. Louvois, the French Minister of War, supports any action that I would request, it would seem. Whether this is out of respect for me or due to his abject hatred of Milord Tyrconnel in Ireland, I am not certain. It matters not if his machinations lead to victory at home, a place that increasingly, I feel that I might never see again. Despite the continued advances of Dutch William's forces, actions at Limerick and the fact that we still hold ground, give me growing confidence that at least a negotiated peace can come. With St. Ruth there, and his leadership and knowledge of war, I almost pity the English and Dutch. The dispatch of St. Ruth to Ireland is tempered however by my own fate. My reputation grows daily with the French. Under any other circumstances I would be proud, of my men and the regiments. On this occasion however I am heavy with despair. The King wishes that the main body of the Irish regiments remain in Savoy, while I travel to the mountainous regions of Catalonia on the Spanish border, with one thousand picked men. Despite my best attempts at relaying my thoughts on the continued work in Savoy, even I can not argue with the King of France.

As I dwell on the matter I feel her contentment, her mocking laughter, as I am forced to draw closer to what I know to be the object of her darkest desires.

CHAPTER EIGHTEEN

Annie Devlin realised that McGrath had been watching her as she opened her car door. Heading back toward Enniskillen, she considered turning down a side road, waiting for the police to pass, then doubling back and scouting around the town some more. But a sudden chill had entered her since leaving the place, a distinct feeling of foreboding. She swore in frustration. Damn place had her spooked. There was something about it. She could not quite put her finger on it. Ever since that moment she had looked for the pub, she thought she had seen a church. When she had looked again, it had not seemed like a normal place of worship. There were no crosses, no welcoming sign. It had seemed barren and isolated... and unfamiliar. The memory had been giving her the creeps ever since. Between fog shrouded villages and the dark winter nights, this story was getting to her. This was ridiculous, she thought. Annie reached for the cigarettes in her handbag on the passenger seat, and then thought better of it, casting the bag onto the floor, increasing speed as she flew along the narrow country road back to Enniskillen.

Reilly pressed his foot on the accelerator, leaving the traffic lights.
"What do you mean it's a pentagram?" he asked his excited passenger.
"The cairns," he said, still tapping on the fragile map. "The cairns mark out the distinct points of a pentagram, an Elder sign."

"That's just a coincidence. The shape is irregular. You'd have to struggle to turn that into a five pointed star," Reilly said, glancing at the map.

"It ties in with everything that Mountcashel has written," Latimer said briskly.

He pulled his shabby notebook from his pocket, with the scribbled notes that he had translated from the journal. "Listen to this."

'I believe, through discussion with my men, and prisoners that live close to this place, that we are encamped upon sacred ground. The five small hillocks that surround our position are, it is rumoured, the graves of ancient druids, whose power, even in death, holds terrible sway over the area. I have never been a believer of such pagan rites, though it is difficult to convince many of the older men of the folly of their unchristian ways. They harbour their pagan beliefs in tandem with their Christian ones, and no degree of threat will dissuade them from their stance. Some also speak of a more recent time when fear stalked this land in the form of a she-demon, whose atrocious acts resulted in her being burned at the stake in the very grove in which I stand, by the Protestant planter who owned the land. Nightmare and ghostly visitation in the night still trouble my pickets and sentries. I begin to wonder, if there is more to these apparitions than simply strong drink, or the sickness of the mind brought about by hunger and poor health.'

Latimer looked up.

"Don't you think that's a little odd, under the present circumstances?" he asked.

"It proves nothing. You're assuming that he didn't have a vivid imagination. I saw no evidence today to suggest that what he records is actually there!" Reilly replied.

"There *was* something there, Joseph. I know it from the way he writes. Mountcashel knew it in 1689 and I believe him," Latimer replied, putting the notebook back in his jacket.

"And what's more..." he continued. "I believe that

something is still there!" he said, glancing through the passenger window at the fields and trees of the countryside.
"What basis do you have for suggesting that?" Reilly asked quietly.
"Let's assume that the cairns mark out a pentagram, an Elder sign of some nature. This can be invoked as a symbol of protection, not necessarily anything ritualistic. Ancient Irish druids used the symbol. I've read that the sign can be used as protection in the occult."
"So you think that the area is being protected from something?"
"No," Latimer replied, sighing, closing his eyes almost in an effort to block out what he really felt. "I believe now, that it's keeping something in!"
They followed the police car in silence until they reached Enniskillen, neither man sure whether to dismiss the apparent ludicrous nature of the discussion, or indeed, to admit that there was a distinct feeling of unease underpinning all their efforts to date.

Mountcashel's Journal, 21st June 1691, Valence, Spanish Border with France

Operations continue on the Spanish border. Amongst our allies are the mysterious 'Miquelets', Spanish mountain men whose belief in superstition and the dark arts terrifies many of our younger soldiers, who are convinced that they are in alliance with the devil himself. It is true that this place is very alien to us all. These mountains hold secrets and, unlike Italy, it is difficult to find passage and even see our destination during days of travel due to the mountainous and barren landscape. It feels somehow defiled and dead.

I discipline those officers who mock the younger men's fears. They have no concept of the darkness that exists behind the veil of our supposed ordered society, which commits more men to die in these campaigns day by day for so little return. In this place, more die through disease and poor food than will ever be killed by a musketball or the edge of a blade.

A. D. GRAHAM

The Miquelets interest me as much as I appear to intrigue them, for I am not angered or frightened by their customs and rituals. The French tolerate them, and perhaps misunderstand my interest as an attempt to ensure their alliance. Instead, my discussions with them have centred on the capabilities of the Elders of their people, in an attempt to ascertain if they have some measure of skill or dark knowledge that might help allay the power that she still holds over me.

Perhaps this is an indication that the dread that ails my dreams can be overcome? These people and their dark ways surely know of the nature of my curse and thus can remove it.

CHAPTER NINETEEN

Under the circumstances, the police had dealt with the two professors in a rather laid back manner. McGrath congratulated himself on not having lost his temper or hit anyone as he left the hotel with Laverty. The two academics had just sat there and agreed to everything, and promised not to do it again. Their lack of conviction or willingness to respond had sent the normally placid Laverty flying into a rage born of frustration, however, as he berated the two men for attempting something that could have seen them both being killed. McGrath, surprising even himself, had remained largely out of the conversation. He could not describe what was wrong with him, only that he had found it difficult, if not impossible, to get out of the car at Newtowncairn when Laverty went to get both the journalist and the two men. He took some aspirin before going into the hotel, though the recurring feeling of unease that he had felt since leaving Newtowncairn had not subsided. Perhaps he was working too hard, he thought as Laverty drove away from the hotel.

"Sarge," Laverty said, his voice laboured.

"What?"

"I said... I asked, why you hadn't spoken back there, with the two professors, I mean," Laverty repeated.

McGrath took a breath. "You... You had it all under control."

Laverty glanced across as he continued to negotiate afternoon traffic.

"Are you all right, Sarge?" he said, his voice failing to mask his obvious concern.

"Yes, I'm fine, kid. Fine."

Laverty concentrated on the road.

"So, they're not going anywhere tomorrow then. That's what they said, yeah?"

"No. That's what they promised. We should keep an eye on them anyway, perhaps?" McGrath said quietly.

Laverty flipped the indicator as the car left the main road.

Latimer swirled the contents of the whiskey glass, then downed the remainder of the liquid, setting the glass on the small bar.

"Why did you tell them that we weren't going anywhere tomorrow?" Reilly asked, his arms folded, watching from the opposite end of the bar as Latimer downed one whiskey after another.

"Because we're not!" he said, signalling the barman with his finger.

"I don't understand," Reilly said. "Don't you want to go back?"

Latimer smiled at the barman, raised his index finger, and pointed to the whiskey optic behind the bar. He licked his lips. "Yes. But we're not ready yet," he said. He was generating quite a bill.

"Not ready?"

"No," Latimer replied. "I need to finish the translation. There are things in there that we need to know. Secrets that I still have to unlock. I couldn't help feeling that we didn't know enough while we were in Newtowncairn, that Mountcashel still had so much more to tell us, and that we owed it to him to hear his story before we went on."

Reilly stared at him. "That's not why we're here, Neil."

"Do you think I don't know that?" Latimer fumed, as rage filled his face with contorted anger, suddenly explosive. He wiped a hand across his sweating face. Reilly's eyes widened in surprise. The barman moved only slightly in a practised motion, careful not to make eye contact with the nutter at the bar. He would soon let him know when he thought that he had had too much to drink.

"I'm sorry, Joseph," Latimer said, suddenly more calm, his breathing ragged. "I'm sorry. I know why we're here. To solve a murder. But I still believe that what we'll find in the journal will unlock the secrets of Pollock's death."

He downed the whiskey and brought the glass down hard again. Suddenly his mood changed. "I've just remembered," he said. "I have a dinner date!" He stood up and rubbed his head again. "I must get some sleep. Would you wake me around teatime?"

"Yes, of course. Is there anything I can do to help with the translation, Neil?"

Latimer stopped in mid-stride. "We'll talk later perhaps, Joseph." He smiled and left the bar.

Reilly ordered a drink, and considered phoning Barbara.

Managing to struggle out of his jacket, unconcerned that the sleeves remained inside out and that he trampled it as he reeled back and forth, Latimer finally sat heavily on the end of the bed. His head lolled and he was almost overpowered by dizziness as he bent to untie his shoes.

The laces tangled and he had to wrench at them, falling back each time to sprawl full length on the duvet. When he finally succeeded, he tossed the shoes into the air, toppling a third and final time while doing so. He never heard them land with a crash on the dressing table, as they broke a mirror...

He must have fallen asleep, he thought. He was dreaming, surely? He considered pinching himself, and then dismissed the thought. He was walking in the field in Newtowncairn again. This time, he was alone. It felt wonderful. The fields and lanes of Newtowncairn had not looked like this before. They were drenched in sunlight and looked idyllic. No fog, no mud, no feeling of foreboding.

Farmers tended their fields; the villagers went about their business. Children played in the town square. Latimer felt that all of his concerns about the place had been unfounded, as if finally realising that Pollock's death had had nothing to do with the village. He strode across the field in the heat.

There was the house that he had seen earlier in the fog. In the clarity of the bright summer's day, it stood out as a strikingly beautiful building, standing guard almost, watching over the villagers and their children. As he stared, a woman left the house and closed the front door. She waved from the driveway, and began to run across the field toward him. Instinctively, he waved back. He did not know why. Who was this woman? Yet somehow, he felt so close to her, as if she had been a friend for a long time. He smiled despite himself, and began to walk slowly toward her, breaking into a run without apparent effort. It felt good.

As he moved closer he could see that she was middle-aged. She looked beautiful. She got closer, smiling and waving, as if she had not seen him for so long and yearned to embrace him once more. As she neared him, her arms stretched out. He felt himself doing the same. They met, and embraced. He could feel her hot breath at his neck, hear her laughter, and feel the happiness exuding from her at his presence. He put his arms around her, as if compelled to do so.

"You've come at last," her soft voice said in his ear. "I thought that you would never come to me, would never help. Now you can set me free... set me free."

Latimer laughed, blissfully happy. In the back of his mind, however, a thought kept nagging, telling him that he was wrong, yet he felt himself becoming enveloped in something more powerful than any emotion that could ever be imagined. Nothing in his thoughts could block the strength of the passion that seemed to be consuming him, as he looked around, at the woman in his arms, at the green fields... the fields where Lord Mountcashel had fought, where his men had died. This was... a dream... a nightmare? Was she doing to him what she had done to Mountcashel? Was this what the general had meant by the feeling that his very dreams were tainted by her presence? Had she controlled his thoughts like this?

Instinctively shrugging out of the embrace and grabbing the woman by the shoulders, he pushed her away from him. Her face began to wrinkle, to age before his eyes, pale skin cracking and falling away, revealing brown, shrivelled flesh. The human face melted, becoming monstrous, as the nose and eye sockets dissolved away, revealing glowing red orbs. The mouth opened, becoming a maw. The jaw distended unnaturally, revealing sharp, spike-like fangs. Latimer cried out...

He awoke and screamed, bolting upright on the bed, bathed in sweat from the nightmare. There was a distinct banging noise. The door.

"Neil. Neil, it's me. Can you hear me?"

Joseph Reilly banged on the door again and again.

"Yes... Yes, Joseph. I'm coming."

He put his feet on the floor, heart still racing, pulsing rapidly. He made to stand up, and collapsed, wincing at a lancing pain in his hip. He tried again, unsteady at first, then stumbling, he moved toward the door.

Reilly looked shocked as he saw his friend, now pale and exhausted looking.

"Hell of a hangover," Latimer said, backing away from the door, swaying slightly.

Reilly stepped in and closed the door, grabbing Latimer by the arm.

"Are you all right?" he asked, suddenly concerned.

"Oh, nervous exhaustion I think. I'm sure that getting pissed in the afternoon without having had a proper breakfast probably doesn't help much either."

He stumbled toward the bathroom, farting loudly.

Reilly winced. "Are you sure that you'll be okay? Your dinner date is in an hour or so!" he called after Latimer as he entered the bathroom.

"I'll be fine, Neil."

Reilly heard the sound of the shower being turned on, and moved toward the desk where Latimer had laid out his notes. The leather bound, battered journal lay on the table, on top of loose piles of apparently disorganised leaves of paper covered with spidery writing. Reilly reached for the book, thumbing through its delicate pages, feeling the soft, gossamer like paper between his fingers. He could scarcely believe that it had lasted this long. Stranger still was the story it contained, in a coded language that few could understand. Indeed, had it not been for Pollock, perhaps no one would ever have been able to translate the general's notes. Reilly sat down, leafing through the foreign code of the journal's entries, hoping for a sign that he could understand, a smattering of French language that he was familiar with. He felt helpless. For the first time in years he could not help Latimer. He leafed through to the end of the book, to the strange symbolic code in the last few pages, hoping at least to find something there that he could untangle, something more tangible than the obscure cipher whose solution seemed only to lie in Latimer's mind.

He stared at the French code, interspersed with the strange angular symbols.

"What are you doing, Joseph?" Latimer boomed from behind him.

Reilly looked up suddenly, completely surprised, the journal snapping shut in his hand.

Latimer stood, wrapped in a towel, water dripping from his hair and body.

"I... I'm just looking at the piece at the end. The piece that you were having trouble with."

"Put the journal down, Joseph," Latimer said, sternly. A vein on his temple was throbbing with anger.

Reilly put the book on the desk, unsure of where to look.

"It's okay, Neil. I was just..."

"You don't understand, Joseph. All is not right here. Don't get involved with that book."

He turned around and began to get dressed.

"I thought if you could show me how to translate it. I thought I could help. That piece at the end, the French code between the symbols. It must mean something," Reilly said quickly.

"I have to go out," Latimer said, walking half dressed across the room to lift the journal.

"We'll talk later if you like," he said curtly.

Taking his cue to leave, Reilly moved toward the door, closing it behind him.

Latimer, still angry, stared at the journal, resisting the urge to open it and continue the translation that had to be done. No, he considered, there was other work to do tonight.

Mountcashel's Journal, 28th November 1691, Catalonia

It is so cold in the mountains. Each morning I awake and feel the stiffness of my wounds in the freezing air as I stare out at snow capped peaks.

Cadores, the Miquelet commander, has guided me to the cave of the witch, known as Midra, the Black Shepherdess. I have no inkling as to why she might be called such, or indeed as to the nature of her supposed flock, though I suspect that any church that she might claim to administer has little to do with the one true God. Out of desperation, I have let her carry out some ancient black rite, whose validity I would have put little faith in but a few years ago. From what I can understand of her ranting, I am possessed by some evil spirit, which even now gnaws at my soul. That much I knew. As to the cure for such an affliction, she informs me that I may never be wholly free of the spirit's power. With the imbibing of some evil brew that she has concocted with my blood, foul smelling herbs and the invocation of diabolic dark rites, however, she assures me that I may sleep without sorcerous influence. Cadores watched the entire affair with the eye of an impartial observer, yet I sense that he knows more than he admits to. I heard the two speak of some Spanish notable whose power over the dead allows him to hold sway over the neighbouring province. It is clear that they fear him greatly, though my Spanish leaves much to be desired and I heard only fragments.

A. D. GRAHAM

I have received news from Sarsfield that our cause in Ireland is lost, and the officers of Dutch William hold the island. The troops previously besieged in Limerick have, for the most part, been allowed to leave and seek French service. I fear now that my country is no longer a thorn in William's side, nor a pawn in Louis's greater game of power struggle and, therefore, that the troops will be treated harshly. They will be used as fodder for Dutch and Imperial guns in the few battles that are left in this terrible war. What have we gained, I ask myself? I know that nothing can be the only answer. Louis's borders may change a little. He will make some gains, though the balance of power will remain unaffected. Only in Ireland does the troops' departure herald momentous change for the Catholic nobility. Our cause is lost, yet strangely I do not grieve for the fallen, or even for the future of the isle. The hand of fate and the witch of Newtowncairn now decide my purpose. I still pray that I might resist her.

CHAPTER TWENTY

Latimer had done his best under the circumstances, but even he had to admit, as he looked at himself in the mirror, that he was no Casanova. He straightened his tweed jacket, trying to make himself a little more presentable. It would not matter, he thought. He was sure that his casual appearance would not offend, either Miss Hamilton or the staff of the restaurant. In fact, when he considered it, he did not think that he would have to do much to impress the female owner of a second hand bookshop who seemingly had not left the place in years. He closed his eyes in concentration, reminding himself that the real reason that he was doing this, despite her extensive occult book collection and his general interest in her, was because of her apparent knowledge of Pollock's last days. He straightened his collar, moving to the desk where the journal lay.

He lifted it and put it in the inside pocket of his jacket, wincing at the thought that he had upset Joseph earlier. He had gone a bit far. Grabbing a hip flask from his jacket pocket he took a swig. In any other circumstances he would have forgotten the incident, apologised to Joseph at some time. But today, here in his room, he felt the pangs of guilt. He had shouted at his only friend, a man whose marriage was on the rocks, who had given up the last chance of making things up with his wife to accompany him on some damn foolhardy expedition to determine who had killed his graduate student, and Latimer had given him the brush off when he had been trying to help.

Damn, he thought, I have to apologise. He pocketed the

hip flask, patted his chest to ensure that the journal was still there, and strode toward the door. He heard a knock before he reached it. He pulled it open. Joseph, surprised at the rapidity of the action stood still at the threshold.

"Neil... I'm..."

"No, Joseph, I'm sorry," Latimer interrupted. "I shouldn't have shouted. I think I was a little drunk. I've had a lot on my mind, and this whole thing is beginning to get to me. I'm even dreaming about it," he laughed, recalling his earlier nightmare.

Reilly smiled weakly.

"It's okay, Neil. I understand the pressure you're under. I was just trying to help, that's all."

"Of course you were, Joseph. I understand that now. Look, let's go to the bar for a quick one, before my date, as you call it." They both laughed. Latimer shut the door behind him and locked it. Both men walked toward the stairs, and the bar.

He glanced at his watch again as he left the hotel. Reilly, after several glasses of whiskey, had elected to go to bed rather than join them for dinner. Latimer was secretly glad that he had turned down the invitation, firstly, because he was concerned that the presence of Reilly, unannounced to Mary Hamilton, might not only cramp his style, but also might actually insult or offend her. Secondly, he was concerned that she would tell him much less than he needed to know, in the presence of someone who she had not previously met and who only Latimer could vouch for. The complications of the last forty-eight hours were playing on his mind. How the hell did he get himself into these damned situations?

He looked up and down the street. Darkness had fallen, and only the lights of oncoming traffic highlighted the fact that the town had not yet gone to sleep. A strong northerly wind bit at the extremities and Latimer cupped his hands to his mouth as he blew on them. Spotting a gap in the traffic, he strode across the road. The inside of Mary Hamilton's second-hand bookshop was still dimly lit. Well, he thought, she either has remembered the dinner date, or is doing a late evening stock take.

He stood by the door and grasped the handle, then thought better of it. A gentleman would never enter unannounced, he thought to himself. He rapped the glass delicately, a little worried as the pane shook within the confines of its rotting frame. He saw movement in the semi-darkness inside the shop, a figure moving toward the door. He could just see her through the glass. The door opened.

"Miss Hamilton, hello. You haven't forgotten, I see," he said.

"I don't normally get this dolled up," she replied, slightly embarrassed by the importance of the occasion.

"Well, I'm glad you did," he said. "You look simply radiant." Latimer took in the make up, the black dress and jacket. She looked nothing like the middle-aged woman that he had spoken with the previous day.

"I feel a little overdressed," she said, noticing his tweed jacket and dark trousers.

"Oh, me. Yes, I always dress like this, but you shouldn't, I mean, that isn't to say..."

"Come in for a minute. It's freezing out here and I'm not quite ready yet," she interrupted, pulling him by the arm.

Latimer reddened, cursing silently to himself that he should have dressed a little more formally. He stood in the shop doorway, the door slowly closing behind him as she scurried off into the back of the shop. He could hear her fidgeting as he glanced around in the dim light, glancing at the rows of stacked books on the floor.

The tiles were scuffed, their colour faded over the years, from what once must have been a dull red colour. Something caught his eye. Then he saw it again, something inscribed on the floor, symbols scratched onto the surface of the tiles. He knelt down, flinching as the bones in his knees cracked, and ran his hand over the floor. Something had been etched there, two lines making up a point, then a curved and angular symbol sitting inside the triangle, something that he had seen before.

He traced its angular lines. Had he seen it in the journal? What did it mean? He ran his finger over the line of the surrounding triangle; it led back into the shop. A thought struck him. He glanced across the floor, looking for a similar mark. At the far wall, he found it. Another apex of another triangle, and another strange, yet markedly different, symbol that it framed.

"What are you doing down there, Mr. Latimer," she said, coming from behind the curtain.

Latimer shot up so fast it made his head spin. He blinked as blood rushed to his head.

"Oh, nothing. You... You have some wonderful spiders. I saw one scurrying across the floor. Massive bugger it was!" he blurted, trying to cover for his actions.

"Yes," she said, with suspicion. "They seem to like it here. They keep an eye on the pests for me," she added dryly.

"Shall we go?" she added, her heels clicking on the floor as she walked across the shop towards him.

"Of course," he replied, regaining his composure and taking her arm, clearing his throat and smiling in a polite fashion.

Being the perfect gentleman, Latimer had insisted upon pulling Mary Hamilton's chair out for her and letting her be seated, to the amazement of most of the other people in the restaurant. Bloody Philistines, he thought, ignoring the whispers and murmurs that his courteous behaviour had provoked.

Mary smiled. "And I thought that chivalry was dead," she said. The action made at least two wives stare at their husbands in a *how come you never do that for me* kind of way.

The restaurant was dimly lit, romantic even, providing a setting that many couples in the area doubtless sought for their evenings out. It was quiet and peaceful, and soft music played in the background. The waiter brought the menu. Latimer asked if he might recommend some wines for her. Mary agreed. Displaying a knowledge of wine that seemingly surpassed his knowledge of seventeenth century Irish history, Latimer, disappointed by the poor selection on hand, chose a red and a white, trying not to notice the embarrassment of the waiter who seemed devastated by his inability to please the man at the table. They ordered starters and a main course. Latimer's description of how he wanted his steak once more confounded the waiter, forcing Mary Hamilton to put a hand to her mouth to hide her amusement.

Having tasted the wine and given his approval, Latimer poured.

"So," he asked pointedly. "Do you like this place, Mary? May I call you Mary?" A stock grin creased his face, making the wrinkles on his forehead stand out in the candlelight.

"Yes you may. And it's quite nice, I think," she replied, in hushed tones.

"You've never been here before?" he asked. "You live in that bookshop across the road, and you've never been here?"

"I don't get out much," she replied, looking uncomfortable as she rearranged her cutlery.

"You don't meet nice men like me that often, I guess," he said confidently. They both laughed as the starters arrived. They chatted as they ate. Not one for small talk, however, Latimer was quickly growing tired of hovering around the boundaries of the questions that he really wanted to ask.

"Tell me some more about Pollock," he said between mouthfuls.

She dabbed at her mouth with the napkin and put her fork down, reaching for the wine.

"Have you found out why he was killed?" she asked.

Clutching his throat, almost choking, Latimer swallowed an unchewed mouthful.

Across the room, by the kitchen door, the waiter heard the sound and was alarmed, until he saw from where the sound emanated. Recognising the smug wine expert who had tried to make a fool of him, he felt a spiteful satisfaction. He sauntered toward the table with elaborate unconcern.

Latimer waved him off with a shake of his hand and downed his glass of wine. The waiter insisted on refilling it, then walked away again.

"Well, you believe in getting to the point, don't you, Mary?"

She watched him as she drunk from the large glass, biting her lower lip in anticipation of the real conversation that seemed to be starting.

"What did he find in Newtowncairn?" she asked again, more insistent.

"Wait a minute, I don't..." Latimer stammered.

"Oh I see," she said, returning to her meal.

"You see what?" Latimer said, puzzled.

"You thought that you'd bring me here tonight, ask me about Pollock, find out what you needed to know, and that would be that!" she said, delicately placing a prawn in her mouth. "You didn't think that I, a poor woman who owns a little second hand bookshop, would be asking more leading questions than you. Is that it?"

She sipped her wine as Latimer sat still

He took a drink. She was building to something, and he was not sure he liked where the conversation was going. Bloody hell, he thought, closing his mouth at last. Yet, as he watched her confidence ooze from her, he sensed pain and sadness behind those dominant eyes, an air of uncertainty and grief that he could not quite understand.

"That's not it at all," he said, looking down at the plate.

"Then what is it?"

Latimer gaped in frustration.

"I'm really not sure whether I can trust you or not," he said, letting the words flow without thinking about what he was saying.

"Now who's being direct?" She laid down the fork, pushed the plate away from her and folded her arms defensively. "Why can't you trust me?" She narrowed her eyes.

Latimer sucked his cheeks, looking around the restaurant as if seeking someone to help him get out of what he was about to say.

"Why do you have a pentagram drawn on the floor of your shop?" he asked. He took a long sip from the wine. Before she could answer, he asked another question. "And how old are you?"

He was sweating. She seemed amused.

"I'm impressed," she said, unfolding her arms at last and leaning forward so that she could whisper. "You plainly know your..." she hesitated, "...stuff." She enunciated the word with her lips as she said it. Latimer found that he could not stop looking at her mouth as she spoke.

He could feel a tangible edge to the atmosphere, as if something was about to explode. Mary looked for the waiter, signalling him as he approached and lifted the plates. She said 'thank you' and smiled as he left.

"Are you a witch?" Latimer said. He felt himself sweating. He could feel it drip from his armpits inside his shirt.

She stared at him. "Yes."

She dabbed with the napkin again, before continuing.

"And in answer to your earlier question, a lady never reveals her age. Though let me assure you that I'm not over sixty." She stared at him again. "I think that answers your question. Were you expecting me to be a few hundred years old, perhaps?"

Latimer gulped.

"I didn't kill Pollock, if that's what you're thinking." She glanced across the restaurant. "Everything that I told you about him is the truth. He was... he was my friend. Unfortunately, for such a short time!" Her eyes began to glaze over.

Latimer was at a loss now to know where to take the conversation. Nothing ventured, nothing gained, he thought. He put his hand on her arm. "I'm sorry. I don't know what you must think."

She patted his hand.

"Tell me why you have the pentagram in the shop," he asked, in a hushed tone.

She exhaled sharply. "Protection."

"From what?" he asked, a chill moving up his spine.

Her voice and manner changed, her face taking on a look of menace tinged with fear. "From her!" she moaned in a deep tone, her lower lip trembling.

They moved closer. They looked at each other in fear and wonder.

"Steak, sir!"

Latimer lurched backwards in his seat. "Yes… that's mine, thank you," he said as the waiter eased the plate on to the table.

With the setting down of his meal, slowly to be followed by the presentation of his partner's dinner, the moment had been lost. In the nervous confusion that Latimer now felt, he was almost afraid to re-establish the connection. He set to cutting his steak. The meat was succulent, the steak cooked medium-rare. He spent more time than was usual cutting each piece, analysing the rivulets of blood that cascaded from them as he sliced, anything but to have to face her again, he thought, but he could not help himself.

She looked straight at him now, had not even lifted her knife and fork yet. She just stared. Latimer was filled with dread. Had he unwittingly stumbled upon the remnants of some exotic and long forgotten Irish witch cult? He was trembling inwardly, unsure of what to say, unable to regain control of the situation. She continued to scrutinise him, dispassionately, as if he was inferior.

"You really don't need to worry, Professor Latimer," she said. Her voice was like silk. Latimer felt himself, against his own better judgement, become a little more reassured.

"Why are you afraid?"

"I think I've been working too hard," he replied, putting down his knife and fork, pulling a handkerchief from his pocket and patting his sweating forehead. He regained some composure.

"Who is she? The one you referred to earlier," he asked. She had picked up her cutlery, began to toy with her food, taking small bites.

"I think you already know that. If you didn't suspect something, you wouldn't be here, would you?"

"There's something in Newtowncairn, isn't there? Something old, so terribly old, and evil?"

"Yes," she said, between mouthfuls. She stopped briefly to take a sip from the wine.

He was unsure whether to tell her about the journal or not, unsure whether to place trust in someone, or something, that he had rapidly become afraid of. What the hell was going on here, he thought. Her presence seemed to fill the room. This woman, who had been so demure not half an hour ago, now appeared so powerful. Was that part of the spell? Was that how these people worked? How could he defend himself, his sanity, against this?

"Look," she said suddenly. "I am not your enemy. I can help you to a certain degree, though you must be careful. You seem to have learned so much already, though I'm not sure how. I'm really not sure at all." She smiled, and Latimer could feel himself gasping.

"Perhaps it is the nature of your interest in such things?" she continued. "Maybe you should confide in me, Mr. Latimer, tell me everything that you know?"

She swallowed a morsel of food.

"I... I... have proof," he stammered. Moments ago, he was sure that he had been entrapped by the Newtowncairn witch, convinced that he had fallen into the same snare that Mountcashel had, accepted that he had no way to escape. Christ, he thought, alcohol must be making him paranoid.

Realisation hit him like a hammer. "You're casting some sort of... some sort of spell on me!" he blurted. "You are, you're doing something, aren't you?"

Customers who had been making small talk looked up

from their modest conversations, at the man in the corner with the quiet woman, the man who was making too much noise and ruining the atmosphere.

She put her hand on his and raised a finger to her lips, signalling him to be quiet.

"I have to be sure that you're here for the right reasons. That she didn't send you."

He was immediately suspicious, then the paranoia lifted and the feeling of isolation disappeared. It was as if the proverbial great weight had not only been lifted from his shoulders, but also now pulled him up into the heavens. He was relieved.

"How the hell did you do that?" he asked, moving his jaw freely as if wires had held it in place and had now been subtly removed.

"Hell has nothing to do with it," she said, glancing around the restaurant, trying to diffuse the nature of the conversation before they attracted attention.

He pulled his hand away, lifted the knife and fork again and began to eat once more, cutting lumps of almost raw steak and washing them down with draughts of red wine, in a vain attempt to return to normality. As he lifted the bottle and motioned to fill Mary's glass again, he regained some degree of control. She accepted the refill.

"You spoke of proof?" she said.

Latimer swallowed reflexively, and reached inside his jacket pocket. He pulled out the journal, smelling the decaying leather as it wafted past his face, as he placed it on the table between them. He could never have predicted her reaction.

She visibly recoiled, sitting back on the chair, as if burned with a hot iron. Her face dissolved into a grimace, a look of disgust and pure fear, as if it reeked of death.

Latimer's eyes widened. He grabbed the book, began to pull it away.

"Where... where did you get that?" she stammered.

"Do you recognise it?" he asked, now intrigued.

"I can smell her all over it."

"Really?" Latimer replied nonchalantly. "I might have spilt whiskey on it earlier. Perhaps that's what you smell?" He attempted to laugh.

"Don't be facetious," she snapped.

Latimer raised his hands in mock supplication, before leaving the journal down. He kept it beside his plate and slowly returned to eating, concentrating on his food. He could sense her fear now, alongside the earlier signs of grief. He almost felt guilty about ignoring it, felt that he should at least speak, though he still felt stung, and humiliated by her earlier actions. He ate the steak heartily, drank freely from the wine glass, ignoring her in an almost smug manner.

"Where did you get that book?" she said, her tone trying to recapture that which she used earlier.

"From James Pollock." Latimer noticed that the commanding effect of her words had been distinctly reduced. When he pointed his fork in an enquiring gesture towards two potatoes that she had left, there was no objection to his helping himself. He munched happily, his words blurred by his eating. "He posted it to me before he died. Do you know what it is?"

She shook her head. "But I know that it is hers!"

"Have you heard of Lord Mountcashel?" he said.

She shook her head again, focusing on the journal, as if its presence could conjure up that which she most feared.

Latimer puffed in a superior manner, lamenting the fact, not for the first time, that so few people knew their history! These people lived here, for goodness sake. What a sad state of affairs, he thought.

"He recorded events from the late seventeenth century in here." He tapped the journal. "Events that I believe relate directly to whatever is still in Newtowncairn. Can you tell me anything of what that might be?"

Mary Hamilton was now but a pale shadow of the confident yet mysterious woman who had been having dinner and casting spells but moments before. It all stemmed from the instant that he had produced the journal.

"How can you tell that she has been near this? It's just a book," Latimer said, not wholly believing the words himself.

Mary's face was different now, almost contorted with fear. "I can smell her upon it. Sense her presence. The scent of death!"

Latimer considered her words, trying to ensure that they both remained calm, and that he remained in some sort of control of the situation.

"Let's eat," he said, putting the journal back in his pocket and returning to his steak. She agreed, slowly returning to her meal, her confidence also recovering now that he had put the offending item away. They made small talk once more, trying to put the moments of revelation behind them.

The inevitable lull in the conversation reappeared after a time. Latimer broke the silence.

"Look. I want to come right out and say something! The obvious implication that I see is that this mysterious woman had something to do with Pollock's death... yes? Was he killed because he had the journal?"

Mary Hamilton drank some of the wine.

"I don't know. I know only that as long as you have that book, we're both in danger."

She finished the contents of her glass.

"Look, Professor Latimer. This has been lovely, really. As I said, I don't get out much, but I must go."

He looked shocked, made to speak, to stop her, though he knew somehow that he would have little chance of success.

"Of course. I'll... I'll see to the bill, see you to your door."

"There's no need," she said politely.

"I'm sure there isn't, Miss Hamilton, believe me! But it would make me feel better, if you don't mind. I'll see to the bill."

She politely agreed, waiting for him as he crossed the still crowded dining room. Moments later, Latimer left Mary Hamilton at her door, somewhat awkwardly. It had been a strange evening. They offered each other their goodbyes, and he strode off into the night.

Mountcashel's Journal, 7th March 1692, Catalonia

I have spent months in the company of Cadores and the Miquelets, to the extent that the French have congratulated me on my assimilation into their society. It would seem that their arrogance precludes their interest in any of the culture of these mountain people. They seem more content that an Irish officer should busy himself with the niceties of the reinforcement of alliances with the irregular troops. The Imperial officers of the enemy use other Miquelet groups for scouting and ambush activities, though Cadores tells me that those bands that have sided with the French are fully aware of the wrath that will be vented on those peoples that do not choose the right side in this conflict. Clearly, these mountain people have suffered before. Their beliefs are dark and blasphemous. Although they had not initially wished to speak of their rites and activities, I see now that beneath the surface of the Christian world that we know, there is a dark depth of blasphemy and depravity. The Shepherdess tells me that the spirit that ails me is ancient and powerful, and that her powers over it will not last long. Cadores says that he believes that she is afraid, that whatever powerful force of evil has touched me at Newtowncairn, it is more than she can hope to stop.

My orders now dictate that I will travel to Germany with a picked handful of Irish officers. It will be painful to leave the remaining men of the regiment but they have gained a degree of experience and recognition and earned their reputation as some of the best soldiers in the army. I have little argument with my orders however. Despite what I have learned from Cadores and the witch peoples, the time has come for me to take my leave of this country. Despite the potion given me by the Shepherdess, I feel that I remain too close to the abyss, and thus play into the hands of the Irish witch. I must leave this place.

CHAPTER TWENTY-ONE

All the hotels in County Fermanagh and the first one I pick has a no smoking policy, Annie Devlin thought, as she headed through the foyer toward the building's exit. She had a nicotine craving, and the more that she looked at the smoke alarm on the ceiling of her room, the more she wanted to reach up, rip it off and throw it out of the window.

She stalked through the foyer, the smell of cooked breakfast wafting beckoningly from the restaurant.

The small man at the desk called after her. "Miss Devlin... Miss Devlin."

She spun on her heel.

"Make it quick," she retorted. "You're keeping a desperate woman from her cigarette," she said, wincing as she had to retrace her steps.

"Yes, it's just that a message was left for you last night." He reached for a small envelope behind the desk and passed it to her.

She pursed her lips impatiently and accepted it.

"Thanks," she said, making for the door. What the hell was this? she thought, as she thumbed open the envelope. A folded piece of white paper sat inside.

She pushed through the revolving door, making her way outside. It was freezing, and she pulled her leather coat about her shoulders. She took the note from the flimsy envelope, unfolding it. A message in black ink, that exhibited signs of having been hastily written. The writing was spidery and hard to read at first. The paper was thick and expensive and smelt of damp, even in the fresh air outside the hotel. There was no signature.

> *Miss Devlin,*
> *You do not know me, though I must inform you that your search for some answers with regard to Mr. Latimer and all that is going on in Newtowncairn, may be drawing to a close. You must come and meet me in the village, in Bennets pub. Tomorrow at 6pm. There I shall supply the answers that you seek.*
>
> *A Friend*

"My God!" she said aloud.

Almost on cue, the mobile phone in her jacket pocket chimed loudly. She did not answer, letting it ring for several seconds. She looked blankly at the note. What did this mean? Was this the break she had been looking for?

She pulled the phone from her jacket, seconds before she knew that it would go to voicemail. It was Sean Watt.

"Hello."

"What's happening, Annie? I haven't heard from you?"

"I think I've just got my first break, Sean. Your timing is pretty good."

"What do you mean, honey?" he said, excitement in his voice.

"Well, so far, I've had no solid leads, even the police don't seem interested in these two, but it looks like I have made a contact in the village."

"Looks like you have?" he responded, concern in his voice.

"Yes. We haven't met yet, but…"

"You be careful, Annie, y'hear me?"

"Yes, Sean. You know I can take care of myself," she answered.

"I know that, luv!" he said. "I think I should send someone down there to help you," he added.

"To look after me, you mean?" she replied icily.

He paused. "Yes, ok. Look, Annie, the guy was murdered, remember?"

"I'll be fine, Sean." There was a note of finality in her voice as she terminated the call. She finished her cigarette and returned through the revolving doors.

Latimer, in contravention of everything that his body was trying to tell him, had sat up most of the night. Betraying the signs of alcohol abuse, sleep deprivation and stress, his face now looked as though it had been through several rounds with a professional boxer.

He knocked cautiously, quietly, on his colleague's door.

Reilly answered it immediately, as though he had been lying in wait. He was fresh faced and obviously well rested. He registered a combination of alarm and amusement at the dishevelled state of the dressing gown clad man who shambled into his room and moved toward the mirror.

Latimer had noted with disgust that his partner shared none of the appearance of over-worked and overhung exhaustion that he was suffering from. Instead, he was bursting with health and barely restrained energy. Slothering on down at heel slippers back toward Reilly, Latimer stood like an unkempt tramp who had been sleeping rough for years. "I wanted to look in your mirror. Mine's broken. Do I really look that bad?" Latimer asked.

"You've been up all night again, haven't you?" Reilly said. "I was about to come and collect you, then get some breakfast. How was dinner? Tell me all the details."

"Don't even go there!" Latimer remarked, striding about the room.

Reilly laughed. "Surely you can't mean that she was able to resist the famous lothario Latimer charm assault?"

"I don't want to talk about it," he said seriously. "But there's more here than meets the eye," he said.

"What does that mean?" Reilly asked, suddenly interested.

Latimer moved his hand in a throwaway manner. "We'll

talk about it later. Right now, I want to stick to what I'm sure of."

He slumped into the seat and pulled the diary from his trouser pocket, together with some folded notes.

"After dinner last night, I sat up and translated the last passage in the diary, at the back, after all the journal entries; the one that's been giving me so much trouble. I've written it out, including my own drawings of the symbols where I can't translate them. I want you to read it," he said, a sense of urgency in his voice. He passed the folded sheets to Reilly.

He unfolded them, began to read. His face quickly betrayed his surprise.

"What is this?"

"I really don't know. If I didn't know any better I would say it was an invocation of some kind."

"An invocation?" Reilly muttered. "A spell?" he replied.

Latimer nodded. "Read it. All that I've translated are the words between the symbols. They make no sense. When I read them aloud, however, they make my head swim."

Latimer paused as he raised his hands and put on a deep voice. "Maybe it's something to do with the mystical power of ancient wisdom!" His attempt at levity was in vain, however, as he remained stern, focused.

"Or maybe you're just completely exhausted from sitting up all night!" Reilly laughed, as he read the words.

Latimer continued. "I'm guessing that the symbols have an important meaning, perhaps related to old dark gods or ancient demonic rites. What I've worked out, in itself, makes no sense. Reading it just gives me a headache. A random collection of tracts, phrases, dark passages. To what end? I do not know!"

Reilly handed the papers back. "This is everything?" he said bluntly. "The entire journal. You've translated all of it?" Latimer nodded slowly. "And you think that this is a spell?" he added.

Latimer stared into the middle distance.

"To what end. What does it do?"

"I have absolutely no bloody idea," Latimer replied.
"You don't believe in this, of course?"
Latimer paused, his lips pursed, remaining silent.
"You're kidding?" Reilly said. "You believe that these words have a kind of occult power?"
"I wouldn't bet against it yet," Latimer replied, wringing his hands together.
"Why the hell would Mountcashel write these down? Are you saying that he was a black magician of some nature, a master of the occult?"
"No, I don't believe that at all. I think that he was compelled to record the spell. It was given to him via a Spanish necromancer in 1694."
"To what end?" Reilly repeated.
Latimer stared at him, and smiled weakly. "I'm not sure."
"And how does Pollock fit into this? Why did he have the journal? Why was he so interested in translating it?"
"Again, I'm not sure. Until a few days ago, I was convinced that he had little interest in religion or anything other than history, never mind the occult."
Reilly sat down on the bed. "So what now?"
Latimer leaned back in the chair, dangerously close, in his exhausted condition, to falling back and landing on his backside. Reilly watched, in anticipation of the worst.
"Well, first, breakfast," Latimer barked, letting the chair come back into its proper position and planting his feet firmly on the floor. Reilly breathed a sigh of relief.
"And then?"
"I've a few things to do, perhaps catch up on some sleep, and we'll go to Newtowncairn tonight," he said, then looked at the notes and the diary, considering. "Or perhaps tomorrow, we'll see. I want to call on the owner of the house that I saw, for purely investigative reasons, of course." He got off the chair and swayed slightly.
"Let's get something to eat."

Breakfast and lunch had both passed uneventfully, between bouts of sleep that Latimer's exhausted body had told him were required. He crossed the busy road, noticing, to his relief, that Mary Hamilton's bookshop was still open. He entered, the bell on the door chiming in its usual fashion. He could not help but look down at the floor, the inscription of the pentagram now clear to him, yet perhaps still hidden to the more casual observer. Perhaps that was her plan?

Mary Hamilton was talking to an older woman. Latimer recognised Agnes from the first time that he had been in the shop. The two seemed to be talking about Agnes's latest purchases and how good they were. Latimer wondered absently if the lady was Mary's only customer. The conversation ended abruptly. Agnes made an excuse and left the shop, smiling politely at Latimer as she passed, as though she suspected that she was interrupting. Oh bloody hell, he thought absently.

He walked stiffly toward the counter. Neither of them spoke.

"I'm sorry," they said simultaneously. They both laughed at the mistake. Latimer was distinctly embarrassed, uncharacteristically at a loss as to how to approach the conversation.

"Look," he began. "I realise that you're afraid of something in that village. My behaviour last night probably did little to help that... I..."

"I'm sorry that I... manipulated you," she said. "I'll make tea," she added. "Come through."

Latimer followed.

They sat in silence as the kettle boiled, unsure of what to say, where to start. Latimer broke the silence.

"I need you to look at something," he said, clearing his throat. "I'm not going to bring the journal out again, though I've translated something in it. I took the liberty of using the hotel's photocopier. I've copied the notes that I made."

He produced the papers from his inside pocket, carefully unfolding and straightening them, copies of what he had given to Reilly to look at. She had looked frightened when he mentioned the journal. He pushed the photocopied handwriting toward her across the round table.

She trembled a little as she lifted them. Since Latimer had produced the journal the previous night, Mary had been a different person, exhibiting less of the strong character that he had first seen.

"I think that it is some sort of spell, though I can't translate the symbols. Do they mean anything to you?" he said, his voice low and soft as he spoke.

She began to read. As the kettle boiled, the whistle blaring in the enclosed space, Latimer watched as shock began to creep across her features.

"What is it?" he asked.

Mary put the papers back on the table, turned to lift the boiling kettle from the heated ring. Her back was to him as she began to prepare the tea, still having said nothing. She placed the mugs on the table and sat down, licking her lips.

"You're right. That is a spell, a very old, very powerful, spell. Where did you find it?"

"It was in the book that I showed you last night. You recognise the symbols that I haven't been able to translate, don't you?" he said.

"Partially. This is from another time, and I'm not sure exactly what it does." She glanced at him. "Perhaps you don't fully trust me yet, if you only brought the photocopy of your notes rather than the original?"

Latimer frowned, keeping his gaze firmly fixed on the table. "You… you didn't like the book, I guess… and I thought it best not to frighten you any further…"

"Why do you think it's there, in the journal?" she interrupted, almost as if she knew the answer.

He sipped the tea. "I believe that Lord Mountcashel was constrained, through some means, to obtain this spell and then return to Ireland. In the event, he died before he could complete his mission. He talks of being compelled to undertake this task, by the Newtowncairn witch. He may even have..." Latimer gathered his thoughts before continuing. "He may even have killed himself to deny her this information."

He watched as Mary put her trembling hand to her mouth. "Mountcashel was smart enough to encode the entire story, together with the tale of his compulsion, the battle of Newtowncairn, his time in France, his disturbed dreams, everything. Even the spell. Pollock worked out how to translate it. I don't know how, but he did. He was brilliant in that way." Latimer paused for another drink of tea. Mary Hamilton, though her shock was apparent, was still listening. Latimer was looking at her, watching for a sign.

"I haven't been entirely honest with you," she said, her voice a little shaken. "James Pollock was my son!"

Mountcashel's Journal, 11th August 1693, Eppenheim

I have received grave news this morning. Patrick Sarsfield has been killed in battle at Neerwinden. I would like to have seen him again. Having left Ireland after the final siege of Limerick, he had fought for the French, as I have. His death is a reminder, not only of our failure in Ireland, but also of my own mortality. And what of the French, who we have fought and died for? They have already left my homeland. Were it not for my loyalty and honour I would desert their cause and flee home. Have they not done the same to us? I try not to dwell on these thoughts. They bring me to the pit of despair once more.

In my darker moments, I think of how lucky Sarsfield may be, that he need no more suffer the pain of loss of his country. I grow weak, plagued by the rotting of old wounds. They begin to stink and suppurate. The wound in my side that I received at the Isere River has begun to weep at night, even though the regimental surgeon had removed the ball and sealed it. I remember him giving me the fragment as a souvenir after he had cut it from my body. Even my wounds from Newtowncairn appear to grow stiff and open after so many years. But the wounds were cleaned, the pieces removed. I walk now with a cane cut by one of the junior officers. My knee clicks loudly with each limping step. I hear them talk of my

ailing condition.
How is this possible? Is it her? From so far away?

CHAPTER TWENTY-TWO

"He's still in there, Sarge," Laverty remarked casually, as they sat in the unmarked police car, watching the hotel and the bookshop.

"How long has it been?" McGrath replied, taking a sip from the steaming paper cup of hot chocolate that he nursed, its warmth providing some respite from the chill in the night air.

Laverty looked at his watch. "Three or four hours, I reckon," he said, as he bit into his hamburger.

"Perhaps it's love," McGrath said, trying not to think of the cold.

Laverty chuckled. The two fell into an uncharacteristic fit of laughter brought about by excessive levels of caffeine and sugar.

"God, that's sick," said Laverty.

McGrath's laughing ceased, as if the humour of the conversation had suddenly evaporated. "Why?" he said, turning to look at his colleague.

"Because they're kind of, well, I dunno, old, really. Aren't they?" Laverty said, chomping.

He felt McGrath's eyes bore into him.

"I would have thought that they were around my age, Laverty."

Laverty coughed as if choking. He recovered, chewed and quickly swallowed.

"I didn't mean that you, I mean… You know what I mean, Sarge, don't you?" he stammered, red faced, slowly realising that talking was making it worse.

"Yes, kid, I know what you mean," McGrath said sullenly.

Latimer had helped Mary Hamilton mop up the tea and brush up the remnants of the cup that he had dropped on the floor, having heard her describe the amazing revelation that he still had trouble believing. He eventually slumped back into his chair, his mind trying hard to catch up with the facts that he was being told.

"How?" He started again. "How could James Pollock have been your son?" he asked incredulously.

As Mary sat across the table from him, he could see her eyes beginning to fill with tears. She put her hand to her face, as if willing herself to tell him a story that she did not want to part with.

"I had... a child when I was younger. I couldn't keep him, for... for various reasons that I... can't... don't want to explain. I had him adopted, illegally perhaps, though I had little choice."

She looked up.

"I could never have known that he would come back to seek me out after so many years, could I?"

Latimer listened, amazed.

"How did he find you? I thought that his parents had been killed in a car accident?" he said, still unsure whether to believe the story or not.

"His adoptive parents were, I believe," she said, trying to choke back tears. "That's what's so tragic about the whole thing. He'd spent most of his life trying to find me. I don't know how he found out about all of this, but he did, and he came looking. Back to the place that I had tried to keep him away from, back here, of all the places that he could have found. He came back here!"

Latimer frowned. "What do you mean that he came back here?" he said.

"My family has lived in Fermanagh for many years, Mr. Latimer," she said.

A VERY IRISH CURSE

Latimer could see that it was now difficult for her to speak. He wanted to move forward and provide a consoling hand for her to hold, yet still he was unsure of the facts, of what exactly was going on; indeed, of what he could do about any of this.

"As I say, my family has lived here for many generations. Lived to serve, lived to serve the witch!" She looked up, her face suddenly burdened with a mask of fear and desperation. Latimer felt like he had disturbed a grave. He could not help but ask the obvious question.

"Are you casting some sort of magic?"

She shook her head.

"No. No, Mr Latimer, not this time. I'm telling you the truth. I promise you that." She suddenly seemed vulnerable. Totally unlike the woman that he had dined with the previous evening.

"That's why he came here? The research was a convenient excuse?" Latimer asked, the tone of his voice changing. He could almost feel anger boiling inside him.

She gazed at him. Her voice croaked as she spoke. "I did not fully understand before. My knowledge of the dark arts has allowed me to remain hidden from her gaze for many years. I never fully realised that she draws us to this place, all of the Hamiltons. Pollock, my son," she continued. "His destiny, had been written in stone since his birth, even if he could not realise it. He was being drawn here... by her!"

"Why?"

"I couldn't have guessed, though I think now that it must have had something to do with this." She held up the photocopied notes that he had brought, now crumpled in her hands.

"She was using him. Perhaps even directing him, for years and years, so that one day he could translate that which she could not!"

Latimer shook his head. It was all too much to take in, in so short a time.

"He came here to find you, and you think that she had...

called him here for some reason related to the journal? How can that be?" he said, still finding the whole thing incredible. "Surely he just came here to find you?"

She was crying openly now.

"I... I knew him for such a short time, and he was taken from me." She looked up. "But, he was a Hamilton, a descendant of the man who tried to destroy her, and it is our curse to serve her. I could not protect him from it. I could not defeat her terrible Elder power, and so I must remain in hiding while she plots her escape..."

Latimer's head was fuzzy, though he was sure it was not the tea. It was beginning to add up, yet he just could not make the final leap. It was too much to believe, to take in. It made some sort of sense, after everything that he had discovered, yet appeared far too convenient.

"But... that means that I've done her work for her. Finished what Pollock began," he mused, growing steadily angry now. "She's used me just as she's used him!" He remembered the dream, his compulsion to come here against the odds. Even poor Joseph Reilly had followed him unwittingly, believing that they were doing the right thing.

He stood up, trembling with anger. "I have to go. I must destroy the notes, the journal, everything. If what you say is true, then I was a fool to come here!"

She looked up, regaining some control over herself.

"Wait... wait," she said, her voice cracking with the effort. She stood, scattering the chairs near the table as she moved toward the back of the room. She opened a cupboard door, below an old sink, and began to rummage inside.

As Latimer watched, he saw her produce a short length of rough wood, about six inches long and as thick as a brush shaft, the broken stubs of short twigs protruding along its length. A row of sharp edged serrations were cut down one side, and the rest of the circumference was intricately carved with signs and symbols. One end was splintered and raw, as if it had been snapped forcibly from the original tree.

"What the hell is that?" he said, before he could think of

anything more delicate to say.

She moved toward him, holding the object in one hand. As she came closer, Latimer noted that it was completely covered with carved inscriptions, symbols that seemed to awaken recognition in him, similar to those he had seen in the journal.

"Take this with you. It will protect you if she knows that you are here. She will reach you in your dreams."

Latimer swallowed nervously, afraid to tell her of the things that he had already dreamt, preferring to cast them aside and ascribe them to alcohol induced torpor.

"What is it?" he asked.

She pushed it toward his hand. "A protection, a druid's totem, made from sacred oak, inscribed with charms. It is very old, and I now pass it to you."

As she did so, he could barely hear her uttering unintelligible sounds that might have been an incantation, moving her hands along the branch, painting patterns in the air. Latimer stood aghast. He felt something, a thrill, a tingle, as if he was in the presence of something very powerful. Then it passed.

He was not quite sure what to say. "Now that you've… cleared your throat, don't you have to recite some mumbo jumbo or something?"

For the first time that day he saw her smile.

"If you keep up your disrespectful attitude toward the dark arts young man, I'll turn you into a fly and feed you to my spiders."

Latimer laughed, and then tailed off. "You… of course, you can't actually…"

"No," she said, "I can't." She became serious once more. "Please. Take it. It will protect you."

Latimer reached for the short, time-discoloured baton, unsure himself of exactly how much it could protect him, but not wanting to offend.

"Thank you, Mary." Instinctively, he reached down and kissed her gently on the lips. She pulled away after a few seconds. She flushed and put her hand to her mouth.

And Latimer decided then not to leave right away. He sat down again at the table and they talked. He shared the history of the area, Mountcashel's involvement, and the more secret history that he had uncovered within the diary. She spoke of her beliefs, of the nature of magic, and of her interpretation of the secret history that Latimer had unravelled. Time passed, though neither seemed to be affected by it, until the light began to fade and night drew in.

"You'd better go, Mr Latimer," she whispered at last.

"I do have one question," he said, getting up, turning to leave his third cup of tea on the table.

"Yes?"

"If you live under the protection of the pentagram. How is it that you were able to leave for dinner?"

"I'm careful," she replied. "I don't venture out for longer than I have to. So far, it seems to have worked."

He smiled, nodded, and turned to go. "I'll be back," he said, his characteristic optimism returning.

He walked to the front door of the shop, and went out on to the footpath without turning around.

As he crossed the road, Latimer considered what he had heard. But Mary's plan had not worked, he thought. Pollock had been directed from the start, in the same way that Mountcashel had, though in Pollock's case it had been throughout his life and he had not even known it. He gritted his teeth, conscious that he had no proof that such a supernatural power existed, yet aware that it seemed to make a strange kind of sense, given all that had transpired. Too much had happened by coincidence.

Firstly, there was Pollock's brilliance. Was that now to be wished away as some machination of a faraway supernatural power? He did not believe it. Then there was the journal; had he been destined to find it, take it, and translate it? It was all too fantastic to accept. And the supposed intent of the witch? Could this person, even supposing that it was not simply human, be capable of such a scheme? That meant that

Pollock's miraculous return to his mother had been designed and played out, yet something had gone wrong, if that helped to explain why he had been killed. Indeed, his own involvement now seemed veiled in the same mist, as if directed by a third party. What if his dream had not been induced by whiskey? He still considered, however, that Mary Hamilton could be making up the whole thing. But then why had Pollock been killed? Had he refused to play ball? Did he know too much? Why had he not said anything about what was going on? Had he ever really known?

His breath came as trails of vapour in the cold of the night. What proof did he have after all, aside from the apparent use of some weird spell? But could that have been a trick of the mind? He patted the oak branch in his pocket. Well, the twig doesn't bloody well prove anything, does it? he thought, as he looked up and down the long street and its parked cars.

"There he is," Laverty said. "Looks like he's going back to the hotel, Sarge."

"Right, keep watch in case he meets the other one and buggers off again!" Laverty blew his nose, aware that the sighting might be the only element of excitement that awaited him tonight.

"Do you think they're likely to try anything again?" Laverty said absently.

McGrath yawned. "No, but we can't take the risk, can we?"

Laverty agreed. It was going to be a long night.

Mountcashel's Journal, 20th October 1693, Paris

We have been present at the sieges of Heidelburg, Wingemburg and Eppenheim. Though the war could scarce have been conducted in any other fashion, we are fast approaching a stalemate of sorts, despite our advances here. Sieges become the daily grind of the armies, an attempt to make last minute gains in the face of a rapidly approaching treaty which both sides know will be based upon territory held at the war's conclusion. So much blood spilt, for nothing?

And Ireland, a crucible for a conflict which decided nothing in turn, under a supposed king who has fled back to France, in exile from his former throne in England. What hope now for my countrymen? What hope now for me? I see now that Ireland was but a pawn in the schemes of the French. I had hoped that intervention might still save our situation there. I was wrong. I am still a soldier however, and I will obey my orders, though the hypocrisy of this war now sickens me.

My dark dreams, stifled for a time by the actions of the Miquelet witch woman, have returned. I run short of the black liquor that she had prepared for me, and grow weary of mind. Am I fated ever to return to the Spanish border to preserve my sanity? It would seem so. My wounds too, have recently become a burden. Though they have healed, to a degree, I ache in the cold evenings here. The German weather, with continuous rain, does little for my body, even if it reminds me somewhat of my home in Ireland. I long to return home. If letters from there are to be believed however, I am now considered an outlaw of sorts. My estates, what was left of them, have been confiscated by the Williamites. The citizens of Bandon, who I tried as far as possible to serve justice to, have claimed much of what they consider their due from the value of my lands. I am despondent. My country is… no more. What is there left to me now? Should I give in to the wretched pull of her will? Should I return to the Spanish border and abandon all my hopes so that she might win this game?

CHAPTER TWENTY-THREE

A curious sense of extreme fatigue had overcome Latimer after he had left Mary Hamilton's bookshop and made his way back to the hotel. He could not quite put his finger on it. He was convinced more by the reality of the hours that he had been working and his age, however, than the dramatic yet perversely more entertaining thought that he had somehow been drugged by the new found bookseller-witch of Enniskillen. He put thoughts of mistrust aside, ascribing them to his exhausted state.

Latimer had meant to call on Reilly for further discussion, and also to start to focus on what they were going to do when they reached Newtowncairn again. It remained important to write down the things that he had learned from Mary Hamilton, in the hope that Reilly at least might be able to make sense of it. He wanted to be convinced that thoughts of occult direction from a powerful source were unsubstantiated circumstantial evidence with no proof... of anything. Reilly would question Latimer's judgement, shake some sense into him, and waken that old sceptical nature again. If not, Latimer's own admission that he was beginning to believe the story might drive him mad.

He reached his room, in need of a drink, although the thought of alcohol made his stomach churn. Not normal, distinctly out of character, he considered. The temporary feeling of nausea convinced him that dehydration was in fact the issue, and all that was required was water. He stumbled into the dark room, moved toward the bed, dropping his jacket on the floor.

There was something different about the room, almost intangible. He was shattered, as if walking in a dream. The desk was arranged differently. Something was missing. He panicked, fell to the floor, crawled across the carpet fumbling with his dropped jacket, searching the pockets, feeling more confident when he felt the slim form of the journal in the inside pocket. That was not it. Not the book. What was it? He put the jacket on again to reassure himself and crawled toward the bed. He lay down, felt himself drifting off into a sleep that he could not resist any longer.

The entity that was Sorcha Ballantine cackled inwardly as it moved a misshapen index finger along the words that Latimer had translated, moving its head involuntarily as they began to take shape in its mouth, enunciating the symbols that Latimer had not been able to form into words. It laughed at how close it had come to its final triumph.

"You had scant trouble?" it hissed, staring at the bespectacled old man cringing in the corner of the darkened room.

"No, Ma'am," he replied. "When I knew that it was time, your preparations enabled me to both enter and leave the town unnoticed. Upon discovering the absence of Professor Latimer, I seized my chance and entered his room. All else was... simple."

She smiled, emitting a deep, throaty grunt of satisfaction, the fragile yet now hideous skeletal frame shuddering demonically with the effort.

"It is time. Bring me the object."

The servant lifted a worn leather satchel from the floor, a satchel that had formerly belonged to Professor Neil Latimer. He moved it toward the oak table at which his mistress sat, close by a tall and menacing black candle.

"Now," it said. "Light it."

A VERY IRISH CURSE

Latimer was walking in Newtowncairn. Was he dreaming again? He was not sure. The sun was shining. Though there was a brisk breeze, it was by no means uncomfortable. He walked toward the old house, across the fields, feeling the crumbling ridges of dried mud under his shoes. It made him feel good, the coolness in the air, the fact that spring was on its way, that the winter skies would soon be making way for the onset of nature's rebirth. He walked toward the house. There was nothing to fear.

"Sarge," Laverty murmured.

McGrath woke with a start from the sleep that he had easily drifted into some time ago.

"What? What's going on?" he said, shifting his bulk as he tried to give the impression that he had not fallen asleep.

Laverty stretched a hand out. "Calm down, Sarge. It's okay. I thought I should wake you. Latimer's room, look!" He pointed up to the window. The room stood out amongst the others. Not only was the light on, but also the curtains had not been drawn.

McGrath looked toward the light. Someone was moving about.

"He's just up late, there's no... What time is it, anyway?" McGrath asked, fumbling for his watch.

"It's after midnight."

"Bloody hell," McGrath replied. "We should have been relieved hours ago. Why didn't you wake me?"

"I was about to when this started. Watch!"

McGrath glanced at the room again, unaware of exactly what it was that Laverty wanted him to see. As he looked at the only lit window in the street, however, he began to notice the odd behaviour of the room's occupant.

Latimer, if it was Latimer, was standing in the room, gesticulating wildly, moving one arm in rhythmic motions as if trying to get a point across to an unseen companion, scratching his head in an obsessive manner. It looked as if he was having a discussion or argument, yet he was constantly facing the window.

"Is there anyone else in there with him?" McGrath asked, puzzled by the activity.

"I haven't seen anyone. Do you think the other guy is in there with him, Sarge?"

"Could be. How long has he been doing this?"

"About an hour. That's what makes it strange. You'd think that he would have got tired and gone to sleep by now. I haven't seen the outline of anyone else in the room in all that time. So he must be talking to himself."

Latimer had been brought through the beautiful hall, decorated as it was with old bookstands and etched reproductions of medieval scenes. He had wanted to look at the books, the antique books, which lined the shelves, yet his compulsion had been overridden by the desire to finally meet her. The light cast by the rising sun reflected off the furniture and ornaments, giving a warm glow to the interior. It was as if the antiques that were on display wanted to tell their story to the historian, who would become entranced by them. He followed the old man upstairs, noting that the steps did not creak, though the immaculate house must surely have been many years old. It had obviously been well maintained by its owner, who appeared to have treated it with the respect that its many years deserved.

The old man directed him toward a study. As Latimer entered, he could detect the smell of freshly picked flowers. The atmosphere was perfect. He saw the woman at the centre of the room. She was tall, perhaps well into middle age, but offered ample evidence that she had taken good care of herself. Only her eyes showed signs of the passing years, of wisdom perhaps. They were a deep blue, and looked at him now with caring, with admiration even, yet he could see a sadness, a loss in them that was difficult to fathom. She seemed happy to see him, brushing a strand of corn coloured hair from her eyes, delicate wrinkling breaking the beautiful outline of them. She rested the paintbrushes against the easel.

She extended a hand.

"Mr. Latimer, I presume. I've heard so much about you," she said, her voice like soft music.

He reached for the delicate hand.

"Miss ..." Latimer stumbled, a little unsure of himself.

"Ballantine. Sorcha Ballantine," she replied, smiling again. "But where are my manners? Please, have a seat."

She cleared some sheets and artist's materials from a nearby sofa, and ushered him to sit.

"Could you bring some tea please, Hamilton?" she said to the old man.

Latimer turned his head sharply. That name! There was something that he should say now. A task that he had to perform. What was it? Why was it significant? Why could he not remember? He closed his eyes. He had to remember, before she spoke. He knew that if she spoke, he would forget. God, what was it?

"Do you like my painting, Mr. Latimer," she said, interrupting his thoughts and the chain of reasoning that he had been desperately attempting to follow.

He opened his eyes. What had he been trying to remember?

"Yes... It's quite beautiful," he said, looking at the landscape that sat on the easel. "You're really quite a talent."

She seemed embarrassed.

"Oh. I don't think I'm that good yet," she said. "It's really just a hobby. Not my real interest at all, but of course you know that already, don't you?"

Latimer looked up. "I'm sorry?" he said, taken aback.

"You know that my real interest is magic!" Her eyes glistened as she said it. "Black magic, you would call it, though, I must admit, the colour does little to describe the power of such endeavours."

He watched her lips form the words. How beautiful they seemed, yet how terrible the words that they made.

"You have nothing to fear from me!" she said quietly. She stood up, extending a hand to him so that he might take it and walk with her. "Tell me about the history of this land, and I will tell you things that you could never have read in your... sources."

He felt the touch of her hand and permitted her to guide him toward the open window. The smell of fresh oil paint lingered as he moved past the easel. Beyond the gently moving brocade curtains, there was the familiar vista of the village below and the acres of farmland that stretched across the landscape.

"We should talk, Mr. Latimer," she said.

He so wanted her to talk. There was so much untold information, as yet unknown lore, which Latimer knew that he wanted to hear. Words began to come to him...

"Why is he pointing out the window, Sarge?" Laverty shouted, concerned by the fact that McGrath appeared to be drifting back into sleep.

McGrath shook himself to consciousness once more. "Perhaps he's just trying to make his point," McGrath laughed, trying to make himself comfortable in what he now considered to be the most painful position known to man.

"This isn't right," Laverty muttered.

They talked and talked, for hours it seemed. On every occasion that Latimer put forward one of his historical foundations, Sorcha was able to refute it, able to point to another event that made his precept seem childish. Her knowledge was amazing. She understood things about history that were like leaps in the dark to Latimer, yet when he considered her points, they were sound. He reminded him of... if only he could remember his name. It began with a 'P'.

She began to counter his refusal to believe in the occult practices of kings and their retinue, speaking with authority.

A VERY IRISH CURSE

He had no sense of time as she spoke. He absorbed each word, never tiring, never losing concentration. His mind was opened to see the truth behind all of the occult literature he had ever known.

Sorcha showed him how such beliefs had existed with the popular science of the time, and had only been destroyed through the advent of the church. He wanted to believe it, wanted to believe it all, but could not make the final leap, and he knew she sensed it.

Tales of the creatures beyond the knowledge of mankind, who had ruled the earth aeons before man. Entities whose power could be called upon in moments of need. Sorcha told him that kings and priests and powerful men, recognised by society as individuals of high moral standing, had once worshipped at the feet of crude idols that represented the images of these dark gods.

"Belief is all," she said finally, finishing her story and opening the glass door to the balcony. Latimer cursed himself in case he had not heard every word of her speech, for having missed parts of it, a gem of knowledge that had escaped him. But he had been in a daze, a mysterious hypnotic stupor of wonderment at her words.

"What are you doing?" he heard himself say.

He watched as she stepped up onto the balcony, then beyond, walking unaided into thin air, floating there, smiling at him.

"Now, it's your turn, if you believe?" she said softly.

"He's opening the window!" Laverty said. "Why is he opening the window, Sarge?" He glanced nervously across the car. His attention passing from McGrath to the window of the hotel and back to McGrath again, as if he was afraid of what could happen.

McGrath snapped his eyes open. Sure enough, it appeared that Latimer was opening the large window on the second floor. There was a small balcony in front of it, though it was purely there for decoration, being a flimsy architectural feature. What the hell was he doing?

"Come, Professor. Why are you afraid?" she said.

"I am not afraid. Perhaps I do not have your faith," he said, aware suddenly of the ground far below.

"After all that we have discussed, after everything that you have witnessed?"

"Perhaps... perhaps because of what I've seen," he said, looking up at her.

Her face had changed slightly. There was an edge to it now. A trickle of fear ran down his spine.

She beckoned to him.

"It's time, Professor!" Her voice was quite insistent. He felt that he had to obey. He could not think of any other way. He had to do it... and do it now!

"You don't think he's going to... jump, do you?"

Both policemen sat and watched, as Latimer, his tweed jacket flapping in the breeze, began to crawl through the open window to balance delicately on the slim steel frame that formed the decorative balcony. Waiting no longer, the officers left the car and began to sprint across the empty road. Laverty, whose youth allowed him to distance McGrath in the effort, began to shout as he reached the hotel side of the street.

Latimer stood on the edge of the window.

"Now, Mr. Latimer!" she commanded.

"Now," he whispered, as his shoes slid on the edge of the precipice. "Now..."

"Latimer!" the voice began to call a warning, a form moving toward him from below.

In the dim recess of his mind, he knew that this was wrong, that it should not be happening. But he was powerless to stop it. How could he prevent himself from doing what had to be done? He knew it had to be done, didn't he? Latimer paused, unable to continue.

Surely there was an object in his pocket he had to keep safe? He could not remember. The wind blew at his hair. Where was it? His hand found a side pocket, the other helping him balance delicately on the ledge. His weight shifted, though, strangely, he felt no fear. He was doing what had to be done, was he not? The wind had picked up. It blew loudly. She was there in front of him, beckoning him to come to her. It was time. Latimer searched with his hand in the pocket, felt a piece of branch from a tree. What was that doing there?

"Latimer!" Two voices were shouting now. Two voices from below, but still she beckoned him. This was... wrong. A voice was telling him that this could not be right, despite everything she had told him. There was a piece of wood. It was important, wasn't it? He clasped his hand around it, felt the outcroppings of twig stumps from the branch dig into his flesh. He squeezed tightly. It was a reflex, a final effort, as sharp pieces of wood burst through the skin of his palm and fingers. His blood felt warm. Latimer winced, imagining how it would seep through his jacket, and ruin it. Pulling it from his pocket, he continued to squeeze. Pain overcame him suddenly and he screamed. Rivulets of dark blood were cascading down his wrist, over his watch. "Latimer!" they shouted from below again.

What was he doing on the balcony? Involuntarily, he fell back, bumping his head against the window, and landing with a hard thump inside the room.

The doctor closed the door to Latimer's room as he walked out into the corridor. "He needs lots of rest, and I've left some medication."

"When can we ask him some questions?" McGrath asked, standing over the smaller man, eyes boring into him.

Laverty stood behind him, keen to get involved.

"Not for a couple of days, I'm afraid," the doctor replied calmly, not allowing the overbearing policeman to intimidate him. "Is he involved in some sort of investigation?"

"Well no, but..."

"Then I'm afraid that I must insist you leave him alone, gentlemen. Mr Latimer, is, it appears, suffering from acute stress, though I do not believe that he is, as you say, suicidal. I can only surmise that the incident is due to sleepwalking."

"Sleepwalking? There's no way!" McGrath replied incredulously.

"Gentlemen, I think you'll believe me when I say that I've seen many potential suicides in my time, and that man," he said jabbing a thumb at the door behind him, "is not one of them. He has no more interest in killing himself than I have in carrying out surveillance on his hotel room." He looked at McGrath.

"With respect, Doctor," Laverty said. "If we hadn't been there..."

"I agree, Constable," the doctor responded, removing his glasses and rubbing his eyes. "Understand this: I have recommended to Mr. Latimer that he stay a while in hospital for observation, though he has refused. I'll be coming back in a day or so. I suggest you give me two clear days to assess his health before asking any questions, or perhaps you'd prefer that I discuss the matter with your superiors."

The doctor gave McGrath an inquisitorial look.

McGrath turned on his heel, with Laverty following.

"What now?" Laverty asked innocently, trying to keep up.

"I'm going to get some sleep, then resume the surveillance," McGrath answered curtly. "Something is bloody well going on here, and I aim to find out what!"

The doctor re-entered the room with Reilly. Latimer lay in bed in his striped pyjamas, reading a local paper and sipping tea. He put down the newspaper.

"Thank you," Latimer said quietly.

"You heard?" he replied, the sound of his lilting Fermanagh accent pleasant to Latimer's ear after the revelations of the last few days.

"It was difficult not to."

"Yes," the doctor said stiffly. "Let's talk about you then, Mr. Latimer. What really happened this morning?"

Latimer looked back at the paper.

"As I said, I don't really remember anything. I can only ascribe the whole episode to sleepwalking."

"Yet you haven't been prone to this before?"

"Never," Latimer replied, scratching his nose.

"He has been under considerable stress, doctor," Reilly chipped in. "This case."

The doctor listened. "Case?" he echoed. "Oh, you're some sort of investigators?"

Latimer glared at Reilly.

"Okay. All right. None of my business," the doctor added slowly. "Yes, well," he continued. "I'll be checking in on you tomorrow. Make sure he takes the medication, Mr. Reilly." They said their goodbyes as he left.

Reilly turned once more to Latimer.

"Are you sure that you're all right?"

"Yes. There's a lot more going on here than we ever considered."

"What do you mean?"

"I believe..." he said, clearly shaken, as he folded the newspaper again and again before discarding it on the floor. "I believe that there is a conspiracy here. We must go back to Newtowncairn. I can't explain it all to you, but we need to go back! It won't be easy, because I don't want the police to know about it."

Latimer paused, awaiting shock, rejection, an argument. He was surprised when he received none.

Reilly nodded. "Okay. I'd like to get to the bottom of whatever is going on here too. You haven't told me everything though, have you?"

"I didn't tell the police, but my notes and satchel were

stolen from here last night!"

"What? Why didn't you tell them? They... we could have got a lead or something."

Latimer shook his head. "There's more at work here than petty theft. Trust me on this one, Joseph."

Latimer began to get out of bed. "Do you still have your map of Enniskillen?"

Mountcashel's Journal, July 20th 1694, Barreges

I have returned to the Barreges region on the Spanish border, to take the healing waters there. My body decays. There is no other word that might describe what ails me. My wounds rot and stink, so long after they were inflicted. Has she yet, from so far, done this to me? Is this some warning as to the nature and effectiveness of her power? The French surgeons look at me strangely, unable to find a cause, despite the judicious application of leeches.

The fine weather helps me a little, though still I find it difficult to walk. At night I think of the men of the regiments and how they fare, though I know that their honour will remain unblemished. For better or worse, they fight for France now, though I know that many of them will want to return home to Ireland and to the families now under Dutch William's dominion there. I try to put thoughts of Arabella out of my mind. I have no wish for her to see me like this. I can not write to her, though I fear that, with the claiming of what lands and property I had, she is destitute.

Cadores, now my Aide de Camp, informs me that the Shepherdess is gone, claimed by some infernal force. I suspect that the dread Irish witch might be behind her apparent disappearance, though Cadores claims that the Necromancer is abroad in the night and has claimed her soul as his own. Is he the man that I am destined to meet? I know not.

CHAPTER TWENTY-FOUR

Annie Devlin looked at her watch again. It was well after four in the afternoon and she was impatient to get moving. She zipped up her jacket, excited at what seemed like the prospect of a break in a story, which so far had promised so much and delivered little.

To hell with it, I'll be early, she thought, pulling at her keys. They snagged on loose threads in the pocket of the leather jacket. As she made for the car she patted her other pockets, making an inventory of the contents. Mobile phone, check, tape recorder, check, CS gas spray, check. Never leave home without it. Despite going through the usual routine, she could not get the thought out of her head that this was some sort of ruse to throw her off the scent, maybe even a trap. She did not want to admit to her feelings, because that would require that she phoned Sean for help and that would in turn mean showing him that she was weak.

The drive was uneventful, though it was difficult to keep to the speed limit in order to stretch the journey time, despite the agonising drive through what passed for rush hour traffic. Eventually she reached the main road leading toward Newtowncairn and decelerated to a fraction above the speed limit. The bright full moon in the early darkness of the winter's night gave a sheen to the close spaced plantations of fir trees flanking the tarmac. What was she doing? A woman, on her own, travelling to the remotest village in Ireland, to meet a contact she did not know, for information, by the light of a full moon. This was crazy? She tried to quell the inescapable fears. There had been worse situations to face in the past, she thought, but she could not think of any at that particular moment. She grasped the mobile phone in her pocket, thought about letting the police know, though that would probably scare off her contact, whoever it was. Consoling herself with the belief that all this risk was worth the effort, she realised that there was no way out now.

McGrath and Laverty pulled into their familiar parking spot facing the hotel. They immediately noted that Latimer's room was lit.

"You think he'll try it again, Sarge?" Laverty remarked.

"I don't think so. He knows we're watching. But if he's determined to top himself, he'll find a way. They always do," he mused morosely, closing his eyes as he remembered the grotesque imagery of so many years of police work.

As the sky began to darken, Latimer emerged and crossed the street.

"He's off to the bookshop again," Laverty said, immediately sitting up in the seat. "Do you think he's likely to try something else?"

McGrath shook his head. "Let's watch for a while yet, before we jump to any conclusions, kid."

Latimer looked carefully for anything odd in Mary Hamilton's reaction to the news. She had indeed heard the commotion on the street, but had thought little of it until she heard the gossip about a potential suicide.

"I had a dream," Latimer said, fixing his eyes on her. "I want you to tell me what it was all about. I want you to tell me why this happened."

Mary Hamilton quivered.

"By your tone, you don't sound entirely convinced that I was uninvolved in this? I don't understand that," she remarked, plainly concerned at the veiled accusation. "Do you think I drugged your tea or something?" She laughed, trying to

A VERY IRISH CURSE

make light of the seriousness of the situation, and the unflinching stare that Latimer directed at her.

"Frankly, I haven't ruled it out, Mary," he said.

She seemed confused. "With what motive? If I had wanted to kill you, wouldn't it have been easier to poison you with an untraceable potion and avoid all the theatrics?"

Latimer paused, considering. "Perhaps. I don't know."

He continued. "That photocopied document I showed you."

"Yes?"

"The original was stolen from my room," he said.

"When?"

"Last night, as we talked here."

Her mood darkened suddenly. "Then we're already too late," she said, her voice breaking.

"We'll see. I'm going to go there, Newtowncairn, and sort this thing out once and for all." He took his bandaged hand from his pocket and rubbed his brow.

"What happened to your hand?"

Latimer paused, unsure of how to respond.

She answered for him. "The totem, the druid's totem. You gripped it and it woke you from her illusion. Didn't it? It did, didn't it?" she cried, the corners of her mouth forming a victorious expression.

"Yes!" he snapped at her. "Look. I don't understand any of this."

"This proves that I wasn't trying to kill you, Neil. You have to believe that, at least?" she said, her smile vanishing.

"Perhaps, though I'm so confused that I don't know now if I'm awake or dreaming any more. It seemed so real."

"Tell me about the dream."

Latimer repeated the pertinent facts of the imagery, the conversation about magic, history, her expertise in all things and her persuasive ability to seemingly make him do what she wanted.

When it was over, Mary Hamilton took a few moments to collect her thoughts before speaking.

"I urge you not to go there. It's too late. She has everything she wanted. A means of escape. She'll inhabit a new host and she'll be free, then we'll die, most likely." She brushed biscuit crumbs from her lap in a casual manner, as if she had already accepted her fate.

"Okay," said Latimer, scarcely believing her attitude. "And what's the worst that might happen?" He dismissed her defeatist attitude. "This isn't over yet. Not by a long shot." He paused, reflecting on what she had said. "Why does she need a host?"

"Her body will be decayed and ancient, used up. She'll need a fresh one. Oh I'm sure there are many in her subservient cult that would give themselves to her. That will be the least of her worries." She looked at him. "If you must go, take the totem. It saved you last night. It can save you again."

He nodded in agreement, grimly.

Latimer looked up again. "One more thing. You mentioned earlier that you could have poisoned me. Left something without a trace. Did you make that up?"

She shook her head. "No. If I really wanted to, I could do that. Why do you ask?"

"Could you poison me to the extent that I wouldn't fight back if, say, my throat was being cut?" His voice was solid as he said the words, as if he finally understood.

"Yes, of course, but I don't see where you're going with this?"

"It doesn't matter. A conversation for another time, perhaps." He paused, and finished his tea.

"Have you a back door, which takes me out to the centre of town?" he asked.

Annie Devlin felt increasingly afraid in the deserted street, but she was determined to face the numbing fear that was starting to gnaw at her. The only lights came from the pub across the road from where she was parked. Glancing at her watch for the twentieth time and opening the car door, she walked confidently across the road, noting that there was little activity inside the pub.

Something caught her eye. Further down the street. It did not feel quite right. She bit her lower lip, unable to shake the feeling that it was something she had seen before. Turning on her heel and walking slowly, her footsteps echoed loudly in the quiet night, the lack of wind magnifying the sound. Out of habit, she pulled out her mobile phone, checking to see if Sean had called, or to reassure herself that she could call someone if necessary. She winced as she noted that there was no reception available. Jesus, she thought, no signal and I'm in the middle of the village from hell.

She glanced up. Of course, that building. The church that had been there, or, she thought had been there the last time. Though, it had been during the day then. She was sure that it had been a church of some kind. Churches and chapels had scared her since childhood. When her father had walked out on her mother, it had hurt more than she had ever admitted to anyone. Her mother had forced her to go to chapel every Sunday. She had been a devout Catholic, and the family had tried to ensure that Annie would be one too. That insistence created the rebellious streak that seemed to have subconsciously developed in Annie's teenage years. An attitude that made her turn against her relations, against the church, against everything. The relationship with her Mum still was not perfect, but at least they were trying to get along now, and her mother had turned back from the drink before the situation worsened and she became an alcoholic.

Moving closer, she stumbled on the uneven footpath. It was not like the small chapel from her childhood. That was for sure. It seemed square, the blocks of stone looked very old and worn by the elements. The doorway was tall and wide, with weathered steps leading to the threshold. The head of the door was crowned with a stone apex, with symbolism above it that she did not recognise. Maybe this was not a church at all, she thought absently, maybe some sort of Masonic temple, or...

"Can I help you, Miss?"

She gasped in fright as she turned around. A large man stood there. The first things she noticed were the oversize wellington boots he wore. Despite her fear, the absurdity of the situation made her want to laugh. The craggy old man looked back at her, as the remnants of white hair blew across his head in the night breeze.

"Oh, hi, sorry... I was wondering if this was a church."

The old man looked sternly at her. "A church?" he rasped. "Yes, a church, that's what it is. It's her church. Perhaps we should go inside. Would you like that?"

Annie shivered as he spoke, his croaking voice making her want to clear her own throat. He spoke to her like he would speak to a child, or a dog. It was the weirdest feeling that Annie had ever felt. Tendrils of fear crept through her as he lifted a gnarled hand, as if to guide her toward the door. Christ, she thought, grasping the gas canister in her pocket.

"I think that's enough now, Tom, don't you. I'm sure Miss Devlin didn't come here to see our church."

The voice was close, as Annie turned around. Another old man? What was it with this place, she thought. Though this one was different. He was dressed in a suit, obviously not a farmer like Tom.

She did her best to regain her composure.

"Thanks for the invite. Tom, is it?"

She backed away, casting her glance back toward her apparent rescuer. "And you are...?" she asked, her confidence returning.

"Why, Miss Devlin," he said, staring from behind heavy rimmed glasses with thick lenses. "My name is Mr. Hamilton. I wrote you a note."

She pushed open the door of the bar. It was heavy, bound in iron.

The lights were low inside. In other locations the effect

might have been nostalgic, romantic even. Here, it was menacing. The bar put new definition into the term 'old style'. She immediately felt the gaze of the patrons fall upon her, the same looks that forty or fifty years before would have discouraged the presence of a young woman in a country pub. There were, however, only a small number of men in the main room. Most sat alone in cubicles, from the farming community by the look of them, all with the same sullen and pained expression. Their interest in her quickly waned as they returned to nursing their drinks. There was no conversation. The atmosphere was underlined by the silence, the lack of conversation. Only one man stood out. The old man, suited and bespectacled, who walked beside her.

"Actually," she whispered, as they advanced toward the bar. "I would have liked to have seen the church."

"All in good time, Miss Devlin," he replied in a hushed voice. "All in good time."

"Why did you bring me here?"

"Why, I thought that, after your little fright with Tom, you might be in need of a drink. He's a harmless old man, really." He snorted as he tried to laugh.

Annie winced.

Latimer did not know how to say goodbye to Mary Hamilton. He was not sure that he would ever be back here. He reminded himself that he was not really sure of anything any more.

"Thank you, for everything," he blurted finally.

"I hope I'll see you again. Do be careful," she said, as he turned and walked away.

Latimer was not altogether convinced of her innocence yet, but he had no option but to continue with the plan. He broke into a run, jogging down the darkened alleyway. He emerged, panting heavily, onto the main street checking the parked cars. A horn blared twice and a taxi flashed its lights. Latimer ran toward it in the darkness. Rain was beginning to fall. For once, he was glad that he had worn his raincoat. He opened the back door of the taxi. Reilly was inside, dressed in a winter jacket, carrying the largest leather hold-all that Latimer had ever seen. "Newtowncairn please, and step on it," he said, smiling at Reilly.

"Right, sir," the taxi driver said, indicating to pull out. "You guys going to do a little hunting tonight, are you?" Reilly looked at the shotgun case. Latimer considered that his friend might just be the most conspicuous person in the world, when it came to appearing nonchalant! He tried not to frown.

"Yes. That's it. We're staying overnight."

"In Newtowncairn, Jeezus. You guys have got balls, I'll give you that." The taxi driver laughed.

"Why do you say that?" Latimer asked,

"The place is haunted. Nobody goes there. Even the people that live there don't like the place." He laughed heartily in the darkness at his own joke. It was enough to stop all further attempts at conversation for the remainder of the journey.

Annie Devlin had not ordered a drink. She wanted to remain sober and hear the whole story. The old man did not pose much of a threat, and if he had an accomplice, she could not see him. The barman and the customers took little interest. Indeed, they would not engage him in conversation. As she listened to him, she noted that the people in the bar spoke in hushed tones, looking away when she stared back at them. Annie had the sense that they knew better than to interfere. She had not quite got over her meeting with Tom, though the atmosphere in the pub did not make her feel that comfortable either.

"I suggest that we leave here, now that you're feeling better," he said at last. "Most of what I have to tell you concerns a woman who lives near this place."

"You didn't say that in the note... Mr Hamilton, wasn't it?" she asked sharply.

"Yes, that's right. Mr. Hamilton," he said, his smile betraying a set of yellow teeth in various stages of misalignment.

She put her hand in her jacket pocket, feeling for the CS gas, looking around.

"Okay, but if this is some sort of trick!" she said.

"I can assure you, Miss Devlin, that I am motivated solely by the truth," he said, his head rocking slightly as if his elderly body could no longer support the weight. He slid off the bar stool that had been supporting him and motioned her toward the door. Annie Devlin had every intention of remaining calm, in control, and confident in the developing situation. She hoped it would be enough as she felt her hand tighten around the spray canister in her pocket.

The taxi dropped the men off in the centre of the village. The village street remained deserted, though darkness, the presence of a pitiful few streetlights and the knowledge gained since their previous visit, granted the scene a more diabolical aspect.

Latimer paid the driver and watched him drive away. The man had offered no further comment, his only remaining wish seemingly being to get out of the village as quickly as possible. Latimer rested his hand on Reilly's shoulder.

"Okay, I didn't want to say anything in the taxi," he whispered sternly. "But why the heck do we have a shotgun with us?"

Reilly felt himself being pushed along the pavement, as if Latimer were trying to hide their presence, directing them away from the few areas that were dimly lit by pale streetlights.

He kept his voice low, while attempting to release himself from his companion's grip. In another time and place, the natural reaction would be to protest, but he forced restraint.

"Firstly, *we* didn't bring a shotgun, *I* did. Secondly, you seem to have forgotten that people have died here recently, and finally, with what you've told me so far..." His voice began to take on an edge as he stopped. "…and with what facts you haven't decided to tell me, I thought it was a necessity rather than an option."

He paused, trying to hold his temper in check. "So bloody well deal with it, can't you?"

Reilly turned on his heel and walked on, shouldering the leather gun case. Latimer stood in silence, unsure how to respond.

"Come on then," Reilly said. "Because I don't have a clue where you want to go!"

Latimer took the lead.

"This isn't right," McGrath murmured suspiciously.

Laverty shrugged. "What? He's done this before. Maybe the Prof and the lady are… you know!"

McGrath's look stopped the poor attempt at suggestion before it had really started.

"No," McGrath said decisively. "No, this is different. I'm going to check it out!" He opened the door, letting a blast of icy wind into the car.

Laverty almost spilt his coffee. "Sarge… what?"

McGrath began to walk up the pavement, then stopped and retraced his steps. He opened the passenger door again.

"Go and check the hotel. Make sure that the other one is still there!" McGrath barked.

"But his car is there, Sarge. It's in the car park. I can see it from here."

Laverty pointed repeatedly. McGrath just gave him the same look.

"Exactly," he said.

Laverty shrugged, and left the car, throwing the cup into a nearby bin. He watched McGrath stride purposefully up the pavement toward the bookshop.

"Exactly? What does exactly mean?" he moaned to himself. "When I have a hunch and it comes through, do I get a thank you? But when he has a hunch, it's all guns blazing, get this done, get that done. Here we go again..." He walked toward the hotel.

McGrath hammered repeatedly on the door of the shop. There were no lights, and no response to his knocking. Something was wrong here. He took a step back and looked up at the first floor, where he assumed Mary Hamilton would be. As he considered what to do next, he heard rapid footsteps behind him.

"Sarge!"

It was Laverty, running across the road.

"Sarge! They've gone. They've gone..." he gasped in exasperation.

McGrath swore loudly.

Despite Hamilton's preference, Annie Devlin had insisted that they take her car. The old man had protested that it was a short walk, no need for a vehicle. Somehow, she felt better knowing that she could assess the situation on arrival reasonably quickly, while still inside the car, allowing her to drive away. She could kick the old man out, if necessary.

Timorously, he contorted himself in the low slung vehicle. Annie had to show him how to fasten his seat belt, and gained the impression, absurd though it was, that he had never been in a car before.

Hamilton's initial misgivings were replaced by abject terror as the wheels fanned road, grit and water. The acceleration pushed him back and made him want to close his eyes. Only the thought of failing his mistress kept him from subsiding into a blubbering wreck below the dashboard.

"Turn here..." he shouted above the noise of the engine, mere seconds later, indicating that she should turn right. She pulled on the handbrake, locking up the back wheels, allowing the car to spin into a right angle, before gunning it toward the open driveway at high speed. Annie Devlin was smiling. Hamilton was not.

The car sped along a narrow lane flanked by overgrown

hedgerows that whipped against the windscreen as they accelerated up the hill. Then she saw the house. It was lit only by the full moon, yet it cast its own weird light, standing naked and alone in the bleak, darkened landscape, its white columns and crumbling masonry testament to its age.

She skidded the car to a halt, her passenger impelled forward by the motion, stopped only by the seat belt that she had insisted he wore. She turned off the engine, pulled a cigarette from her pocket, and fumbled for her lighter.

"Might I say, that... you... drive like a maniac, madam," Hamilton said, his hand on his chest in an apparent attempt to aid him getting his breath back.

"Let's go," was her only response.

Hamilton wobbled toward the steps of the house, astounded that he was still in one piece.

The interior was spacious and well decorated. Even the hard to impress journalist liked the décor, the level of detail, and the antique themes.

"So where is the lady of the house?" she asked, staring at Hamilton, who seemed happy to let her wander about the well lit hall, soaking up the atmosphere.

"She'll be with us presently, Miss Devlin," he muttered. "Perhaps you'd like to have a seat in the front room. I can make some refreshments."

She agreed, and followed his directions into a well-lit room decorated mainly in white, with lush settees and hanging green plants that cast eerie shadows across the clinical whiteness. Annie could smell paint in the air, though not from the décor. It seemed to be artist's paint. She sat down, sinking into the sumptuous settee.

Minutes later, the lady of the house arrived. Annie Devlin tensed slightly. The woman had made an effort, but the generous layers of make up that she had applied could not disguise the fact that she was very old. Her grey hair had been brushed as much as possible, in a way to hide the fact that most of it appeared to be falling out. She tottered painfully, so much so that Annie wanted to get off the seat in order to help her. She watched as the wrinkled face flinched with each step.

"No need to get up, Miss Devlin," she said, her voice betraying her discomfort. "I have very little time left to me, and it's just possible that you might be able to save my life."

Latimer had still not got over the presence of the shotgun. He pulled his raincoat closer over his shoulders, to keep out the freezing chill of the night.

"You know how I hate those things, Joseph."

Reilly sighed again. He is still going on about the bloody gun, he thought. "I'd rather have it and not need it, than need it and not have it," he replied curtly.

Latimer slowed down. "That's quite good. Did you get that one from a book?"

"A film, actually," he replied. The two laughed, easing the tenseness that had been generated between them, until Reilly stopped. "The last film that I saw with Barbara."

Latimer frowned. "I'm sorry that I dragged you into all this, Joseph," he said.

"I'm still not exactly sure what all this is, are you?"

"Well, I've got a better idea after talking with Mary Hamilton," he said. He slowed his pace. "She's really a witch, you know?"

Reilly looked shocked for a moment, then he found his composure again. "Of course she is, Neil," he said, a vein of sarcasm bubbling just beneath the surface of his tone.

Latimer sighed again. "I really don't think that we'll need the shotgun here," he repeated, changing the subject.

"Well," Reilly whispered. "I hope that you're right!"

McGrath was mad. Laverty had given him the car keys as soon as they had returned to the vehicle. The look on McGrath's face had been enough to convince him that holding on to them was not such a good idea under the circumstances. McGrath screeched the car around another bend.

"I think you need to calm down, Sarge. I mean really," Laverty said, pushing against the roof of the car in an attempt to avoid being whacked against the inside of the body, concerned that McGrath had finally snapped after the mounting pressure of recent days.

"They aren't going back to that village," was all that McGrath would say, over and over again, as if it was all that mattered to him any more.

Laverty had no option but to agree and hang on.

Puzzled by the situation that was unfolding, Annie Devlin had simply tried to be understanding, in a most uncharacteristic manner. The older woman certainly seemed full of information. She would not elaborate on how exactly Annie could save her life, so she had decided to pursue the real reasoning behind why she had been invited to come there. At least it looked as though the CS gas that still nestled snugly in her jacket pocket would not be needed. She got out a notebook and her tape recorder.

The old woman looked on. "I'd really prefer if you just took notes, dear," she said as she sat down, a brown freckled arm reaching shakily for a cup of tea that the old man had just poured.

Annie acquiesced, not wishing to cause upset at this late stage.

"So what can you tell me about Latimer?" she said, declining Hamilton's suggestion that she might take sugar with her tea.

"Firstly, let me introduce myself. My name is Sorcha Ballantine. I have lived here for many years, longer than you can possibly imagine. I could tell you stories of this land and its peoples that stretch far back in time. Most of them you wouldn't believe, I fear. Some... well, even your Mr. Latimer would find a little incredible, I feel."

She smiled, and toyed with her cup.

"How is he linked to what's going on here, to Pollock's death, I mean?" Annie asked, determined not to drown in meandering reminiscences.

"Oh, he's vital to everything, dear," she responded. "He could be the entire future, if he would only let himself go, understand what has to happen, and become part of something bigger."

Annie was confused, and her expression showed it. "What's his relation to the drugs story here? I don't understand all this. Are you connected?" she asked, now desperate for answers.

"Drugs?" Sorcha Ballantine spat the word as if it was infected. "None of this has anything to do with the machinations of small time criminals, dear!" she said, enunciating each word in succession, her voice seeming to grow more powerful.

Devlin squirmed in her seat. She had to admit that she was scared now, despite the earlier signs of there being nothing wrong. She put the pen and notebook down, reaching her right hand into her pocket again, feeling the reassurance of the gas canister.

Ballantine took another drink. "Don't you want your tea, Miss Devlin?" Suddenly, her voice was like liquid again, less caustic, almost like her mother used to speak to her when she was young, Annie thought. She shook her head, trying to clear the fuzziness that was forming.

"No, I don't think that I want any," she replied, her voice sounding weak and distant. She pulled her hand from her pocket.

"Of course you do, dear," Ballantine said softly, watching her, rubbing a crooked wrinkled finger around the top of her cup as she spoke. A faint, resonating hum filled the air.

Annie shrugged and reached for the tea, drinking deeply, then replacing the cup in the saucer.

"I think now..." she said, her eyes narrowing in concentration. "We should talk... about..." She felt groggy, as if she was drunk.

"What, dear?"

Annie looked up in response into a face of pure malevolence and evil, a countenance tinged with hatred, its limbs hideously misshapen in a mockery of humanity… and then it vanished, and the old woman was there, though she swayed in Annie's vision. It was time to get out of here. Annie moved off the chair, her mind intent on directing her body out of that room and away from the house. Her body slipped, disobeying the instructions that she knew were being sent from her addled brain, sliding down to the floor. The jarring thump made her scream. She tried to get up, watched the two occupants of the room swaying in her peripheral vision. She felt sick…

Hamilton caught her as she was about to topple. In an effort that would earlier have appeared impossible for his wizened physique, he lifted her in his arms. Sorcha Ballantine stood and sighed, running her hand along Annie Devlin's body.

"Take her downstairs and make the preparations. Our friends will be here soon."

Latimer and Reilly had begun to walk along the path that led to the large house positioned off the road. They knew that the answers to the riddles that had been underlining all of their endeavours to date would lie there. Latimer broke the silence.

"I know that you don't really understand what's going on here, Joseph, but I want you to trust me." He could think of nothing else to say. He had to tell Joseph what he knew. "I've been here before, in a dream."

Reilly did not answer. In the darkness, Latimer could sense that, even now, Reilly was raising his eyes to heaven in a 'here he goes again' manner.

As they reached the top of the lane, gravel crunching noisily under their boots, Latimer stopped. The exterior was unlit. Inside, the rooms were also in darkness. The lack of illumination and the condition of the exterior suggested that the place was empty, possibly derelict. Latimer was more startled, however, by the presence of a red sports car in the driveway, lit by the light of the full moon that looked out of place against the dilapidated façade of the house.

"I've seen that car before," he whispered.

There was no reply.

"Joseph... Joseph?" Latimer said, moving around in the darkness.

"I'm here," came the reply. "You lost me on the track."

Reilly no longer had the shotgun case shouldered, Latimer noted. In fact, he had ditched it completely and now carried the gun cradled in his arms, broken open, ready to be closed and fired at a moment's notice.

"Are you expecting trouble?" Latimer asked.

"I'm taking no chances. We've been through this," Reilly replied, in a 'no arguments now' manner that concerned Latimer.

"That car. I know it from somewhere," Latimer repeated, pointing in the moonlight.

"Yes, it's Annie Devlin's," Reilly replied. "She drove it to Pollock's funeral."

"I remember now." In the silence, he remembered all the reasons that he had come here, thinking how his intentions and motivations seemed to have been subtly altered. At Pollock's funeral, she had made a show of how all this might even be his fault. Made him feel guilty... over what? Why was she here? What did she think she knew? It was not fair. Why did he have to be hounded by this journalist? Was she going to print more damned lies? Sully his, and worse for all concerned, Pollock's good name? He wondered idly if he were anything but a pawn in another's game.

"Let's go," Latimer urged, moving toward the dark house.

Reilly followed him.

"Okay, here's a stupid question, but one that I think is relevant," Latimer said quietly in the moonlight. "But do you think that when we knock the door, and someone answers, that you're going to have a good reason why you're prowling around in their garden with a shotgun?"

Reilly considered for a moment in silence, and then replied, "I don't think it's going to be an issue. Look."

Latimer glanced toward the front door. It was slightly ajar, the light of the moon revealing some of the details inside the hall, details that he was sure he could remember from a dream. As they moved up the crumbling stone steps, Latimer's heart was pounding. He watched as Reilly levelled the gun, moving slowly, methodically, toward the opening. His colleague did look impressive. Either he knew what he was doing, or he had been watching too many violent movies lately! Wanting to say something, he decided against it. They were too near the house now, to risk being discovered by foolish talk.

The door creaked noisily on rusted hinges opening into a wooden floored hallway. It was incredible. Even in the moonlight, Latimer could see that the hall matched an interior he had seen before, but that he had never physically known. It had been in his dream. He wanted to pinch himself to make sure that he was right.

Reilly moved toward the back of the hall.

"Wait," Latimer said. "Where are you going, Joseph?"

"No idea," he responded. "This was your plan, remember?"

In other circumstances, Latimer might have found the comment funny. As it was, he was terrified. Reilly found a door and tried it. It opened into a darkened room. He reached forward and seemed to find a switch. Instantly, the room was bathed in a pale yellowish light.

"Kitchen," whispered Reilly, his voice steady.

"This is breaking and entering, right?" Latimer asked as he pushed past Reilly into the room, his loud whisper disturbingly loud in the darkness.

"Pretty much," Reilly replied, in full agreement.

"Let's hope our friendly policemen fell for the ruse then!"

"I think so, long enough for us to check the place and get

out of here," Reilly said.

"I'm not sure that these are your standard country fayre ingredients," Latimer said, walking around the cracked tile floor, staring at the large glass jars that adorned the timber shelves. He moved slowly from jar to jar, unsure whether to accept that the contents were real or not.

"These are body parts," Latimer said at last, swallowing hard, trying to control the genuine catch of fear in his voice. "And I think that at least some of them are human!" he gasped.

Reilly followed him, resting the shotgun on his shoulder. "I recognise some of these," he whispered. "In South American tribal rituals they use a lot of this stuff." Latimer stood with his mouth open in wonderment. "This must be what she uses for her..." He trailed off as Reilly looked up, not quite sure that his colleague would believe any of his story. The witchery, the woman who supposedly lived here. The things that she had done. She had killed Pollock, hadn't she? He shook his head in disbelief. Why had they come here again? What had he done? There was scant consolation to be gained through reasoning that even if the police did not think he was either completely mad or up to no good, they would never believe any of this. As soon as his conviction that there might be a plot here centred on some sort of ancient evil, started by a witch of all things, came out... He recoiled at the impression that his story would create. With luck, they would insist on psychiatric counselling. Oh, what the hell was he doing?

He temporarily set aside his dilemma as he looked at the obscene contents of the containers once more. "Why would anyone keep this? For rituals?"

Reilly nodded. "I suppose so. Perhaps to concoct whatever they used to paralyse Pollock before they killed him."

Latimer stopped at the far end of the room, his back to Reilly. What had Joseph said? How could he...? Joseph could not have known...

"I've never mentioned the fact that anything was given to

him before," he said slowly.

"What?" Reilly replied surprised.

Latimer turned, his face reddening with anger.

"How did you know anything about Pollock's autopsy, the way he died? I've never mentioned it!"

"You must have," Reilly blustered.

"I didn't," Latimer replied, his expression darkening.

Latimer began to walk toward him.

Pulling the shotgun from his shoulder, Reilly let the barrels fall neatly into his free hand, shutting the mechanism as it fell. The audible click echoed loudly. Reilly let his right hand find the trigger.

"Don't come any closer, Neil," he said, his eyes bright. "I mean it."

Latimer continued to walk toward him, his face twitching.

"What's going on, Joseph?" he growled.

Reilly pulled the trigger.

Mountcashel's Journal, July 30th 1694, Barreges

Only now, at the end, do I see the nature of her snare, my fate and the hellish purpose of this demonic undertaking.

I was unaware as to whether the visitation was a dream or some trance. I remember writing strange symbols at the behest of a dark shadow or cloaked man in my room. Amidst the sound of strange incantations, I wrote and sweated in the darkness. Now as I wake, the symbols and cryptic letters cover the page in my journal in front of me. My hands are mired with strange smelling ink. I do not understand. What is this plan that she has put in place? Who was the visitor? Is my will my own? He spoke his name as he bade me write, though I can not now pronounce it. I feel her claw like fingers from afar, pressing upon my heart when I try to break free of her, clutching at my breast when I try to run away.

July 31st 1694, Barreges

A VERY IRISH CURSE

I see now, that she seeks release, deliverance from the chains that bind her there, and only this demon from the blackest pit can aid her in her quest.

I had to give the order to Cadores three times before he would agree. Then, with tears in his eyes, he swore that he would carry out my final command. I have dismissed all my other officers. Tonight, Cadores is to kill me and burn what remains of the journal and the strange writings that I have been forced to record. Let that be an end to the matter. I know only that she wants what is written there. She will not have it. I have ensured that she will never have it.

I have recorded my last will and testament, and left what little I have to my surviving relatives. My only regret is that I shall not now be buried in Ireland. Beyond that, I no longer fear death.

Mountcashel

CHAPTER TWENTY-FIVE

Despite his best attempts at communication with his Sergeant, Laverty had had little success at deflecting McGrath's frantic attempts to reach Newtowncairn as quickly as possible. Having arrived there, however, neither policeman actually knew what to do, since there was no vehicle to look for, and this time it was dark. McGrath was reluctant to talk, and Laverty noticed that he was becoming increasingly agitated. Having decided to use the tried and tested method of speaking to the locals, Laverty had left the car and went to the only building with any lights on, the local pub.

Can't be fans of the police service, he thought as he emerged, with only the experience of a few hard, silent stares and a total lack of substantial information to benefit him further. He walked slowly back to the car and knocked on the driver's window. McGrath opened it. He was shaking.

"Should we do a search on foot, Sarge; get the torches out of the boot?" he asked.

McGrath agreed nervously, slowly getting out of the car.

"Anything wrong, Sarge? You don't seem to like this place much?"

McGrath ignored him and opened the boot. The two men reached for high visibility coats and torches. Laverty pulled the Glock automatic pistol from his holster and checked the ammunition load. He did not expect any trouble, he reassured himself. He put on the yellow jacket and checked the torch.

"We'll try that field, shall we, Sarge?" he said. "Where we saw them last time. That one with the house at the far end, yeah?" Laverty was becoming concerned now. What was wrong?

McGrath suddenly stopped trying to zip up the coat, his violent convulsing becoming worse. He began to shake his head vigorously.

"Okay," Laverty responded urgently. "Take it easy."

The crack of a gunshot rang out. Both policemen turned their heads to the source, surely not far from the area that Laverty had just mentioned, a house, on a hill.

He ran to the driver's side, noting that the keys were still in the ignition. He jumped into the seat.

"Let's go, Sarge," he shouted. "Let's go!"

McGrath quietly closed the boot and began to walk around the side of the car, where Laverty had just got in. He undid the catch on the holster that held his revolver in place as he did so.

Latimer felt the shotgun pellets slash through the air near him as Reilly pulled the trigger. They blew a large hole in the glass window behind his head. Even now, through his semi-deafened state, he could still hear the sound of loosened shards of glass falling onto the path outside. He stood aghast, the smoking barrel of the gun but a few feet away.

Reilly stood in front of him, sweating, panting deeply, breath after frustrated breath.

"No closer, Neil. That's just one barrel. There are two, remember?"

"You'd kill me too then, Joseph?" Latimer said, his attempts at keeping a calm timbre to his voice failing miserably. Realisation hit him like a sledgehammer. "Like you killed Pollock!"

Reilly took another deep breath. "Yes. Yes I would. There's so much you don't understand about what's going on here," he said, his voice clear and distinct, almost relieved, as if a burden had been finally lifted from his shoulders.

Understanding slowly dawned on Latimer. "How long

have you been involved with her, with these people," he asked, suddenly staring back at Reilly. "How long?"

Reilly regarded his former friend with a high degree of contempt.

"It's not about being involved, Neil. It's not that simple. All this mindless drudgery that we live with, day after day, generation after generation, can't you see that we have had our time, that we've gone as far as we're going to go. What she offers is something new, a different way that the dregs of humanity living in squalor in the cities and towns of this world would have little time for. But us, Neil, we who understand that she brings power and deliverance if only we will obey her, understand her, worship her. The beings that sit outside our pathetic world are waiting for the chance to come back, to come home again."

Latimer stood in amazement. He could scarcely believe this. In a weird way, however, it started to make sense. His earlier idea, that fantastical witchery had guided him here, some notion of destiny – that had been all wrong. It had been Reilly who had guided his thoughts, nudged his emotions in the right direction, and even made sure that he took all the right turns, made all the correct decisions. And now they had the spell. Latimer snorted in disgust and frustration. Part of it was directed at himself. He had been duped. No, worse, he had let himself be fooled by a man who he had thought his friend, and a woman whose evil had led them both to this place, at this precise time.

"I don't know what she's promised you, Joseph, but it's a lie. I've seen the product of her work. Terrified people, trodden upon by her immortal madness, too afraid to leave their protection, too afraid to admit the truth to themselves. Why did you have to kill Pollock?" he said, trying to control the anger and frustration that he felt, feeling his hands become drawn into fists as he felt his face flush with fury at his utter helplessness.

Reilly grinned, made an attempt to laugh. "Pollock wouldn't do as he was told. He wouldn't do what she wanted.

Don't you see? She can end all this pain and misery, bring a new dawn to the world. Don't you understand? The way people live now, in abject poverty while the rich take the fruits of labour, exploit them, around the world. She can change that; change it all. These people have nothing to lose when it all falls apart. For them, the breakdown of society would almost be a blessing. They look forward to a cigarette and a pint." Reilly was raving, spittle forming on his lower lip. "What the hell kind of life is that?"

Latimer had had enough. "You're more screwed up in the head than I ever gave you credit for, you murdering bastard," he hissed, behind clenched teeth. "To think, I once called you my friend!" He felt so angry now, wanted to charge Reilly, wanted to kill him and put an end to this. But he had to control himself. This was not the time. He had to be clever. Don't end up like Pollock, a voice in his head kept insisting.

Reilly shook the shotgun, threatening Latimer that he would not permit any action. "Pollock wanted to be part of it, Neil. You have to believe me. He did. At least, at first. Then something happened to him here. I don't know what, but it changed him utterly. He wouldn't continue with the work, the translation. I... we realised that he had to be disposed of, destroyed. By that stage, there was only one other man in the world who could finish it."

Latimer watched him gloat.

"I don't know how you found out so much so quickly. The journal must have been good, damn good. Mountcashel tells a wonderful story. Perhaps a little too much information. And, of course, there's that other witch you mentioned. I really must check that out!"

Latimer gnashed his teeth. "You even lay a finger on her and I'll..." He closed his eyes, calmed. Mustn't give anything away, he thought. Christ, this was not happening. Was Reilly threatening Mary now? He had never even suspected this, never considered how Reilly might be involved. It was insidious. He had to stay calm, and wait for the right moment.

His eyes closed as he tried to regain his composure.

Realisation was now hitting him like a brick to the skull. He stared at his former friend. "You broke into Lisa's house. You were looking for the journal the entire time. But... but you couldn't have translated it anyway, could you? You used me, you son of a bitch. You used me, and I didn't even suspect it, never even considered that you were involved with her, with that abomination. You gave her the idea to use me. You told her that it could still be done. Didn't you? You used me to finish the work, to translate that bloody spell. To what end? So that she can be reborn, or something, lead you and your murderous monstrosities?"

Latimer wanted to tell him more about Mary Hamilton, about how Pollock, against all the odds, had found his mother. Would that endanger her still further? Would telling the truth now only make matters worse, especially if he could not get out of the situation and escape to warn her?

Reilly licked his lips as he nodded, agreeing with everything that Latimer had said. "It's time that you met the mistress of the house. Perhaps she'll explain to you... before she kills you. Let's move!" Reilly barked, ordering his former friend toward the door.

Laverty wound down the car window.

"Let's go, Sarge. What's wrong with you?"

He looked up as McGrath's face became distorted with malevolence. He watched in disbelief as McGrath began to pull his revolver, slowly, from his holster.

"Sarge! What are you doing?"

McGrath, seemingly fighting with himself, sweating at the apparent effort of the act, began slowly to raise the gun.

Laverty's mouth was open. He could not believe what he was seeing. What was McGrath's problem? He fumbled for the keys, stuck them in the ignition and turned them.

The car started immediately and he slammed his foot on the pedal and moved the gearstick into reverse, just as McGrath fired. Laverty ducked instinctively as the bullet hit the windscreen in front of him, shattering it as he pumped the accelerator, spinning the wheels as the car lurched backwards. He changed gear, driving away at speed toward the junction, drifting across the road as the tyres screeched in protest. His heart was thumping in his chest. What the hell? What was McGrath doing? What was he doing? He punched broken glass from the windscreen in front of him, snatched a glance in the rear view mirror. McGrath had disappeared.

He stopped briefly at the junction and turned left, in the direction from which the gunshot had come. Call it in, his mind told him, for God's sake call it in.

Laverty stammered into the handset. Damn, it was switched off. He pushed the button; nothing. He pulled it free, the loose cable dangling as the disabled radio came away from its cradle. McGrath must have tampered with it. His mind screamed for him to keep driving, to get out of there. Alone, without hope of backup, there had to be a way out. He thought about the gunshot, about McGrath's reaction. The Sarge had not been the same since he had gone to that damn house, and that was where the shot had come from, wasn't it? If he was going to sort McGrath out, he needed to get some distance between them. Laverty handbraked the right turn into the open driveway, gunning the vehicle up the gravel path.

McGrath cried as he sat in the hedgerow. What had he done? What was wrong with him? He had fired at his partner. Fired a shot. Something, someone, had told him to stop Laverty going to that house. McGrath's brain was on fire as he tried to remember, but he could not. Part of him was sure that he had been there before and spoken with a woman there. Something clicked in his head. No, it had not been a woman. Had he seen something else there? He had to warn Laverty, had to stop him. He stood up, re-holstered the pistol, and began to run down the dark street.

Latimer had been led to the entrance of the cellar. Typical, he thought, it was all playing out like a bad horror movie. Except that in this case, real people had been murdered. A surge of anger flashed through him again. His best friend had killed Pollock. There simply was not any justice.

"I can't believe this, Joseph. We were friends, weren't we?" he said beginning to move down the narrow staircase, trying to reason with Reilly. "This isn't you. It isn't. You're being used, Joseph, can't you see that? Everyone here is being used." His voice betrayed the emotion that he felt. He had to get through to Joseph. Surely it was not too late?

Reilly remained silent as he proffered the shotgun barrel, indicating that Latimer should continue to move down the winding staircase. The smell from the room below struck Latimer's senses. The smell of decay. Light streamed from the underground room as he moved, step by step, closer to the source of all the misery that had unfolded here.

He was, however, completely unprepared for what he actually saw. Velvet wall hangings decorated cold stone walls. Naked flames spurted from torches mounted in sconces, and large red candles burned on top of tall steel posts that rested on the floor, casting an eerie light as they flickered and created shifting shadows. A large altar, ornately carved from a single stone block, dominated the centre of the room, together with the base and gnarled roots of an ancient tree at one end. The air was dry. It made Latimer's breath catch in his throat as he inhaled. An old, bespectacled man stood solemnly, watching Latimer's entrance. On the altar lay Annie Devlin, her wrists and ankles bound to the four corners of the ornate block with thick rope, her blouse and bra ripped open to reveal her breasts and pale skin. Latimer considered her bikini line as she lay there, and was that a tattoo of a rose? He brought himself to his senses.

"Just what is going on here?" he shouted in alarm at what he was seeing, and in an attempt to bring a semblance of normality to the nightmare that he was witnessing. Then he saw her.

Floating above the scene, illuminated by the flickering flames, clad in a white shift, was a hellish figure that served to remind him of all of the nightmares that he had ever had. Latimer felt his jaw drop as he saw her, saw it, existing as a form of life that should not be. The figure was human in form yet coloured a dull brown, its arms and legs misshapen, impossibly thin and gnarled. It must have been human, once. Now, its flesh peeled and cracked as it tensed and moved. He saw its face, the teeth prominent, the flesh taut, clearly outlining the contour of its skull. Then he saw the eyes. The eyes were very much alive, blue and radiant, yet so devoid of flesh that they rolled, oily and spherical, in what was left of the face. He had seen those eyes before, in a dream. They looked at him, and he saw what was left of the jaw muscles move. He wanted to cry out in terror, but found the simple act of breathing effort enough.

Laverty had been driving so fast that he hardly had sufficient room to brake to a stop. Only at the last moment did the headlights pick out the red sports car in the driveway. He swore, and pushed his foot down urgently on the brake. The back end of the police vehicle slid at a right angle as Laverty fought for control. He felt the car slide on the stone chippings, felt himself lose control temporarily, until finally the brakes took hold and he came to a halt, inches from the other car. He let his head rest on the steering wheel. That was close, he thought, then he remembered the events of the last few minutes. He sat upright, checked the weapon in his holster and undid the seatbelt. His mobile. He fumbled for his phone, pulling it out quickly. No signal! How could there be no signal? Now, of all the times… He threw the phone violently against the dash and raced quickly for the house. The bravado that he had experienced earlier was slowly being replaced by the hope that the occupants of the place had a phone.

Despite Latimer's fright, he was able to get a hold of himself, as Reilly nudged him in the side with the barrel of the shotgun. He moved slowly into the room, noting that Annie Devlin seemed unaware of her surroundings, her gaze fixed on the ceiling. Perhaps she was still in shock, he thought, trying to think of a million reasons not to look at the floating abomination in the corner. He forced himself to concentrate on the fate of the journalist rather than let his mind acknowledge the presence of something that he could only consider inhuman, otherworldly. He closed his eyes, hoping that it was another dream.

"Professor Latimer," he heard it hiss, noting from the edge of his vision how it floated from its original position, to a point between the gnarled remnants of the tree and the altar that the prostrate Annie Devlin now lay upon.

"Look at me, Professor. Don't you remember me?"

He heard the voice change slightly, subtly, a difference in tone that emerged as she, it, spoke.

He looked up, opened his eyes. The thing had changed, had slowly become a woman, an old woman, but unmistakably related to the witch that had inhabited his dreams, that had urged him to jump, to fall and to die.

"You…" he muttered. "I know you. You tried to kill me!" he said.

She laughed. "Yes, Professor Latimer." The voice had become almost human now. "But you were too strong for me, weren't you. Do you remember the conversation we had that day, by the window?"

"Of course I…" he blurted, then corrected himself. "That was just a dream," he said, standing straight, as if he could win her over by simply talking. The reality of the situation that he was in, that they were all in, was hitting home. He cursed himself for even contemplating that Mary Hamilton could have been wrong.

"Perhaps," she said. "But everything that I told you was

true, and you believed it." Her voice was silken, throaty, alluring.

Latimer had to take his eyes away from her, toward Annie Devlin, her breasts rising and falling as she breathed slowly.

"What do you want with her? She hasn't done anything."

"Oh, Professor Latimer," the witch said. "Annie is very important to me. You could say that I'm about to become a new woman." She nodded toward the old man that stood by the altar. From a nearby sheet-covered table, he produced a long, serrated blade. Latimer recognised it as obviously ceremonial in nature, with an ornate iron hilt.

"You can't be serious?" he said, light glinting from the blade. "To what end? What good can the continuation of your evil bring? Can't you just die?"

"Oh no, Professor," she said. "No. My kind can, and will, live forever, and now that you have helped me untangle that which I could not do myself, I will be free from the curse that has kept me tied to this place for the last four hundred years. Tied to the damned tree of those druids, and their sacred places."

Realisation struck Latimer. The tree on the map. Even Mountcashel had worked it out. The cairns. An ancient curse had tied her here, kept her in this place. The sum total of what power she had left could only be used in Newtowncairn. That was why she needed to escape, needed the spell. And, in his ignorance, he had translated it for her! Damn! He had to play for time until he could think of a way out of this. Looking behind him, Latimer noted that Reilly still held the shotgun, alert, ready for him to dare to make a move.

He licked his lips and began to speak. "So you duped Lord Mountcashel, all those years ago. But he was a little smarter than you gave him credit for?"

That got her attention, he thought. He felt the sting of her stare as it burrowed into him. In a single instant, she had changed again, become the misshapen thing that represented her true form.

"Yes! What a fine game he played. He cheated me

through death. But at last, at last I shall be free. Thanks to you!"

"And what about Pollock?"

What was left of her lips curled into a snarl. Latimer continued. "He didn't want to play the game, did he? So you poisoned him and had your murdering lackey here kill him?" He jabbed his finger toward Reilly. "Was it worth it? Was it?"

She calmed, and began to laugh. A terrible hacking cough-like sound that Latimer imagined could only come from poisoned, half-dead, lungs.

"Of course it was!" she hissed, the eyes boring into his soul. "I believe that you have something that belongs to me!"

Latimer shuddered before he realised what she was talking about. Slowly, he lifted the journal from his pocket. He looked at the leather cover, decayed and ancient. All of this had transpired because of him, and because of this book. The old man approached, took it from him without a word, and slipped it into his own jacket pocket.

A rustle of wind shook her frame as she began to utter demoniacal words.

Latimer felt pain in his head and limbs as he stumbled and tried to stay upright. He groaned and swayed sideways. What was she doing? Was this the spell that would release her? He gasped and cursed, unable to move.

"Proceed," she said, floating down toward the old man, lifting the sacrificial knife, moving toward Annie Devlin who remained motionless.

Laverty drew the Glock automatic pistol from his holster as he moved through the ground floor of the house. There were no lights on, nobody here and, most important of all, no phone. For God's sake, how much worse could this get? A quick glance into the kitchen, and the shattered window, warned him that the shot must have come from there. What was in those jars? He fought the urge to vomit. Right now, there was not time to check it out. He could hear muffled voices coming up through the floor. He knew that much.

He was sure that there must be a cellar. He found the entrance below the main staircase and opened it quietly. Lights, voices and other noise appeared to be coming from below, down a winding staircase. As he made his way down, he was certain that one of those voices belonged to Latimer. Couldn't be, could it? Yes, it was his voice. Another voice was clearly audible, its tone changing as the conversation went on. This had to be cleared up. Mainly because it looked as though McGrath was not going to be able to do anything!

Laverty reached the bottom of the stairs, bathed in sweat. The conversation had stopped. Could he hear moaning? Was it Latimer? This was it.

Laverty's entrance onto the scene appeared to cause a flurry of panic amongst most of the occupants of the room. It was unexpected. Latimer's eyes lit up immediately, despite the pain that he was being subjected to, as he fell to his knees.

"Laverty," he groaned. "Shoot her!"

Confused, Laverty had initially scanned for anyone who was armed. Holding the automatic pistol in his right hand, with his left supporting his aim, he had pointed it at Reilly, who still carried the shotgun, and only now began to turn around.

"Okay, let's put the gun down first..." he began. If only he had not glanced up. As he did so, he caught sight of the witch, floating beside the altar, resplendent in all her demonic glory. Evil incarnate, decayed and deformed.

He cried out in shock, took his eyes off Reilly, and in that instant did not see that the man facing him had swung his shotgun round and pulled the trigger.

Latimer watched helplessly as Laverty took the full force of the blast in his chest at close range. He flew backwards and landed heavily on the steps, his pistol beside him. The smell of cordite filled the air within the small chamber. Latimer's pain was subsiding. Had it just been a brief lesson for him, a means for him to be kept quiet? He considered briefly making a lunge for Laverty's gun. He crawled toward the bleeding figure, every movement resulting in agony. Perhaps the policeman was even still alive? He heard the sound of the shotgun being reloaded.

"Stay where you are," Reilly's voice hissed, as he locked the barrels back into place and pointed the gun.

"He might still be alive," Latimer said agonisingly.

"Just get back!" Latimer watched as Reilly moved toward the policeman. At the altar, he noted that matters were proceeding as if nothing had happened. Eager to get on with the ceremony, the witch had taken the sacrificial dagger and now floated behind Annie Devlin's head. She slowly began to raise the blade, reciting guttural incantations from the remnants of her mouth, whose very sound conjured up images of dread within Latimer's mind.

Reilly stood up, framed in the doorway of the entrance to the cellar.

"I'm afraid he's dead, Neil," he said in a matter of fact tone.

Latimer gritted his teeth. "How many people does that make now, Joseph? How many people have you killed for her? Isn't this enough?"

Reilly licked his lips. "That just leaves you."

Latimer shook his head slowly, backing away toward the altar, hearing the noise of the witch's spell as it took form to his right.

"What about Barbara?" he said. "You've lied to her. What about her?"

Reilly smirked. "It was a marriage of convenience," he said. "There was nothing there for me. It was merely a cover so that I could continue the work that had to be done here. That's all."

Latimer cursed and shook his head. "You're such a bastard, Joseph. Truly!"

"Perhaps," he said, smiling as he levelled the shotgun.

Latimer watched as the four bullets impacted on Joseph Reilly's upper body from behind. The sound rang in his ears as he saw two of the rounds exit from his torso. As his former friend fell, he saw McGrath framed in the doorway at the bottom of the stairs with a smoking revolver. He was pale, ghastly looking, saliva dripping from his mouth, as if he had overcome some desperate trial through sheer force of will alone. Latimer found himself forming the words again as the incantation to his right seemed to stop.

"McGrath! Shoot her! For God's sake, shoot her!"

Latimer looked to his right, to where the witch appeared to be smiling.

He glanced back at McGrath, who was slowly bringing his arms down, bringing the gun down.

"Oh, Sergeant McGrath won't shoot me. Will you, Sergeant?" the thing said in a silken voice.

Latimer watched incredulously as McGrath shook his head in an involuntary manner, as if he were being forced to make the movement. He watched helplessly as the old man began to walk slowly past the altar, toward the shotgun.

McGrath's head hurt. All he could see was red. He had followed Laverty as best he could. He had heard another gunshot and something in him had snapped. He had sprinted through the mud and gravel to the house, followed Laverty's route, and done what he thought was right, after seeing his corpse. Yet still he was so confused. Now that beautiful woman, Sorcha Ballantine, was standing in front of him. He could see little else, except Professor Latimer. He remembered him. He had something to do with all this, didn't he?

"Now kill Professor Latimer. He is of no further use to me!"

Her order was plain. He was not sure what to do. It was easier to do what she said, wasn't it? He began gradually to move his aim toward Latimer.

Latimer had been shot at, saved and was now back where he started! Twice he could have had the upper hand. And now, twice, he was about to lose it. This time permanently. This was it, he thought. It was all over. Strangely, his thoughts drifted back to Mary Hamilton, of how the old man who now moved across his field of vision toward the shotgun must be related to her in some way, if what she had said in her story were true. Mary Hamilton, he thought, a moment of realisation coming over him. He closed his eyes suddenly, aware of how stupid he had been.

Latimer put his bandaged hand in his pocket, feeling for the totem, the baton that Mary had given him. One chance!

His movement was fluid, most uncharacteristic for him, as he pulled the stump from his pocket and turned around, taking two rapid steps toward the witch. She glanced at his action, too late. She had little idea as to what he was doing, never mind considering how she might stop him, until it happened. He launched himself at her and plunged the baton, stake-like, into her chest as hard as he could. The force of the action pushed her back onto the tree stump, a gnarled and burnt oak tree, Latimer saw clearly as he rammed the druidic totem home. He watched as the thing's jaw dropped, as the atrophied muscles of its face tautened, as its foetid breath dowsed him. Black blood covered his hands, burning them. Talons ripped at his jacket and face as he watched her writhe, her jaw distending impossibly wide, flesh rupturing and breaking around her mouth and horribly black teeth. The high pitched wail echoed through the chamber until it was reverberating off the walls. The flames flickered. Her hands clawed at his face again, scratching it, trying to find his eyes. Latimer yelled in determination, forcing the improvised weapon deeper into the deformed flesh, letting the black ichor-like blood that leaked from her carcass almost scald his hands and face.

"Die, you bitch!" he heard himself shout as he plunged the totem, now coated in gore, again and again into the thing, until it moved no more.

He felt the old man behind him, on the other side of the altar, holding the shotgun, pointing it at him, his hands shaking terribly.

"What... what have you done?" he gasped.

Latimer began to move away, the inky black lifeblood of the witch dripping from his hands, noticing that McGrath, in the corner, had now lowered his weapon and stood confused and paralysed. The old man had moved to the far side of Annie Devlin, in an attempt to get a better shot at him. Latimer turned and watched as the thing that had been the witch's head lost contact with its body and rolled down the tree stump onto the floor. He wiped the blood from his hands. It was sticky, and had caused red lesions to form where it had contacted his flesh.

The old man raised the gun. Two shots rang out. Latimer yelled, his eyes closing with each bang, as he watched the old man fall, saw the shotgun fall from his hands onto the floor, as he looked at McGrath, his revolver now raised as it blasted the old man.

The force of McGrath's bullets carried Hamilton into two of the steel posts that carried thick candles. He knocked them over as he went sprawling, the naked flame making contact with the dry, red material that lined the walls. As Latimer glanced at McGrath, now standing steadily, with the revolver pointed at his target, he rapidly became aware of the fire that was beginning to grow on the far side of the room. McGrath continued to pull the trigger on the empty revolver, the click-clack of the hammer striking the empty chambers.

"Ease down, McGrath. It's over. We have to get these people out of here!" Latimer said, more calmly than he felt as he moved towards him, trying to avoid slipping on the blood on the floor, and pulling the policeman's hands down.

"Latimer!" The voice shouted shrilly from behind him. He glanced around at a furious Annie Devlin, trying in vain to escape her bonds while attempting to cover herself up. She had come out of the trancelike state that she had been held under, upon the death of the witch. All at once she saw her state of undress, the fact that she was bound to an altar, and the increasing ferocity of the fire amongst the dry, flammable material of the wall hangings. To her side, orange tongues of flame were rapidly spreading up the wall as thick smoke rose from the top and billowed across the ceiling.

"Get me the hell off this thing!" she yelled as she writhed, coughing as the smoke began to thicken.

Latimer looked from McGrath to Devlin, to the fire, which was now growing beyond control. He ignored them all, moving toward the man lying sprawled on the floor.

"Latimer!" Devlin screamed, incensed at being ignored.

He retrieved the journal, putting a hand in front of his face to protect him from the searing heat and the rapidly spreading flames that were now catching at the other wall hangings around the chamber. He replaced it in the pocket where he had kept it these past days.

McGrath had regained most of his senses and moved to untie the journalist. Latimer helped, and carried her off the altar. She pulled her blouse across her chest as Latimer tried hard to look elsewhere.

"Let's go."

"I'm bringing Laverty's body," McGrath said, in a downcast tone. It was a requirement rather than a statement. There was no time to argue, and even less to ask if the whole episode had been some sort of communal nightmare.

Latimer let Annie Devlin find her feet, though she immediately collapsed against him. She was weak, and her legs gave way as she struggled to take in the events. It was clear to him that she would have to be carried and that he had to make the hard decisions. He needed to take charge. As he watched the fire grow, engulfing the room, spreading to the remains of the witch, with the heat beginning to become unbearable, Latimer realised that there would not be enough time to pull Reilly's body clear. He lifted Annie Devlin awkwardly and began to ascend the stairs, biting his lower lip as he felt his back creaking. McGrath followed with Laverty, even as the heat of the flames began to scorch them.

As they cleared the top of the stairs, Latimer noted that the fire had taken on new life as it reached the witch and the remnants of the oak tree. The roaring flame spurted from the cellar, cleansing the rooms with twisting tongues of bright fire that leapt to curtains and furniture and raced across the ceilings. They rushed through the hall to the outside of the house before letting their charges down. Even as they made it to the garden, the first lines of sparks were chasing across their clothes.

Latimer watched as a frantic McGrath worked on Laverty, but it was too late. He had already lost too much blood. Coldly, logically, Latimer reasoned that with the nature of his wounds at such close range, he would have suffered little. McGrath, in tears for the second time that night, put Laverty in the police car and proceeded, to Latimer's surprise, to begin work on what appeared to be a broken radio. Latimer guided a groggy Annie Devlin to her car. Pulling open the door, he nestled her in the passenger seat.

Semiconscious, she was still in shock.

"Do you know what happened in there?" he asked.

She nodded. "Yes, I... I was conscious, though I... couldn't fight her. I couldn't do anything. Nothing!" Tears came. Latimer put a comforting arm around her. She had been sure that she could face anything before. But this had been different; more than she had been ready to deal with.

"I still don't really understand all this," she said, between bouts of sobbing. "I'm sorry," she murmured.

"So am I, Annie. So am I," Latimer replied as he watched the fire take hold of the house. He looked through the windows as the flames began to sweep rapidly through the interior, as if they had waited long centuries for a chance to purge the rotten timbers, as if there was a deep-seated need to cleanse and purify. He patted the object in his jacket pocket. The journal. The real recollection of Lord Mountcashel, and the events of the Battle of Newtowncairn.

Latimer walked toward the house. The fire was clearly

visible in the hallway. The hall that he had seen in his dreams, and had walked through with Joseph Reilly. He pulled the journal from his pocket. He felt empty, drained of emotion, and ignored the terrible heat. It was as if he could not feel it. His own cleansing fires had taken away so much, a friend who had not been a friend, a student who had been so much more. Yet, he considered, he had learned so much. Had it all been worth it in some twisted way? There were sinister dark corners in this world, things that no man should know, beings that should not be. He prayed silently that he might live the rest of his life without ever experiencing such terrible sights again, in ignorance of such knowledge.

"What are you doing?" Annie Devlin asked from the car. Latimer looked around. She had found a cigarette, her hands shaking violently as she raised it to her lips.

He stood, staring at the flames, despite the searing heat.

"Some secrets are too terrible to tell," he said, casting the journal into the fire.

He whispered to himself. "I prefer to remember you in my own way, Lord Mountcashel. Let history tell your story. The truth is too terrible."

Latimer turned his back on the house and walked toward the car.

CHAPTER TWENTY-SIX

UNIVERSITY PROFESSOR INVOLVED IN DRUGS SCANDAL AND MURDER
By Annie Devlin

Professor Joseph Reilly was killed in a shootout with armed police last week, sources admitted today. Professor Reilly, who it is now confirmed was involved in a crime syndicate based in the County Fermanagh village of Newtowncairn, was also believed to have been involved in the recent death of James Pollock. When cornered by police, the resulting shootout also resulted in the deaths of Constable Michael Laverty and Silas Hamilton who was thought to be an accomplice of Reilly. Police also report that a number of citizens in the village have lived under a web of fear because of the gang's propensity for violence. It is believed that some locals are so afraid that police are setting up counselling services in the area. Local politicians are astounded that matters have been allowed to get so out of hand, while the police state that if only more witnesses had come forward, the problem might never have become so serious. Sources in Professor Reilly's former university had little comment to make, other than their perception of a hard working academic, which could not, it now seems, have been more wrong. Enquiries continue.

Pollock, A student from the university, who has now been cleared of any involvement with crime in the area, was one more innocent bystander caught up in the recent upsurge of violence.

Latimer smiled wryly as he read the newspaper. At least she had left Barbara out of the whole thing. He knew, however, that some unscrupulous journalist would eventually find her. He had explained the entire affair to Annie Devlin. Well, he thought, as far as he could, and as far as she would accept, without of course mentioning Mary Hamilton. She would, he felt, have been a lot less understanding had she not seen what she had seen. As it was, he felt that she would remain emotionally scarred for the rest of her life, as would they all.

McGrath, in characteristic fashion, explained the whole thing quite well to his superiors, though remained racked with guilt at the death of his partner, despite Latimer's best efforts to explain that he had been under a spell of some nature. He would never believe that, and Latimer knew that he would carry those demons for a long time. He only hoped that he would not throw away his career in his attempt to deal with them, and that he would accept his invitation to visit Mary Hamilton at some stage.

Latimer knew that bringing Mary Hamilton out into the light would have answered many of the queries that people still had, though he also knew that she was not ready for such attention. No, he thought, Mary would remain his little secret.

The phone rang. A solemn John Moore began to describe the arrangements for Reilly's funeral. Latimer responded in clipped phrases, not really having the stomach for the whole affair, bearing in mind how little of Reilly's remains had ultimately been recovered. Moore, always concerned after the welfare of his team, had tried to understand what Latimer had told him, had tried to piece together the evidence. Without the journal, however, he had as much trouble understanding it as Annie Devlin still had. So, Latimer embellished and invented where necessary, and made things fit with what both McGrath and Devlin had ultimately decided to say. The truth would have been too unwholesome and, indeed, unbelievable. Moore, too, would have to accept Latimer's version of events.

"Neil, are you still there?" Moore barked over the phone.

"Yes, John. Still here."

"Look. I'm golfing this weekend in Portrush. Care to join me? It would do you good, I think."

Latimer smiled. "Thanks for the concern, John, but no, not this weekend."

"You have a prior engagement?" he asked, concern in his voice.

"Yes. Sort of. I'm going back to Enniskillen."

"What? After everything that's happened. You can't be serious!"

"Yes, well, it can be relatively quiet down there. I won't be anywhere near Newtowncairn, if that's what you're worried about."

"Glad to hear it. Where are you going?"

"Well, I wanted to call in to a little bookshop I found there."

Latimer smiled, and took a swig from the whiskey glass.

The End

Printed in Great Britain
by Amazon